The Adventures of
Johnny Vermillion

BOOKS BY LOREN D. ESTLEMAN

Kill Zone

Roses Are Dead

Any Man's Death

Motor City Blue

Angel Eyes

The Midnight Man

The Glass Highway

Sugartown

Every Brilliant Eye

Lady Yesterday

Downriver

Silent Thunder

Sweet Women Lie

Never Street

The Witchfinder

The Hours of the Virgin

A Smile on the Face of the Tiger

*City of Widows**

*The High Rocks**

*Billy Gashade**

*Stamping Ground**

*Aces & Eights**

*Journey of the Dead**

*Jitterbug**

*Thunder City**

*The Rocky Mountain Moving Picture Association**

*The Master Executioner**

*White Desert**

*Sinister Heights**

*Something Borrowed, Something Black**

*Port Hazard**

*Poison Blonde**

*Retro**

*Little Black Dress**

*The Adventures of Johnny Vermillion**

*A Forge Book

The Adventures of
JOHNNY
VERMILLION

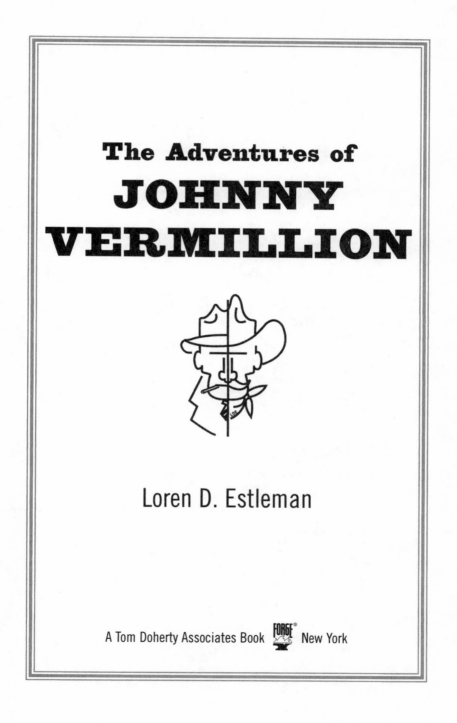

Loren D. Estleman

A Tom Doherty Associates Book FORGE® New York

THE ADVENTURES OF JOHNNY VERMILLION

Copyright © 2006 by Loren D. Estleman

This book is printed on acid-free paper.

A Forge Book
Published by Tom Doherty Associates, LLC
175 Fifth Avenue
New York, NY 10010

www.tor.com

Forge® is a registered trademark of Tom Doherty Associates, LLC.

Library of Congress Cataloging-in-Publication Data

Estleman, Loren D.
    The adventures of Johnny Vermillion: a novel / Loren D. Estleman.—1st ed.
        p.   cm.
    ISBN-13: 978-0-765-30914-3
    ISBN-10: 0-765-30914-9
    1. Theatrical companies—Fiction.   2. Bank robberies—Fiction.   I. Title.
PS3555.S84 A65   2006
813'.54—dc22

                                                                        2006042532

First Edition: June 2006

Printed in the United States of America

0 9 8 7 6 5 4 3 2 1

For Robert C. Jones,
a gentle giant with the wit of a banished elf

Our interest's on the dangerous edge of things.
The honest thief, the tender murderer,
The superstitious atheist, demirep
That loves and saves her soul in new French books.

—ROBERT BROWNING,
"Bishop Blougram's Apology"

· I ·

The
Prairie Rose
Repertory
Company

1

Most of what follows took place in the West.

Not just any West.

It was the West of legend and suckling-memory, where drifters caked head to heel with dust swilled red-eye whiskey at long mahogany bars, punching holes in the tin ceilings with their big Colts to impress their half-naked, quartz-eyed hostesses; where buffalo rolled thunder across gaunt desert, grass ocean, and the great mountain ranges where the earth showed its tusks, stopping only to splash in the wallows and scratch their burlap hides against the cowcatchers of the Central and Western Pacific and the mighty Atchison; where red-lacquer Concords barreled down the western face of the Divide, pulled by teams of six with eyes rolling white, whips cracking like Winchesters above their heads; where glistening black locomotives charged across trestles of latticework oak, burning scrubwood in greasy black streamers and blasting their arrogant whistles; where highwaymen in slouch hats and long dusters pulled bandannas up over their faces and stepped suddenly from behind boulders, firing at the sky and bellowing at shotgun messengers to throw up their hands and throw down the box; where all the towns were named Lockjaw and Busted Straight, Diablo and Purgatory and Spunk.

A West where gamblers wore linen and pomade and dealt aces from both sides of the deck and derringers from inside their sleeves; where cowboys ate beans and drank coffee around campfires to harmonica music, and everything was heavily seasoned with tin. At sunup, drowsy and stiff, the cowboys drove undulating herds of grumbling, lowing, high-strung longhorns past ridges where feathered warriors balanced their horses square on the edge, bows and lances raised against the sky while the brass section blared and kettle drums pounded. Gun battles cleared busy streets in a twinkling and bullets rang off piles of rock in the alkali flats with a *p-tweeeeee!*, kicking dust into the eyes of lawman and outlaw alike. The U.S. Cavalry was invincible, and bandits and gunfighters were celebrities, trailing battalions of paparazzi in brown derbies: Custer had yet to stand on his hill, Jesse to turn his back on Bob, and Wild Bill to draw his fabled hand. All the wagon trains came with concertinas, and all the undertakers and hangmen looked like John Carradine.

It was a West where prospectors, cotton-bearded and toothless, led mules over foothills riddled with shafts, Russian grand dukes shot buffalo from Pullman cars, bandidos wore their ammo belts crossed and flashed gold teeth in duplicitous grins and called everybody Gringo; where women baked bread in gingham and looked cute in buckskins and spilled like ripe peaches out of corsets and sequins and wore feathers in their hair. Train robbers shinnied up telegraph poles, tapped into the lines, and rapped out misleading messages to citizens' vigilance committees on the barrels of their six-shooters. Posses sprang up like cottonwoods, lynch mobs stormed jails, fiddlers played "Little Brown Jug" at church raisings, and legions of tintack piano players knew all the notes to "Buffalo Gals" by heart.

A West, this, where cattle barons gathered in clubs and railroad magnates sat in parlor cars to smoke cigars and plot mayhem; where assassins in their employ took target practice on grangers and Chinamen and shot at the heels of tenderfeet to make them dance. Where tall saguaro cactus grew everywhere, even places where it had never existed; where saloon mirrors were in inexhaustible supply and every bluebelly sergeant was named O'Hara and wore his hat brim turned up in front. Men rolled cigarettes and spat into cuspidors. Most of the lumber went into saloons and gallows and markers on Boot Hill.

Sam Grant was in Washington, soldiering his way through his troubled second term, chain-smoking General Thompsons, drinking Hermitage by the case, and wishing he'd never heard the name Bill Belknap. Lily Langtry was on tour. So were Lotta Crabtree and Jenny Lind, and Edwin Booth was performing as Prospero in Denver. Judges Bean and Parker adjudicated in Texas and the Indian Nations. Ned Buntline guzzled Old Gideon, philandered with married women, and wrote reams of frontier claptrap that sold millions in New York and San Francisco. Wyatt Earp was in Dodge City getting a tooth pulled by Doc Holliday. Chiefs Crazy Horse and Gall rested on the Powder River, watching old Sitting Bull smoking up dreams with a blend of open skepticism and hidden contempt. These things are matters of history and bear no direct application to our tale, but they help set the stage for the rip-roaring action to come.

It was a West of ruthless ranchers, patient housewives, crooked sheriffs, courageous pioneers, eager hellcats, leather-lung bullwhackers, scheming carpetbaggers, spinster schoolteachers, blacksmiths, gunsmiths, wheelwrights, farriers, dressmakers, swampers, grave diggers, and prostitutes with hearts of gold; also of ice and iron. One out of three men answered to Frank or Jack or Billy, regardless of whether his real name was Henry or Leander, the women all seemed to be either Sadie or Jane, and any cowpuncher worth his found knew which one to kiss and which to marry. Everyone seemed to walk around wearing a sandwich board advertising his or her true nature: card cheat, music-hall lecher, bushwhacker, army deserter, wife beater, husband poisoner, snake-oil merchant, newspaper rat, whiskey trader, reader of French novels. All wore the uniform of his station: the top hat tilted at a disreputable angle, the garish waistcoat, the rhinestone buckle on the pointed shoe, the leaded walking stick, the boots with flaps over the toes. But it was also the West of elaborate obfuscation. Dry-goods stores sold muffs with pistol pockets in the linings, spring-operated wrist holsters, and knife scabbards to be worn on lanyards around the neck. Unescorted women walked the streets in safety, but the theaters and ballrooms dripped with murder. It was possible to purchase arsenic in quantity and pistols small enough to conceal in the palm of one's hand. The West's reputation for politeness and hospitality was based on the threat of imminent death for transgressors.

It was the West also of rampant optimism. The consumptive in search of a cure, the criminal in quest of redemption, the failure in pursuit of a fresh start, the bigamist in flight from his wives; each found a fresh page upon which to start his journal anew. A world bereft of records, fingerprints, and the ubiquitous camera, and a blank amorphous map labeled the Great American Desert, offered panacea to a variety of ills. Not since Alexander fled the shadow of his father into the vast reaches of the Known World had our solitary planet so plainly beckoned to the wanderer to cast aside his burdens and press on.

It was the West of Daniel Boone, Kit Carson, and Billy the Kid; but it was also the West of William S. Hart, Roy Rogers, and John Wayne. It was big enough to encompass the bombastery of Buffalo Bill and Cecil B. DeMille and the skullduggery of the bloody brothers Harte.

This was Johnny Vermillion's West; a West that should have been, but never quite was.

2

Tannery, Nebraska, was a good place to sin, and now it's gone.

A few overgrown foundations, a well fallen in and filled with top-soil and chaff are left, and they're invisible from the traffic whirling past on the state highway. But for a few years, before the buffalo vanished and the farmers took their trade west to Omaha, Tannery roared like a young bull.

It boasted fifteen saloons, buck-toothed whores, a Masonic Temple, two banks, and a theater called the Golden Calf. This last seated six hundred, with triple-decked boxes nearly all the way around, but it stood vacant during the warm months when the hides were ripe. Stacks of them two stories high surrounded the tannery itself, attracting flies and repelling visitors not directly in-volved with the industry. The larger theatrical troupes passed the place by from May to November, leaving the citizens to manufac-ture entertainments of their own. A sporting lady known only as Roberta once rode a tame buffalo named Ambrose into the tap-room of the Metropolitan Saloon and halfway up to her quarters on the second floor when the stairs collapsed under the weight; but show me a ghost town without a buffalo-riding whore named Roberta in its past and I'll show you a town that plain bored itself out of existence. Our story is more original than that.

Nothing in the short stormy history of Tannery ever compared to the night the Prairie Rose Repertory Company performed *The Count of Monte Cristo* at the Golden Calf. People who claimed they were present that night were still talking about it years later, after the town had been dismantled and reassembled on the south bank of the Platte under the name Plowright.

Sadly, Plowright proved no more durable in its second incarnation than it had in its first. The spring runoff following the disastrous winter of 1886–87 swept the entire town downriver, drowning one-fifth of its population and scattering the survivors from Ohio to Oregon. But journals and letters carry the story, and aged participants close to the principals were candid in their memoirs.

During the frosty autumn of 1873, in response to a telegraphic exchange between Tannery and Kansas City, Isadore Weaver, proprietor of the Golden Calf, posted the first new bill to garnish the front of the theater since Mabel North, the Yankee Belle, had trilled "Listen to the Mockingbird" to the accompaniment of a live canary on its stage the Saturday after Easter. This was sensation. By the time he brushed out the last blister, a crowd had assembled, exhaling clouds of steam as they read the legend aloud:

FIRST WINTER TOUR

J. T. VERMILLION'S

PRAIRIE ROSE REPERTORY COMPANY

PRESENTS

"THE COUNT OF MONTE CRISTO"

(ADAPTED BY MR. C. RAGLAND FROM THE CLASSIC NOVEL

BY ALEXANDRE DUMAS *PÉRE*)

FEATURING

MR. J. T. VERMILLION

MISS APRIL CLAY

MAJOR EVELYN DAVIES

MME. ELIZABETH MORT-DAVIES

MR. CORNELIUS RAGLAND

ONE PERFORMANCE ONLY

A separate notice was plastered across the bottom, informing interested readers that the play would take place Saturday, November 7, at 8:00 P.M., and that all would be admitted for the sum of fifty cents.

"Never heard of any of 'em," huffed Lysander Hubbard, publisher of the *Tannery Blanket* ("We Cover the Plains"); the poster had come by rail and not from his shop. "What've they done, I wonder?"

Stella Pardon, who ran the general merchandise with her husband, blew her red-lantern nose into a sturdy handkerchief. "Honestly, as long as none of them shot Lincoln, what does it signify? I'll be there, with or without Loyal."

That, demonstrably, was the general sentiment. Weaver pasted up a SOLD OUT notice three days later.

On the Friday before the performance, the westbound U.P. panted to a halt beside the Prince Albert Memorial Depot and stood with steam rolling off its boiler while porters unloaded trunk after trunk onto the platform. Each piece of luggage was stenciled with the theatrical company's name in large, easy-to-read letters. Taking shelter inside this Stonehenge from flying snow, the five new arrivals introduced themselves to the consumptive young staff reporter for the *Blanket* and a large sampling of residents and transients that had been gathered there for more than an hour.

The chief spokesman, identified as Mr. John Tyler Vermillion of Chicago, was a tall fellow a year or two shy of thirty, slim as a trotter. When he removed his hat, a fine soft black one with a broad brim, his longish fair hair whipped about him like a young Byron's. He wore silken moustaches and an imperial in the hollow of his chin, and even the yoke-shouldered buffalo hiders present acknowledged him uncommonly presentable. Existing photographic portraits indicate chiseled bone and eyes of that crystalline shade of blue that always reproduces pale in black-and-white. He must have made a fine figure that day in his gray ulster and beaver collar, Wellingtons shining on his narrow feet. Even Stella Pardon's eyes glistened like steamed plums.

"May I present Miss April Clay," said he, sweeping every gaze with his hat toward the woman who had just joined them from aboard the day coach. "She will be playing the unattainable Mercedes; and may I warn you, gentlemen, she remains in character offstage as well as on."

A chuckle coursed through the group, warmest in the throats of the "gentlemen" thus admonished. Bowler, badger-piece, and filthy slouch hat came away as one, in some cases exposing crania covered since All Hallow's Eve. For Miss Clay was a dainty daub, in the language of the day; a strawberry blonde with skin like milk, dressed to the fashion in a tweed traveling suit and cape, with an adorable little hat pinned to her upswept hair. She was then in her twenty-second year, five feet four in tiny patent leathers with a hint of heel. Her eyes were hazel, slanted gently (her grandmother, it was said, was Russian), and as large as asteroids.

"Where did you appear last?" inquired the young man from the *Blanket*.

The wind gusted. Miss Clay swayed and placed a slender hand in a suede glove against the reporter's waistcoat for support. She asked his pardon, withdrawing the hand. "The Tivoli, in Kansas City. I assayed the role of Viola in Mr. William Shakespeare's *Twelfth Night*. I was Maria as well, and briefly a sailor."

Her voice was astonishingly low for one of her stature. The reviewer for the *St. Louis Enquirer* had compared it to "a bassoon in heaven's ensemble."

"Three parts in one play? How did you remember all the lines?"

"The sailor was nonspeaking," said Mr. Vermillion. "We are a small company, but versatile. Each of us seldom portrays the same character twice in succession, and we often perform double and triple duty. In the hierarchy of the stage, repertory is solidly working class. In that, we are very like your own fine panners and prospectors, sifting the streams and prowling the hills all round for gold."

Someone in the audience pointed out that Tannery was a buffalo town, not a mining camp. The leader of the troupe was unabashed.

"Your noble stalkers and skinners, if you will, conquering the brute and refining its outer shell for personal comfort. We come before you, ladies and gentlemen, to distract and amuse, to provide a brief holiday from the trials of daily existence."

Applause crackled. He bowed and swung his hat. "Madame Elizabeth Mort-Davies, who has charmingly agreed to strain credulity and appear as the hero's silver-haired mother."

Mme. Mort-Davies' hair was, in fact, a rather alarming shade of violet, piled high and caught cruelly with combs; it was not observed to move even when the wind toppled a large valise from the mountain of luggage. She was nearly as tall as Mr. Vermillion, straight-backed and buxom, and fifty-five if she was a day. Matrons were her specialty, but she had been known to don a beard for Polonius, and strain credulity to cracking to allow Miss Clay to abandon the ingenue for a smaller part that offered more challenge. Saturday night, she would also pull a set of false whiskers as the venal warden of the Chateau d'If.

Her husband, introduced as Major Evelyn Davies (emphasis on that first long *E*), formerly of the Queen's horse guard, stood a head shorter and round as a barrel hoop in a buffalo coat and morning dress, dove-gray gaiters on his square-toed boots. He wore white handlebars and carried a gold-headed stick. His responsibilities included the beleagured Edmond Dantes' aged father and also the Abbe Faria, Dantes' fellow prisoner.

"Finally, Mr. Cornelius Ragland, the plain sturdy band that holds together our quartet of gems. Tomorrow night you shall know him as the villainous Danglars, and perhaps recognize him among an army of coachmen, stewards, and prison guards. However, impersonation is not the sum total of his genius. He is the playwright who distilled Dumas *Pere*'s great work into three manageable acts, with time for intermission."

Young Mr. Ragland was plain as tin, but far from sturdy; he made the hollow-chested journalist look burly by comparison. Stoop-shouldered, bespectacled, with ears that stuck out conveniently to prevent his hat from settling onto his shoulders, he appeared miserable in the cold, and his suit of clothes was far from clean. At every glance he belonged to that genus of sickly male described as Too Fragile for this World.

"What do *you* play, Mr. Vermillion?" someone called out. "The Chateau Deef?"

The leader of the troupe laughed with the others. "It will be my privilege to ask you to accept me in the person of Edmond Dantes and his alter ego, that mysterious, haunted fellow, the Count of Monte Cristo." He bowed deeply, and those in witness could do naught but clap their hands. Frontier audiences were notoriously generous.

Isadore Weaver arrived, crimson-faced and puffing, apologizing for certain entrepreneurial details that had delayed him at the Golden Calf. He made the company's acquaintance and explained that accommodations awaited them at the Railroad Arms; a brace of stagehands was on its way to transport their costumes and stage properties to the theater. Mr. Vermillion seemed prepared to resume orating, but Miss Clay tugged at his sleeve and asked the fellow from the *Blanket* for the time of day. Among the crowd on the platform there was a furious scramble for pockets. The reporter alone came up empty-handed and bewildered by the situation.

Miss Clay smiled and produced a battered turnip watch and chain from her little reticule. "It's a handsome timepiece," she said. "I couldn't resist a closer look."

Blushing, the young man accepted its return, along with her sweet apology. Miss Clay, explained Mr. Vermillion, was a gifted parlor magician whose father had studied under Monsieur Robert-Houdin in Paris. His listeners applauded the charming demonstration of legerdemain, and not one noticed the blue-icicle gaze he fixed upon the pretty conjurer.

When the fire curtain rose Saturday night, bearing with it its wallpaper pattern of advertising ("TROPICAL FRUIT LAXATIVE, THE GENTLE PERSUADER, AVAILABLE AT BOYLAN'S

DRUGS"; "ELY & SONS PRESENT SUMMER AND WIN-
TER SUITS FOR MEN AND BOYS"; "SHARPS METALLIC
CARTRIDGES BY CASE OR GROSS, ORDER AT PARDON'S
GENERAL MERCHANDISE"), a capacity crowd cheered every-
thing, even the set.

The set, at least, benefited heavily from anticipation. Back then,
itinerant actors traveled much more lightly than the Broadway
road companies of the present day, depending upon theaters to
supply all but their costumes and makeup and some hand properties specific to the production. The Golden Calf appealed in
turn to its patrons, who built and painted sets and donated odd
sticks of furniture, some of which came from the trash heap behind the Old Cathay Saloon after its biweekly brawl. As a result,
the home of Edmond Dantes in Act I was more reminiscent of a
Victorian jumble sale than of the play's French Empire setting,
and when Edmond bearded Danglars in his own den in Act III,
a number of sharp observers noted that the villain appeared to
shop in the same places as his mortal enemy. But it was the performances that mattered.

Whatever his thespial challenges—he tended to speechify, and
Mr. Ragland's script indulged that tendency—Mr. John Tyler
Vermillion of Chicago cut a dashing figure in tights and delivered
his soliloquys in a ringing tenor, punctuated by clashing blades
and much athletic hopping about during the fencing scenes. Miss
April Clay captivated the women with her courage and the men
with her decolletage; a bit of modest lace in the last act, and a dash
of talcum to her temples, supported the passage of years. Poor Mr.
Ragland was a weak and unconvincing swordsman, but spoke his
lines with a serpentine hiss (and a bit of a lisp) appropriate to the
dastard of the drama. All agreed that the Madame and the Major

were rather fine, and the choice of material fortunate. During the quiet stretches, a great many fewer shots were fired into the ceiling than usual.

At intermission, those consulting their programmes for the first time were startled to learn that Miss Clay and Mme. Mort-Davies had disguised themselves as prison guards to dispose of Faria's earthly remains. It had been assumed those mute parts were played by men of the cast.

The *Tannery Blanket* and its readers joined in declaring *The Count of Monte Cristo* a successful opening to the winter theatrical season. The review would have claimed the entire first column had not someone robbed the Pioneers Bank & Trust midway through the second act.

3

It is an established fact of American town life that one neighborhood is singled out as the best among three adjoining, that one of two identical houses is regarded as superior, and that traffic is heavier on one side of Main Street than on the other. The Pioneers was the more successful of Tannery's two banks simply because its competitor, the Planter State, stood on the side where Grand Street entered Main at a right angle, interrupting the pedestrian flow. Even rugged settlers, once settled, tend to follow the path of least resistance. That path led to Horace Longnecker's institution three doors down from the Golden Calf Theater.

Alvin S. Geary was on duty the night of the robbery. As the cashier in shortest residence, he'd been ordered to come in that night to correct a shortfall of sixty-two cents in Friday's deposits, an assignment accepted with ill grace. Geary suspected Old Longnecker had pocketed the difference in order to force Geary to surrender his ticket to *The Count of Monte Cristo* to Longnecker's married daughter. He was sufficiently bitter to attract suspicion, but his refusal to change his account eventually persuaded City Marshal Fletcher to broaden his search.

According to Geary, he had the deposits spread out on the large worktable in Longnecker's office, counting the notes and coins and comparing the sums to figures in the ledger, when he heard the street door open and close. Certain he'd locked it securely, Geary stepped into the lobby to investigate and found himself facing a cloaked figure pointing a large revolver directly at his chest.

The intruder gestured toward the office. Hands raised unbidden, Geary backed inside, followed by the visitor, who produced an oilcloth sack from a coat pocket. No explanation was required. The cashier took the sack and scooped the money into it. The figure with the gun took back the sack, gestured for Geary to sit down behind Longnecker's desk, and backed out, reversing the key in the office door and locking him inside. The episode was over in less than five minutes, with no words spoken.

By the time Geary broke free, some thirty-four hundred dollars in notes, gold, and silver had vanished without a whisper.

The bandit wore a soft dark hat with the brim pulled down and a coarse scarf wound around his lower features, with a bulky coat that hung to his heels. He stood under the average height and the coat was far too big for his slender frame; the sleeves were turned back twice and the revolver appeared too heavy for the delicate wrist that stuck out of the right. Geary had the impression he was a youth, aged no more than sixteen.

"You're stout enough," said the marshal. "You ought to have tried to outwrestle him."

"Not for Old Longnecker's money. The gun was stouter."

Marshal Fletcher was forty and unpleasantly fat, a fixture in outlaw tales of this type. Picture him in a horizontal heap behind his desk, batting at flies with a paper fan given out by the local undertaker, soup stains on his vest and egg crusted on his badge of office. A fly lands on his neck; he swats, but he's too slow, and the insect takes flight, insolent and drowsy in the heat from the potbelly stove. A pot of coffee has simmered there since morning—when it's poured you could tie a knot in the stream. There is the usual gun rack and the usual bulletin board shingled with plug-uglies and offers of reward, with no restrictions as to their condition upon delivery.

Lazy fat men are commonly dismissed as cowardly and stupid. This was not true in Fletcher's case, although in most circumstances he preferred to sit still and acquire the reputation than stir himself to correct it. Against that, he had a drawer full of fans given him by the undertaker, and a board stuck in Boot Hill for every one. A fly is not a desperado.

Once he was satisfied of Geary's innocence, the Law in Tannery took the obvious next step and presented himself at the Golden Calf.

The cashier had insisted that the robbery took place at five minutes past nine, nearly an hour before the theater let out; but Fletcher knew a bit about the comings and goings of actors in performance, even if he didn't care for entertainments of that nature. He'd read somewhere, possibly in the *Police Gazette,* of Edwin Booth absenting himself from *Richard III* in New York City long enough to get smashed at the Knickerbocker bar and staggering back onstage just in time for his cue. He reckoned that an experienced imbiber would be twenty minutes at such a task; the Pioneers bandit had needed just five to remove thirty-four hundred and change.

Fletcher sheltered no prejudice against theater people, only strangers. He was a community booster, confident in the belief that most serious felonies were committed by people from out of town.

Summoned to the lobby, Isadore Weaver was unhappy to learn that the marshal intended to interview the cast of the splendid play that was then whirling and crashing toward its final curtain. He was unhappier still that Fletcher wished to detain all six hundred members of the audience until they'd been questioned and released. He became obstreperous on the second point. A compromise was reached: The public would be allowed to go home after leaving their names with the head usher and information on where they could be reached. The owner beckoned to that fellow, told him what was needed, and conducted the marshal backstage.

The Golden Calf retained two dressing rooms, each generously proportioned according to the standards of the time. Mabel North, she of the duet with the canary bird, had had one all to herself and her partner in its cage, but the Farrell Family of tumblers, high-wire performers, and dog trainers had crammed themselves in eight to a room, plus six poodles. Gallantly, the male portion of the Prairie Rose Repertory Company shared the smaller of the two chambers and gave the other to Mme. Mort-Davies and Miss Clay. Marshal Fletcher smoked a cigar in Weaver's office and questioned them one by one, starting with the men.

He found Mr. Vermillion cooperative and pleasant. Wan Mr. Ragland was nervous; many of his responses were mumbled and unintelligible and had to be repeated for clarity, but Fletcher was experienced with uncertain youth and did not reckon it a mark against him. He positively disliked the apoplectic Major Davies, who challenged him constantly, thumping the floor with his stick and answering every question with one of his own. Fletcher had to smack Weaver's desk hard with his hand to startle the man into submission. All three assured the marshal they had not left the theater from first curtain to last, nor witnessed any of the others leaving.

Vermillion smiled. "Do you understand repertory, Mr. Fletcher?"

"Marshal. I think I do. You shuffle yourselves like cards and play each other's parts."

"And whatever parts are called for beyond the first and second leads: grooms, nurses, Lord High Mayors, lunatics—spear-carriers, we call them. Most plays have five or six such characters, nonspeaking usually, but essential to the business onstage. Some have dozens. We play them all. There isn't time to step outside for a smoke, much less rob a bank."

Fletcher struggled upright. "Who said anything about robbing a bank?"

"A theater is a leaky old barn, Marshal. Rumors fly in and out like sparrows."

Ragland, too, knew Fletcher's purpose; the audience had been lined up as far back as the stage, waiting to give the head usher the information he wanted and get out. He'd overheard them talking on his way there from the dressing room.

Asked if he also was aware of the situation, Major Davies thumped his stick and demanded to know if his wife was to be subjected to this infernal inquisition.

Miss Clay resembled a little girl with her makeup scrubbed off and a silk scarf over her head, a smart coat covering her robe. She was sweet and answered questions readily. Mme. Mort-Davies, who had had time to fix her face and hair and put on street clothes, provided direct responses, offering no details beyond those requested. Their sessions went swiftly.

At the end, the marshal felt he had a clear picture of what each player had been doing at the time of the robbery. A score of interviews conducted at random over Sunday convinced him that none of the players had been outside the view of six hundred witnesses long enough to have committed it; but lazy men, once they've overcome inertia, are thorough. Before he led a posse out of town in pursuit of a lone fugitive, he directed three full-time deputies to search the theater, the company's rooms at the Railway Arms, and their many trunks and bags for the missing money, which contained too much gold to conceal on the person. The Prairie Rose arsenal of fencing foils and stage pistols was impressive but hardly conclusive, as everyone owned firearms. Their props were numerous and varied and included a bicycle. The bandit's attire, so vaguely described by Mr. Geary, might have been anywhere among the dozens of costumes and accessories so tightly packed in pasteboard drawers and placed upon thin wooden hangers, or nowhere at all.

Neither the search nor the posse was successful. On Monday morning, butt-sore and lighter by several inconsequential pounds, Marshal Fletcher apologized to the players for their inconvenience and escorted them to the depot. As the train pulled away, he saw his employment future leave with it. For once, the swarm of flies that overhung Tannery had given way to a cloud of doubt concerning the local system of law enforcement. Every merchant in town had lost some portion of his profits while the Count of Monte Cristo was busy settling old scores, and all Fletcher had managed to do was discourage him and his party from ever coming back to free the town from its travails.

Eight miles due west of Tannery and a brief, kidney-rattling buckboard ride north of the U.P. tracks lay the hamlet of New Hope, now entering the late stages of dissolution. An establishing shot lingers significantly on a plank sign with a black X painted through "NEW" and "NO" lettered above in the same dismal shade. The town's founder had undertaken to swindle E. H. Harriman in a business transaction, and without pause to reflect, the dyspeptic force behind the Transcontinental Railroad had altered the construction by a quarter-inch on the surveyors' map. New Hope withered.

As their transportation slowed to negotiate the prairie-dog town that had taken up residence on the broad single street, April Clay frowned prettily in the shade of her parasol.

"Johnny, it's deserted. There's no one to protect us from Indians."

Vermillion, seated facing her on the bench opposite, reached out and patted her knee. "Of course there is, dear. You've met Gunderson."

Their driver, a representative specimen of frontier color introduced as New Hope's mayor pro tem, wore a Union forage cap and the greatcoat of a colonel in the Confederacy. He'd appointed himself to fill the vacancy left by the founder's suicide.

"It's a damn Whitechapel in the desert," declared Major Davies, gripping his stick. "There are *rats* in the *street*." He was always in bad cess when his wife was absent.

"Those aren't rats, old fellow. They'll keep the rattlesnakes out of our beds."

"You don't mean we're to stay here overnight!" April glared defiance—a showstopper in the third act.

"That depends on Liz. She doesn't pedal as fast as she used to."

"She rode the high wire in Atlantic City in sixty-three," said the Major. "My part against yours she'll be here by dark."

"Even so, there's no train before morning. I've slept outside on Blue Island. We'll survive."

"It will be an adventure," said Cornelius Ragland.

All eyes turned to the fragile young man, who had not spoken since before they left the train. He sat next to Gunderson on the driver's seat. His eyes, large as pears in his thin face, gleamed through his spectacles.

"Corny's our pioneer," Vermillion confided. "There's nothing for him back East but the sanitarium."

They drew rein before a gaunt barn in a community of dun-colored clapboard. Gunderson hopped down among the obligatory tumbleweeds and reached up to help Vermillion unload their single trunk; all but it and April's leather train case had remained aboard the train, bound for their next port of call.

"Oh, Johnny, a *barn?*"

He bared his polished teeth. "I think you'll be pleasantly surprised."

Inside, a lantern burned on a table inside a circle of barrel stoves, an island of warmth in the dank vastness smelling of grain. There were chairs, a pile of bedrolls, a picnic basket, and a foil-wrapped glass neck sticking up out of a galvanized bucket filled with chunks of ice. The Major drew out the bottle of champagne and squinted at the label. "New Jersey." He let it slide back.

"The French have yet to discover the charms of Nebraska." The leader of the troupe uncovered the basket, took out a tinned ham, a loaf of bread, and a jar sealed with beeswax.

"Them's peach preserves." Gunderson twisted the corncob pipe in his gray beard. "I couldn't get the cheese."

"Quite all right." Vermillion handed him a small drawstring bag. Silver clanked. "We're waiting for the rest."

The mayor pro tem left, and the company sat down to their meal, filling tin cups with water from a canteen. They saved the champagne for later. April avoided the ham, but took her bread in small pieces spread with preserves. Ragland ate with appetite, Vermillion with exaggerated fastidiousness. The Major said American peaches were no substitute for Sussex marmalade.

Nearing dusk, they heard a noise outside. April drew a derringer from her reticule, a fine Remington with silver plating and ormolu grips. Vermillion opened the door and peered out, then spread it wide. "Merely our prodigal daughter. You may stand down, dear— although I must say that piece looks more comely in your hand than the Colt."

"That horrid thing. I'm sure if I pulled the trigger it would flip me over onto my bustle." She returned the weapon to its pocket in the lining.

Mme. Mort-Davies entered, pushing her bicycle. She'd strapped down her generous bosom with canvas and pulled on a heavy ribbed sweater and tan riding breeches of the kind worn by Western Union messengers, gathered tight to her calves with high lace-up boots. She made rather a homely man with her abundance of hair gathered up inside a tweed cap. Her cheeks were flushed from the cold.

"About time, my pet. Thirty minutes more and you'd have pedaled all this way for nothing."

She fixed her husband with a stony gaze. "I've made it clear to Johnny these wagers of yours don't include me."

"In any case I didn't agree to it." Vermillion plucked the oilcloth bundle from the bicycle's wicker basket while Ragland went to work with a wrench. In three minutes the front wheel and basket were off and the entire vehicle was packed in the trunk. Vermillion waited until he finished, then dumped the bundle out onto the table. Packets of banknotes lay among the silver dollars and glittering gold double eagles. April sighed.

The Major was the first to speak. "Next time, we must get inside the vault. I made more than this at the Old Vic."

4

Who is Johnny Vermillion?

The history of the American theater makes no mention of him or the Prairie Rose, and his name occupies barely a footnote in the constantly mestasticizing library of Western outlawry, with inaccurate information appended. For answer, we must depart from the written record and borrow a technique from the medium of film.

The color bleeds to sepia and we observe a sprawl of maverick construction on the swampy shore of Lake Michigan, far more impressive for its size than its architecture; for it appears to be without limit. Grain elevators tower above its few wooden stories of houses, shops, barns, and municipal and county buildings, the first generation of brick warehouses on the lake, and long horizontal columns of depots built of native sandstone. There are stacks and chimneys, of course, and smoke lies in coppery layers like the sunset. Locomotives chug high and low and all about like toy trains. Superimposed on this, a virile legend: CHICAGO 1844.

Not, perhaps, the Chicago we expect. The eye searches in vain for the stockyards, slaughterhouses, and gingerbread mansions of iconic memory; they are yet to be built. This is an agrarian center, serving wheat and cotton and flax to the East on rails still shining and fresh. Its days of butchers and barons and grotesque wealth lie twenty-five years in the future. But it is a young force, brawny with plans.

We are drawn, as by the Ghost of Christmas Past, over roofs, past lines of washing, and through a window on the third floor of the Winston Hotel, which will perish, along with its mahogany and crystal and miles of green velvet hung in swags, in the Great Fire of 1871. We cross the glistening tessellated floor of the ballroom, littered with confetti in heaps like cornstalks, and stop at last before an Empire chair supporting the prosperous corpulence of Scipio Africanus McNear, assistant city comptroller and chairman of the local Democratic Party. His collar is sprung, his waistcoat unbuttoned to provide egress for his grand belly. A tower clock chimes four; all his colleagues have retired to their beds, leaving him to smoke a final cigar and sift through a pile of telegrams congratulating him upon the election of James Knox Polk to the presidency of the United States. He has been a tireless supporter of the gentleman from Tennessee ever since John Tyler gave up his own bid for reelection, and McNear has delivered Chicago to the Democrats at the expense of fifty tons of coal distributed in the South Side and a number of fractured skulls in the disputed precincts. He expects much from Washington in exchange.

However, the telegram we find him reading is not from a crony, but from the head of surgery at St. Patrick's Hospital downtown:

YOUR SON BORN TWO TWENTY THREE A M EIGHT POUNDS
SEVEN OZ STOP MOTHER CHILD WELL RESTING STOP AWAITING
NAME

Boss McNear, as he is pleased to be known to the press and public, has a pawkish sense of humor. Chuckling, he produces the pencil he used to tally the vote and scribbles a name on the back of the telegram: "John Tyler McNear, Esq."

He reckoned he never knew a better day, and that fate demanded a steep price. In 1860, the year the Republican Party gave Abraham Lincoln to America, McNear's wife, Geneva, a daughter of one of the city's founding French families, was killed when the streetcar she was riding jumped the tracks; she was pregnant with a daughter, who perished also. McNear was serving as a state senator, and came home from Springfield to find himself a stranger to his fifteen-year-old son, a dreamy sort of lad who had spoken French exclusively until he was five. He was promptly shipped off to a boarding school in Rockford. There he failed consistently at mathematics, humiliating his father, the former comptroller, but scored well in history and drama, where his performance as Dr. Faustus on the school's amateur stage drew an enthusiastic review from the *Rockford Evening Gazette*. McNear, who did not attend, consoled himself that the young man might become a decent orator, but his hopes were shattered when John was expelled for theft.

Summoned before his father to explain himself, he confessed that after his exit in Act IV, he'd removed a number of valuable items from pockets in the cloakroom, and that a silver snuffbox belonging to a patron had been found in his rooms. McNear beat him severely with his belt, and later beat him again when the school superintendent wrote to report that Master McNear had not committed the crime in person, but had seduced the young lady who played the Good Angel into performing the task while he was soliloquizing onstage; the young lady had come forward upon her own, hoping that the truth would lead to Master McNear's reinstatement.

"You filthy pup!" sputtered the old man, when his arm faltered. "Is that what they taught you up in Rockford?"

John Tyler, it's said, touched his torn lip with a handkerchief. "Actually, I believe it was in your suite at the Winston, the night the party nominated Douglas. I learned a great deal that evening."

That evening, Scipio Africanus McNear suffered the first of several strokes that would force him to retire from public life at the age of fifty-eight. His investments during the cattle boom that followed the War Between the States allowed him to live the life of a wealthy invalid on Lakeshore Drive, with nursing care around the clock, and to pay his son an allowance to keep him away from home. Then came the fire. When the company through which he'd insured his pens and meatpacking plants defaulted on all its claims, the prospect of an impoverished old age brought on the stroke that killed McNear on the eve of his seventieth birthday. His former colleagues contributed to a collection to bury him in Mt. Carmel Cemetery, sparing him a pauper's grave on Blue Island.

John Tyler did not attend. He spent the day of the funeral in a banquet room at the newly rebuilt Palmer House Hotel, treating his friends to a champagne supper with the last of the money given him by his father. For years, he'd used his mother's maiden name, Vermillion. None of his guests knew of his loss, and his women friends, who imagined they shared the secrets of his heart, were not aware he was related to one of those vulgar political creatures their fathers condemned at garden parties.

His descent from that point was vertical.

His male friends were not disposed to help him out. For some time, objects of value had had a habit of going missing when he was present—a watch here, an unattended banknote there. Such trinkets were considered dispensable in their set, and their principles differed sharply from those of the previous generation. Like John's, their family connections had released them from military service during the war: Honor, to them, was rather a remote concept, like the elaborate burial practices of the early Egyptians, and they looked upon it with the same combination of amusement and contempt reserved for last year's collar. When they confronted him, they were contented to accept his markers, just as they were when any of their peers lost at cards or arranged a loan to hold them over until their next allowance. Some of the items were returned, in fact, and some debts repaid. But after he was locked out of his rooms for nonpayment of rent, the reality of his financial condition barred him from both their company and their hospitality. Turned away from their doors with nothing but the clothes he stood up in, Johnny Vermillion perceived that his country was headed in a harsh new direction, to a place whose customs were dictated by money, and not by whether one's French ancestor had sailed with Drake or fought the British at Ticonderoga.

It was a lesson for which he'd been prepared all his life. From an early age, he had witnessed the comings and goings in his father's house of ward leaders and building contractors, bearing satchels of cash to and from Boss McNear for favors asked and services rendered. He'd spent the summer before his mother's death running errands for the Democratic Party, and had seen the unsheathed greed on the faces of elder statesmen whose pen-and-ink likenesses graced the sober columns of the *Chicago Sun* when tariffs were discussed and hospitals under construction. Money was the ammunition of the Industrial Revolution; whether it was acquired with a pistol or scooped in buckets from the public treasury seemed less to the point than getting it and spending it. He had not so much a disrespect for the rights of property as a lack of awareness that any such rights existed.

The loss of Geneva Vermillion McNear, a creature above and apart from the soiled coinage that kept the political system tinkling like a player piano, had severed whatever connection this sensitive, good-looking, queerly observant boy had maintained with the catechism of *Peré* Argulet, the spiritual guide of his youth at St. Patrick's. The boy was a clever thief by birth and an uncommonly skilled one by education. He'd stolen far more from his acquaintances than they ever suspected—they'd blamed carelessness and attrition—and pawned it to support a standard of living somewhat greater than his father's subsidy had made possible. Now he was denied access.

His female friendships, although less altered (his father, a strikingly handsome figure before the overindulgence of his middle years, had given him a straight nose and a narrow waist, his mother her fair hair and all the charms of the Parisian court), offered even smaller hope for shelter. Many were married ladies, and those in single circumstances had strict landladies and rigid curfews. He had neither the training to enter a profession nor the endurance to withstand sixteen hours of physical labor daily. The spark of dramatic ambition that had glowed briefly at school had long since guttered out. That left either vagrancy or thievery from strangers. Prison fare, he'd heard, was bad for teeth and ruinous to the complexion, and certain other rumors that had come his way concerning life inside he found not worth the candle. The wastrel's way beckoned.

By the winter of 1872, he was sleeping on streetcar benches and begging for coins. A successful day's panhandling bought him a "flop" for the night on Blue Island. This was a dirtfill in a canal leading from the lake and a hotbed of malaria, saloons, brothels, and that variety of lawyer that existed mainly to give abortionists and white slavers a reason to feel superior. The island itself was in a constant state of erosion, retarded only by the addition of fresh manure swept from the streets. To take a turn there was virtually impossible without kicking up a bone belonging to some indigent buried by the city. Even the Great Fire had gone around it as a waste of destructive force.

On a pewter-colored morning in late November—it might have been early December—Johnny awoke to a prod from an impatient toe and stirred himself to clear the doorway where he'd sought shelter from the wind an hour before. The visitor, however, made no motion to step past him. He was a stout, ruddy-faced party in a tall Mormon hat with an eagle feather in the band and a preposterous fringed coat trimmed with an otter collar, crumbs in his moustaches. Johnny thought he looked like a third-rate hotel waiter reciting *The Song of Hiawatha* in concert. The waiter fixed the man at his feet with an alcoholic glare.

"You look as if you'll clean up well enough." He held up a silver dollar. "How would you like to be an Indian?"

The man's name was Buntline, plainly a *nom de caprice* under which he practiced professionally. To hear him speak, in a four-wheeler

growling over brick pavement into the heart of furious construction downtown, he'd been just about everything *but* a hotel waiter:
naval officer, newspaper publisher, duellist, inciter to riot, temper-
ence lecturer, popular novelist, and, currently, producer and playwright. Johnny shared the carriage with four other recent recruits
in varying degrees of sartorial and hygienic neglect and learned
their employment was temporary. A bill posted outside Nixon's
Amphitheater had promised a spectacle involving authentic fron-
tiersmen and genuine red Indians. However, there had been an
oversight, and although the former were available, the latter were
not. Until such time as the real article could be procured, he explained, "you gentlemen present will wear feathers and paint and
carry on like wild dogs for the sum of two dollars per week."

Scouts of the Plains opened under Nixon's roof, a canvas rig as
temporary as the nonspeaking cast, on December 18, led by an
uncommonly beautiful former scout and buffalo hunter named
Cody. He was two years younger than Johnny, with the identical
straight figure and even features, and wore his chestnut hair to his
shoulders, a closely cultivated Vandyke, and buckskins tailored to
his measure. An execrable actor who stammered and forgot his
lines, he was nonetheless a powerful presence; beside him, his fellow rude thespians, a man called Texas Jack and Buntline himself,
faded into the painted prairie backdrop. The effect upon the audience, male and female, was electric. Johnny himself, behind the
clay-colored pigment that smeared his face, developed a bit of a
crush on Cody that evening; a manly one, to be sure, with no sug-
gestion of unnatural attraction, but a crush just the same. But he
was not so besotted as to fail to study the phenomenon and isolate
its ingredients. In forty years in public life, Boss McNear had prided

himself on his ability to make stew from toads, and this, too, was his legacy. Cody himself seemed unaware of his charms, which was a contributing factor in its success. Years later, touring the great cities of the New World and the capitals of the Old, the star would learn to apply them to queens, kaisers, and Sioux chiefs, real ones; by which time Johnny Vermillion could provide lessons of his own.

The play was folderol, an amateur freak show seasoned with "blanket-stretching" tales from the border told around a synthetic campfire and a slapstick Indian raid with rubber tomahawks and popping stage pistols, and a sensation. Notwithstanding withering reviews in all the Chicago papers, the engagement sold out and was held over for weeks. Johnny was bored to stupefaction by the unscripticed antics of his fellow "supers" and himself, and not a little embarrassed by them. But his salary allowed him to sleep indoors and eat regularly, and he put his time in the wings to good use, analyzing the stuff of mass popularity. Although he and Cody never exchanged a word, Johnny observed that he never left the theater after a performance without a different attraction on his arm, decked in ruffles and touched with scent, parasol in hand. The young man from Blue Island out of Lakeshore Drive bought a suit of clothes in a secondhand shop, a decent fit, and let his hair grow, even though he could afford an occasional visit to a barber. He was content to have it trimmed only when it curled over his collar, a Byronic effect. He knew from instinct he could not pull off the part of a backwoods Adonis; his accent was solidly Midwestern, and his French too good.

The show closed out its extended run and prepared to embark on a tour of the eastern states. The "Indians" were not invited, possibly because New York's Bowery and the Tenderloin of Boston promised their own sources of two-dollar-a-week performers. Johnny wasn't disappointed. He'd determined to exploit his skills as a mendicant and borrow money to open a show of his own.

5

He had, of course, no prospects among his former friends, from whom he'd stolen hundreds. Wasting no time in lament—a foreign emotion—he took the five-dollar gold piece he'd received in severance from an ebullient and unusually munificent Buntline, sewed it into the lining of his new suit coat, and boarded a boxcar bound for St. Louis.

In the restless years following the end of hostilities between North and South, not all of the pioneers who ventured West did so aboard day coaches and wagon trains, the latter already fading from the landscape in the glare from the flashpans at Promontory Point. Something in excess of fifty thousand maimed and impoverished veterans sought berths in freight cars and on the naked rods between the wheels hoping for work on the frontier. A rare whole man in that company of cripples, many of whom were younger than he, Johnny felt shame—for the fathers who were either unwilling or unable to secure their sons' exclusion from the draft. He concealed his unbroken condition in the fluttering shadows.

Fortunately, conversation was limited to a barter system of smoking materials and flasks of paint-strip whiskey, and one lively auction over a paperbound novel, filthy and tattered, begun by an entrepreneurial fellow who wore a bandanna over one side of his face, ruined by grapeshot on some forgotten field; boredom was the overpowering complaint on that endless trek. The story—*The Prairie Rose, or A Maiden's Journey Among Savages*—eventually sold for two cents and a half-consumed plug of Levi Garrett's. Johnny admired the title.

In St. Louis, he spent his stake on a shave, a bath, laundering, a press, and a room above a printing shop on Pike Street. A wallet lifted in bustling pedestrian traffic yielded a slim bounty, from which he paid his landlord, the printer, to provide him with twenty-five cards printed on good stock:

J. T. VERMILLION, ESQ.
The Prairie Rose Repertory Company

The printer fingered the notepaper upon which the order was written. "What about an address?"

"I hope for better quarters presently."

The first to receive his card was a banker named Argyle, whose name Johnny had read in an advertisement in the *Dispatch.* Explaining that he had no appointment, the visitor sent the card into his office through Argyle's private secretary, a thin young man, pale as porcelain, who wore his spectacles on a black ribbon pinned to his waistcoat, and sat down to read *Frank Leslie's Illustrated Newspaper* and wait. At the end of two hours, during which a procession of roseate gentlemen in boiled collars passed in and out through the private door, he was granted an audience of five minutes. He found Argyle, an emblem of the type in white side-whiskers and a liverish hue, behind a leather-topped desk looking quizzically at his card. Introductions were brief, and Johnny lost no time in placing his proposition before the banker.

"Young man," said Argyle, "the theater is an unstable enterprise. This institution—"

"Pardon the interruption. Are you not related to Walter C. Argyle, the Chicago financier?"

"Walter was my brother. He is deceased." The liver went gray around the edges.

"The same Walter Argyle who threw himself beneath the wheels of the Michigan Central at Union Station in eighteen fifty-nine?"

"A tragic accident." He stole another glance at the card. "Vermillion. The *Chicago* Vermillions?"

"On my mother's side, actually. My father was S. A. McNear."

There was now no trace of healthy organ meat in the banker's face. "I—I understood he had no offspring."

"That was his conceit. I was a disappointment. However, I apprenticed to him for three months in fifty-nine. Your brother was a valued contributor to the party, right up until his partners learned their own contributions got no closer to the Douglas campaign chest than his office. The money never surfaced. There was talk of an unknown accomplice, but those rumors died out, as they will when there is no foundation. I hope I'm not upsetting you with these unhappy recollections."

Peter Argyle was a man with a keen grasp of the realities. It was this instinct that had led him to St. Louis, and to shift his allegiance to the Republican Party a full year before the election of Ulysses S. Grant. Without further conversation—indeed, before the five minutes allotted to the interview had elapsed—he signed and handed the young man a bank draught in the amount of five hundred dollars.

St. Louis, it developed, was fertile ground for past guilty associations. Johnny was not always successful. He retired from one second-floor office when the man behind the desk rose and offered to propel him through the window, and there was an anxious moment near the levee when the newcomer had reason to be grateful for the rough education he'd received on Blue Island; he blacked the eye of one attacker and scaled a fence to elude his partner. Others were more cooperative; some negotiated. At the end of his first week on the Mississippi, Johnny Vermillion had reason to close old accounts with his late sire and to open the door to a suite of comfortably furnished rooms on Fifth Street. The time had come to begin assembling his troupe.

Here, as it had in the form of Buntline's toe, fate prodded him. Struggling against the pedestrian flow on Market Street following a successful interview with a regional vice president of the Santa Fe Railroad, he bumped into a petite lady in a becoming white dress, tipped his hat to her in apology, and fought his way upstream for a hundred yards before he realized a roll of banknotes was missing from his inside breast pocket. The railroad man had paid him in cash. Instantly he reversed directions and gave chase.

The lady was fast on her feet and graceful, but had shown faulty judgment in her choice of dress; like a marine rescuer fixing on the ripples where a swimmer has gone down, her pursuer kept his eyes on the white vision fluttering in and out among the duns and grays and blacks of business dress, toppling hats and jostling old gentlemen off their canes as he plunged ahead to close the gap. By the time he caught up with her, rounding the corner of Third, he'd lost his own hat, and his hair hung over his eyes. The scream he stifled by clamping his hand over her mouth and pushing her into a doorway was genuine fright. He stuck something into her ribs, or rather the stays that bound them.

"A knife is a wicked weapon," he whispered. "You have something that belongs to me."

She made a noise full of *m*'s against his palm. Pinned against the door by his weight, his hand covering the lower half of her face, she was warm, and tense as coiled spring. She glared fire at him from under a white hat with a sweeping brim, the veil pinned up on one side. It was a most becoming hat. He could feel her heart beating clear through him.

The tension went out of her body all at once. She nodded. He withdrew his hand and turned it palm upward.

Suddenly he stiffened. The object she drew from the reticule wound by its drawstring around her wrist pressed hard against his abdomen. It made a crisp *snick* when she thumbed back the hammer.

"A pistol is a wicked weapon," she said. "I'll have yours."

He laughed and showed her the harmless card case in his other hand. Stepping back, he opened it and held up a card.

She read it without taking it. The silver-plated derringer remained in place. "Where is your theater?"

"All over this great land. Tell me you have not dined."

April Clay, neé Klauswidcsz, was the daughter of Polish immigrants, although she insisted her grandmother had belonged to a noble family in St. Petersburg. Her father was a prodigal, and had not been heard from in ten years; her mother had been dead for two. April was currently supporting herself at the Steamboat Theater, assisting a magician billed as Gandolphus the Great, with whom Johnny assumed she had a romantic arrangement, but apparently not a satisfying one financially.

Johnny could hardly believe his good fortune. Here was a beautiful young woman with stage experience, her own demonstrated talent for sleight of hand, and none of the cumbersome baggage of honesty. If she could act—but what did that signify? She would look comely in ruffles and tights.

They ordered the sauteed duck at the Planter's House, with a dessert of roasted peaches served in champagne sauce—his first taste of that delectable libation since the day of his father's funeral, and a harbinger of change. By the time the coffee was served, she had agreed to invest half of the money she had separated from Johnny into their joint venture, and also to pay the bill, as it had been the only cash he'd had on his person.

He suggested they seal their partnership in his rooms, over the remaining portion of their bottle of wine. She declined sweetly. Commerce, she explained, was a difficult undertaking without the additional complication of a personal relationship. Thus, from the beginning, was set the tone for the association. He saw her to a hansom, and did not realize his card case was missing until he returned to his rooms.

The next stage of recruitment presented more challenge. They needed character players, capable of comedy and drama, and versatile enough to support a multiplicity of roles. The dignity of age would supply authenticity and gravity, but good health was crucial, to withstand the rigors of travel under often primitive conditions. Add to this the necessary cavalier approach to probity and virtue, and the difficulty increased. During the long days and nights that followed this declaration of their requirements, both Johnny and April wondered, fleetingly, whether honesty weren't the simplest policy after all, if not strictly the best. It was a passing consideration as noted, gone with the sunrise.

Separate and in tandem, they haunted the theaters and melodeons of St. Louis, taking in matinees and evening performances and comparing notes afterward. They avoided the popular shows in the bigger theaters, concentrating instead upon the barely respectable houses on the tattered fringes of the entertainment district, with no lines at the box offices and FINAL NIGHT plastered in an indolent diagonal across the performers' names. This was Desperation Alley, where the weak and defeated straggled behind the herd, to be picked off by predators. It was also, unfortunately, a burial ground for the hack, the charlatan, and that pathetic breed of entertainer that should have never been allowed closer to the proscenium arch than the third row of the orchestra. The pair endured more banana-handed jugglers, broken-arched dancers, tone-deaf singers, overcautious acrobats, and harelipped elocutionists in one six-block area than in all the theaters of the East; April confided that she'd have put them all out of their misery (and hers) if her little Remington only had the range.

Success came to them both simultaneously—or almost.

Johnny sat through a dreary afternoon bill at the Empress, a cramped collar box of a music hall that had survived the riverfront fire of 1849, and still smelled of char, as well as generations of cooked cabbage; tearing his programme into a string of paper dolls to keep himself from screaming profanities at the abominations onstage. With two acts remaining, he'd reached the end of his patience and got up to leave, only to be arrested at the door by a series of perfectly round vowels projected from behind the footlights. He turned around and watched a corpulent old fellow, in full dress with top hat and the scarlet sash of a dignitary, proclaiming his passion for a woman taller than himself and straight as a plumb, dressed in the simple gray of a mature maidservant with a white apron. The placard on the easel downstage right was redundant to the action: THE DIPLOMAT DEPOSES. The woman waited, hands folded before her apron, until he finished—and declined his proposal of marriage, wringing a collective gasp from the scattered audience, and general applause as the curtain rang down on the old gentleman with head hung low.

The performance impressed Johnny less than the response from the orchestra; he found it mannered and laughable, as was its subject. *The Diplomat Deposes* had been around for years, an old dependable harness horse of the stage. His own school turn in *Dr. Faustus* had followed the one-act piece, and he had sat through three hideous versions in the last ten days alone. That a pair of actors whose best years were demonstrably behind them—he reckoned their combined age would stretch back to the Revolution—should manage to wring such a reaction from so jaded a gallery was remarkable. That their position near the bottom of a fifth-rate bill in a tenth-rate theater placed them in straits he considered approachable was encouraging. As a stagehand shunted the placard to the back, exposing the next and last, Johnny made haste to record the two names in his leather notebook.

Ablaze with his discovery, he was exasperated not to be able to find April. The old dragon who stood sentry in the lobby of the women's hotel where she lodged reported that she'd been out all day. Their preferred table at the Planter's House, where they met regularly to commisserate, was occupied by a middle-aged German couple with faces as sour as *braten*. He decided that April was scouting an evening performance, but could find no mention of where in his notes. He returned to his rooms and paced the floor until the hour when the theaters let out.

Back at the Planter's, he drank a quick brandy and ordered another. It had not yet arrived when April swept in, ravishing in green satin, her cheeks afire with excitement. She was seated opposite him before he had time to rise. They both started speaking at once; stopped, laughed distractedly, and started again: "I've found what we've been seeking."

Johnny played the gentleman and sat back to hear her out. She'd been talking less than a minute when he lunged forward and grasped her wrists, cutting off both her circulation and her narrative. "Don't tell me their names," he said. "I shall guess. Major Evelyn Davies and Mme. Elizabeth Mort-Davies."

Nothing in their association, including accosting her on the street and threatening her with a knife, ever so astounded her in his presence. Her mouth formed an adorable crimson O and her unforgettable eyes widened to their full extent. He struck a mental photograph of the expression, and was loath to dispel it with an explanation; but theirs was a professional enterprise, with no place for egoism outside of costume. Through an oversight, Johnny and April had duplicated each other's effort, attending both the matinee and evening performances of *The Diplomat Deposes*. It was proof of the unity of their vision that both had recognized the object of their goal when it presented itself.

Ambuscaded at the stage door following the next day's matinee, the Major and the Madame were sufficiently motivated by the beauty and charm of their admirers to join them for supper. Once again, dessert—pears this time, pan-fried and drizzled with maple syrup shipped at fabulous expense from New England—worked its magic. The Major, who claimed service with Queen Victoria's horse guards before the Call drew him to the London stage, was hesitant in regard to the larceny, as his knowledge of law enforcement was based upon the compact efficiency of Scotland Yard, but by that time it was clear he was not the one who made the decisions in that union. Mme. Mort-Davies quizzed them closely concerning practical details. She'd been an acrobat and high-wire artist until age alone had directed her into spectacles less demanding physically, and she was far more interested in mechanics than risk. Accord was reached, and of morality no mention was made. Exchanging observations later in private, Johnny and April agreed that the Davieses' account of their years on the circuit had been edited to remove a veritable cross-country crime wave of petty proportions.

She lifted her glass. "To the Prairie Rose."

He shook his head. "That would be premature, and bad luck. We still need a second lead: a Tybalt. The prospect of Major Davies bounding about with a foil would provide comic relief where none is required, to say nothing of its effect upon the boards. We must appear to be legitimate."

"Oh, dear. More auditions."

"Take heart. Now that we're four, we each need attend half as many."

Fate spared them even that ordeal. The next morning Johnny, deeply regretting last night's overindulgence, stumbled out of bed in his nightshirt to answer the door and found himself facing a physical manifestation of his own fragile condition. The young man on the landing was a half inch shorter, disregarding his stoop, and underweight; sunlight seemed to shine through him as if he were made of bone china. His ears stuck out from his cropped head and a black ribbon dangled from his wire spectacles.

"Mr. Vermillion, my name is Cornelius Ragland. We've met."

"I think you're mistaken." Johnny was on his guard. This fellow in his shabby suit, holding a shabby hat before him in both hands, bore all the marks of an extortionist, with his guilty evidence stuffed inside the even shabbier leather portfolio pinned under his left arm. Perhaps he'd been betrayed before he'd even begun.

"I am Peter Argyle's private secretary. I showed you into his office some weeks ago."

Johnny was certain now of his suspicions. He did not remember the fellow, but Cornelius Ragland appeared easy to forget even when he was standing in front of one. Argyle had been the Prairie Rose's first reluctant investor; perhaps he'd left his transom open during their transaction, and here came his secretary to turn the tables. He did not represent Argyle. The banker had gotten off easy at five hundred dollars. He stood to lose far more by exposing their arrangement.

Abashed by Johnny's silence, the visitor stammered ahead. "I— I couldn't help but remember your card said you were with a theatrical company. I've been asking around for you ever since that day. Your address wasn't on the card."

He drew the portfolio from under his arm, dropping his hat in the process. There was some funny stage business during which he dropped one, then the other in trying to retrieve it. Johnny wondered if he ought to crack the fellow on the head with a water pitcher while he was bent and search his case. Perhaps it contained Argyle's canceled bank draught.

He was muzzy-headed, however, and did not act. Upright again, Ragland untied the portfolio and sorted through the mass of foolscap inside. "Here is *Sleepy Hollow,* and *The Count of Monte Cristo,* and two of Dickens', abridged of course. A full staging would consume several hours."

"*What* are *Sleepy Hollow* and *The Count of Monte Cristo*? What manner of game are you playing, Mr. Ragman?"

"Ragland." Red spots burned on the stranger's cheeks. Johnny guessed he was consumptive. "They're adaptations, Mr. Vermillion. Stage plays, based on great novels. I'm a playwright."

"I thought you were a secretary."

"That's temporary. I—I've heard that repertory players are always in need of material. I thought—perhaps—" He muttered something apologetic and turned to leave. The tips of his ears had turned as red as his cheeks. He'd mistaken stunned relief for rejection.

"One moment, Mr. Ragland."

The young man turned back swiftly, nearly losing his hold on his bundle of loose pages. He let his hat fall in order to grasp the case with both hands. Johnny's misery fled before an urge to laugh. Ragland amused him to the bone.

"We're a small troupe. We ask everyone to pull a deal more than his own weight. If—and I mean *if* according to Mr. Webster's definition of the word—if we decide to use your scribblings and employ you to scribble more, we will expect you to perform other duties as well."

"What would they entail?"

"Have you studied fencing?"

6

Cornelius Ragland tested the tensile strength of the Prairie Rose. April Clay was bemused by the naïve, eminently seductible young man who claimed Baltimore as his home, but whose infirmity had prevented him from serving with the Southern Confederacy. Major Davies, who distrusted all things French, including their support of the South, thought him a bad risk. Mme. Mort-Davies, a trouper since her birth in the Gold Ribbon Theater in Atlantic City, saw potential in his guilelessness, but wondered if he had the stamina to withstand a prolonged tour. Johnny Vermillion brushed aside all objections.

"This conversation is pointless," he said. "I've told him he's hired."

"We don't even know if he can act," said April.

"I don't know if *you* can, dear. You've all expressed your opinions as artists of the stage, which is an attitude I encourage. However, you've overlooked young Mr. Ragland's principal value to our company of players."

"His writing talent?" The Major blew out his moustaches. "A monkey can scribble."

"*The Diplomat Deposes* is evidence of that. I'm not referring to his literary skill."

"Certainly not his presence," said Mme. Mort-Davies. "He is barely there."

"That can be manufactured. But you're right; it isn't that either."

"What, then?" demanded April.

"He and I are roughly the same height."

This announcement was met with the silence of self-recrimination. With proper coaching, particularly as to posture—identical costumes, and an expert application of makeup, Johnny and Cornelius could stand in for each other onstage while the man the audience thought it was watching stole away to perform elsewhere. In the flurry of rehearsals and arrangements, the troupe leader alone had remained on mission.

"Mind he doesn't turn sideways," grumped the Major. "He'll vanish into the backdrop."

They engaged the tumbledown Empress Theater for their debut. It was located near the levee—a factor of prime importance—and the rental fee agreed with their budget. The purchase of duplicate costumes, and of material for the versatile Mme. Mort-Davies to add certain features to those costumes that could not be duplicated, had strained their resources, to say nothing of the cost of hand properties. These included foils, a brace of duelling pistols, and a Colt revolver large enough to impress patrons in the back row and cashiers at close range. The costumes were Elizabethan. The Major, a superstitious old thespian, held that no successful season had ever begun without a Shakesperean comedy; he would not budge from the position, and so Cornelius Ragland's original scripts were laid aside in favor of selections from *Twelfth Night,* scaled down to the size of the company. April squealed in delight. She'd seen Ada Rehan on tour in the role of Viola and since then had worshipped at her shrine.

"You'll have more than her measure your first time out," Johnny said. "I'll warrant Rehan never played Maria in the same production. You'll make a fetching sailor as well."

He assigned the Major to the role of Sir Toby Belch, with a walk-on as a priest. The Madame—Lizzie, as Johnny made bold to address her—fitted Shakespeare's description of Oliva quite nicely, and would wear whiskers as Viola's sea-captain friend. Cornelius, who had no stage experience, was confined to the part of young Sebastian, which would be challenge enough; although he would double for Johnny as Orsino for one brief scene.

"And who will you play other than Orsino?" April asked.

"So far as the printed programme is concerned, I shall appear in a variety of undemanding roles apart from the lead, but the programme is a fraud. I shall perform only two."

She asked what was the other. He smiled.

"You won't find him in the dramatis personae."

Rehearsals were intense, and twofold: This troupe must not only block out movements and commit the Bard's lines to memory, but also practice switching costumes backstage. Many a long night was spent in a swirl of flying fabric until, within seconds, countess became captain, lady fell to maid, knight ordained himself priest, Viola's brother became her lover. This last transformation was performed with the most ease, as they had managed to procure duplicate costumes for Orsino and Sebastian, and the pair had only to exchange sashes to complete the substitution. With the plume of Johnny's hat covering half of Cornelius' face, and with his back turned toward the audience for most of the scene, the illusion was satisfactory. Madame Lizzie, a gifted scold, berated the former secretary to stand straight and dissemble his stoop. She was also a talented seamstress, and with scissors and string had reengineered all the one-of-a-kind costumes so that they came off with a twitch and refastened in a twinkling.

Bald head streaming, the Major groped in vain for a handkerchief. He'd forgotten he was dressed as a priest and that the cassock had no pockets. "At this point, we could empty five safes during the first performance."

"We'll start with one, during the last," Johnny said. "We're virgins, don't forget."

Twelfth Night—An Abridgment opened at the Empress the second week of October 1873, to uninspired reviews from a press that had seen Henry Irving in a full-scale production of the same play. Audiences trickled in, as did water; the sky wept through all six performances, the roof leaked, and at times it seemed more seats were occupied by buckets than people. None of the city papers mentioned the show's closing, at the end of the Monday matinee. They needed the space to report the daring daylight robbery of the steamboat *Czarina Catherine* by a lone bandit that afternoon. The vessel had docked at St. Louis to take on fuel and passengers, one of whom, described as a tall man in a long coat with the collar turned up and the brim of his hat turned down, produced a large revolver in the purser's cabin and demanded the contents of the safe. The purser, alone at the time, complied, and the mysterious stranger left carrying six thousand dollars in a satchel, an amount deposited for the most part by professional gamblers hoping to squeeze one more profitable season out of a mode of transportation made obsolete by the railroads.

The owner of the Empress, more tidy in his dress and grooming than in his finances, clucked over the Prairie Rose receipts, a disappointing four hundred dollars and change. "You didn't even make back your investment."

Johnny was sanguine. "St. Louisans are overentertained and jaded. I expect a warmer welcome out West, where diversions such as ours are rare. And the weather will be kinder in the dryer reaches."

"People starve to death on the plains."

"You underestimate our little party. We intend to develop a system for living off the land."

You've seen it before: a succession of stoked boilers streaking toward the screen, intercut with close-ups of charging wheels and plunging drive rods. On the soundtrack, short cello strokes imitate the chomping of pistons and steam whistles blast from the brass. Depot signs loom at us from the far perspective: KANSAS CITY; OMAHA; SIOUX FALLS; CHEYENNE; SALT LAKE CITY. Quaint old-fashioned broadsheets spin and stop long enough to display headlines: BOLD ROBBERY OF THE FARMERS TRUST (*Kansas City Times*); LONE BANDIT HOLDS UP STOCK SHOW (*Omaha Herald*); WELLS, FARGO OFFICE RAIDED (*Sioux Falls Journal*); CATTLEMAN'S BANK STRUCK BY DESPERADO (*Cheyenne Leader*); MORMONS FORM VIGILANCE GROUP FOLLOWING OVERLAND OUTRAGE (*Deseret News*). Solitary figures in big hats and bandannas appear and dissolve, gesticulating with a revolver (can there be just one?). They are tall and short, comically fat and thin as water, substantial and slight. We pan past actors in elaborate costumes making faces, fencing, and soliloquizing, across a row of frightened clerks and cashiers raising their hands, around an auditorium filled with people clapping hands, dissolve to a pair of hands scooping piles of money into gunnysacks and satchels. Stacks of banknotes and gold coins grow before our eyes. Bottles of champagne foam over in the dressing room of some frontier theater—steer horns hung among the generic collage of playbills and atomizers—where our little band has gathered to commemorate the success of their inaugural tour. And out.

We leave them, reluctantly, for another establishing shot of Chicago. This time, the stockyards and slaughterhouses are in place, and a great many more buildings constructed of brick, so we'll have no more nonsense about great fires. We dolly in toward an imposing edifice of gray stone and a brass plate mounted at eye level, engraved with the omniscient eye of the Ancient and Honorable Fraternity of Free and Accepted Masons and this legend:

PINKERTON NATIONAL DETECTIVE AGENCY
"We Never Sleep"

Well, you knew it had to make its appearance sometime.

The window we creep through on this occasion belongs to a small, sparsely furnished office and a man seated behind a desk, industriously clipping an L-shaped hole out of a newspaper with a pair of shears. He places the cutting on a stack to his right, stuffs the rest of the newspaper into a wire wastebasket packed already to bulging, and slides another newspaper off the stack to his left. The only decoration in the room is a portrait, overpoweringly large in a massive gilt frame, of a resolute face with a Quaker beard on a sloping body buttoned tightly into a three-piece suit, glaring over the man's shoulder from the wall behind the desk. We shall meet him in the flesh presently.

The man doing the clipping is named Philip Rittenhouse, and he is not popular at Pinkerton headquarters. Numerous times he has made use of his authority to cancel leaves of absence upon short notice, and his humor is of that sarcastic bent that rarely endears. Moreover, he is an ugly man. Absolutely clean-shaven, including his head, he has deep hollows in his temples that throw his brow into prominent relief, pale and gleaming like polished bone. His nose has a predatory hook ending in a barb, and although his teeth are quite good, he bares them only on one side when he smiles, like a dog snarling over its dish. Thick lids sheath his eyes; it is because of these that a departing operative referred to him as "Reptile house." Those who stayed behind have shortened it to "the Reptile."

He has, in fact, only one admirer in all the Pinkerton National Detective Agency, and that is Allan Pinkerton himself, the subject of the portrait on Rittenhouse's wall. For the Reptile is an uncommonly fine detective. Seldom leaving his office, working almost exclusively by wire and through the post, moving his field agents about like pieces on a board, he has broken a coal miners' strike in Pennsylvania and brought to justice sixteen fugitives whose names marred the lead columns of newspapers throughout the United States and its territories for months. This in itself might have attracted the old man's attention, but not necessarily his affection. *That,* Rittenhouse has secured by refusing to communicate with the press when a major case is closed, referring all requests for interviews to Mr. Pinkerton or one of his sons. The challenge in the agency is to rise to a level approaching genius without casting a shadow across the face of its legendary founder, and the bald man in the little office has met it to the degree that if one of Mr. Pinkerton's male offspring developed a dislike for him and demanded his father to choose between them, Rittenhouse himself would not place a wager upon the decision.

He has contributed significantly to the stack of cuttings, diminished substantially the pile of unmutilated newspapers, and altered the shape of his wastebasket beyond all hope of restoration, when the patriarch of the Pinkerton clan, somewhat grayer than his painted image but if anything more resolute in appearance, opens Rittenhouse's door and steps inside. He never knocks, and none of the doors in the building contains a lock to bar him from entering its remotest corner.

Pinkerton observes Rittenhouse's project. "I'd wondered about that item in your budget: subscr-riptions." If anything, the old man's Glasgow burr has increased in prominence during his three decades in America.

The Reptile's manner is familiar, but respectful. "You mustn't be a Scotchman in this. They whisper in my ear from a thousand miles away, and seldom raise their rates. Unlike paid informers."

"Rest your eyes from the small print a moment and tell me what you think of this." Pinkerton draws a square of yellow flimsy from his watch pocket and places it between the stacks on the desk.

Rittenhouse does not pick up the folded telegram. A man with inexhaustible patience for details, he has none for redundancies. He asks what's in it.

"It's from Mr. Hume, of Wells, Fargo, and Company. He wants us to look into a robbery that took place at a freight office in Dakota Territory last month. The bandit made off with thirteen thousand in gold." He waits, but no response is forthcoming. "That's bandit, not bandits. There seems to have been a r-rash of this lone wolf sort of thing out that direction."

"Hume is their chief of detectives. Good man. Why does he need our help?"

"His hands are full with gangs: the James-Youngers and the Reno brothers and this fellow Brixton and his band. Hume's people are spread thin. That leaves a gr-reat many holes for a one-man crime wave to slip through."

"Shall I close them?"

"Not your usual way, Philip. Stagecoaches are on their way out. This agency's personnel is committed to the railroads and banks, so there will be none of this broadcasting agents about like seeds just to close one case. One man is responsible, and one man may ferret him out where an army may not. I want you to go to Sioux Falls and handle it personally."

"Very well."

Pinkerton's thatched brows twitch upward. "I thought you might offer argument. You've been a fixture here since before they laid in the gas."

"That's just it. I haven't had a holiday in three years. That's unhealthy."

"This is no holiday. Field work is exhausting, to say nothing of dangerous. It is also deadly boring; interviews with uncertain witnesses, dead ends, waiting hours for suspects who never appear. You must have the constitution for it."

"I've been exhausted and bored right here. A little danger sounds to me a nice tramp. I'll make arrangements immediately."

"Draw what you need from Dorchester downstairs. I want reports by the week and a thorough accounting first of ever-ry month. Stay in boardinghouses wherever possible. I fail to see why a highwayman should take his chances with the Wrath of Pinkerton, when running a hotel allows him to do the same thing with impunity."

"Shall I draw a bedroll as well, and sleep out under the stars each night?"

But Rittenhouse's superior is impervious to his sting. "Don't forget to requisition a pistol, though I caution you not to use it. Going into the field does not make you a field man. When you have your evidence and a location, turn them over to the local authorities for apprehension. Mind they give credit to the agency."

Following the old man's departure, the Reptile thinks for a moment about underwear and Pullmans, then makes inventory of the cuttings he's taken. They are from newspapers in St. Louis, Kansas City, the *Tannery Blanket,* Omaha, Sioux Falls, Cheyenne, and Salt Lake City; the week-old copy of the *Deseret News* arrived only that morning. He skims through the dense paragraphs once more, noting names, dates, and other salient material on a writing block in his own encryption, then drums the scraps together and slips them into a pasteboard folder upon which is displayed the Pinkerton Eye and a notation in his own tidy hand: *Solitary Thief.*

From those same publications, he's cut also dramatic reviews calling attention to a series of entertainments presented by a troupe of traveling actors skilled in the special requirements of a small company saddled with large casts of characters. These, too, he reads again, makes notes, and places the cuttings in a second folder labeled *Prairie Rose.*

Closing the cover, he lifts his lip on one side to show his teeth. "One man." He slides the two folders inside a leather briefcase that has seen all its wear so far traveling back and forth between that room and his cold-water flat on South Clark.

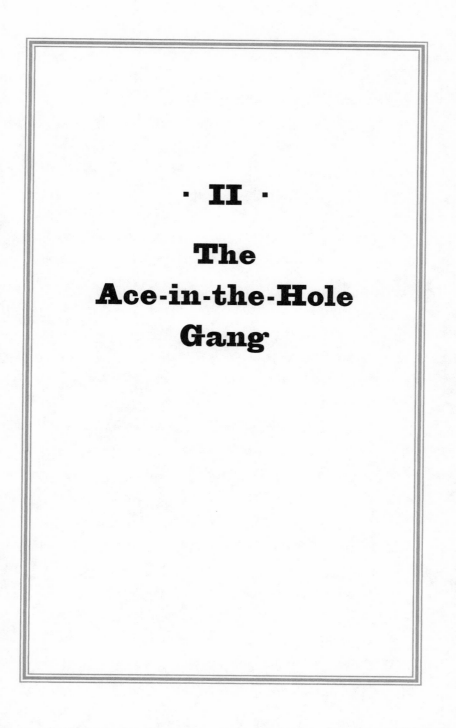

· II ·

The
Ace-in-the-Hole
Gang

7

Before we forget Marshal Fletcher of Tannery, wise beyond his weight, let us move in tight on the bulletin board in his office and linger for a moment upon one of the prognathous, razor-challenged faces posted there. It's a peculiarly savage likeness of a type once epidemic on the covers of *Action Western* and *Flaming Lariat*: jaw sheared off square at the base, boot-scraper beard, eyes like dynamiter's drill holes in granite. The name beneath the pen-and-ink sketch is Black Jack Brixton, and it should come as no surprise that he's wanted dead or alive. His activities include assault, armed robbery, murder, and burning entire towns to the ground.

Dissolve to a real face, strikingly identical, in glorious Technicolor on a screen thirty meters wide: Brixton in the flesh, under a gray Stetson stained black with sweat, a blue bandanna creating a hammock for his aggressive Adam's apple. His expression is intense. He is watching something we are not privileged to see until we cut directly to the explosion.

In the enormous ball of smoke and fire and dirt, we pick out flying sections of steel rail and shattered oak ties, uprooted trees, and what may be a human body, flung high and flailing its limbs like a piece of shredded licorice before it disappears under a heap of earth and sawdust and pieces of sets left over from previous productions.

As things clear, we see a locomotive hurtling toward the destruction. The engineer's face, leaning out of the cab, pulls tense with shock. A sooty fist hauls back on the brake lever. The steel wheels shriek, spraying sparks. The cowcatcher grinds to a halt inches short of the bent and twisted ends of the rails. Steam whooshes out in a sigh of relief.

"Yahoo!" cries Brixton, smacking his horse on the rump with the ends of his reins and firing his six-gun into the air for added incentive. The animal bolts, leading the charge down the hill.

"Yahoo!" cry his subordinates, galloping out of the dense stand of trees on the other side of the tracks. More bullets fly.

As several men board the train to pacify the paying customers, the rest take charge of the engineer, his fireman, and the fat conductor. They are herded out onto trackside and Brixton threatens at the top of his voice to blow their heads off if the guards in the mail car fail to open the door by the count of five. On "four," hammers click. The door slides open then and the guards emerge with hands high. Foolishly, one lunges for the revolver in his holster. Brixton shoots from the hip. The guard snatches at his abdomen, drops his weapon, and tumbles to the cinderbed.

A bundle of dynamite makes its appearance. A match flares; the fuse is ignited. The spark travels ten feet and the door flies off a black iron safe embossed with a gold eagle. Sacks of coins, bars of bullion, and bales of banknotes—big, square, elaborately engraved certificates, much more impressive-looking than our modern bills—vanish into canvas bags and saddle pouches. More cheers and shooting as the horsemen clatter away.

These are a few minutes in a day in the life of the Ace-in-the-Hole Gang, infamous in newspapers in both the East and West and in a flood of cheap novels printed in Chicago and New York City. Somewhere in a cattle camp or saloon or velvet parlor with a piano, an uncertain baritone is singing its ballad to a melody plagiarized from "Blood on the Saddle."

Like so many others of his day, Jack Brixton's story began in Missouri, where he rode with the Bushwhackers, holding up Union trains, blowing windows out of banks filled with Yankee gold, taking target practice on Jayhawkers, and generally giving civil war a bad name. Witnesses say he left that crew because he considered Bloody Bill Anderson too lenient.

Accounts of how he spent the years between the end of the conflict and the spring of 1874, when his trail crossed with Johnny Vermillion's, are mostly hearsay. He's said to have rustled cattle in Texas, hunted Apache scalps in Arizona, shot a couple of dozen Mexicans south of the Rio Grande, and introduced the sport of lynching to Wyoming Territory. It was about the time the Wyoming story got around that people started calling him Black Jack.

It was a name no one called him to his face. Transients and newcomers to the gang found that out right away, at the butt of his Smith & Wesson .44 American, a weapon endorsed also by Jesse James and Wyatt Earp for use as both a firearm and a bludgeon. Brixton had a superstitious horror of nicknames. Frank "Hole Card" Handy, the gang's original leader and also the inspiration for its name, had been so called because of the Butterfield derringer he carried for emergency use in a special holster sewn inside the crotch of his trousers. Drawing it one night during a dispute over a hand of poker, he shot off the end of his penis and bled to death before he could be brought to a doctor. His successor, Apache Jim Weathersill, who was no part Indian but had been rechristened to avoid confusion with the better-known Jim Weathersill of the Turkey Creek Outfit, took a double load of buckshot in the belly from a pimp who'd mistaken him for the original Jim, and Redleg Johnson, the most athletic of the Ace-in-the-Hole boys, miscounted his coaches while loping along the top of the Katy Flyer looking for the mail car and ran off the end of the caboose to a broken neck. Brixton had come to the conclusion that living up to one's professional name involved ceasing to live at all. He considered it bad luck to pass one of his wanted posters without slowing down to obliterate the "Black" with a fusillade of lead.

In addition to his daring, ruthlessness, and bad temper, Black Jack Brixton was notorious for his escapes from the law. He'd been captured in Missouri by McCulloch's cavalry, by the sheriffs of several counties in Kansas and Colorado, by a succession of town marshals (which he didn't count), and by a deputy United States marshal in the Indian Nations, and had wriggled free every time, a phenomenon he credited to his talent for dislocating both wrists. No matter how tight the manacles, he had only to slip his bones out of joint to slide them over his hands and off. He'd employed this trick so many times his wrists had a habit of slipping out on their own, often at inopportune moments, as when his gun arm gave out under the weight of his big American in a bank in Grand Junction and he shot Mysterious Bob Craidlaw, his best man, in the foot. After that, he'd acquired a pair of Mexican leather cuffs with brass studs and buckled them on tight before going to work; Mysterious Bob acquired a permanent limp.

Bob kept his own counsel to the extent that no one in the bank apart from Brixton and himself knew he'd been shot until the gang reunited in a line shack twenty miles from the scene of the robbery, when he pulled off his boot and poured out a pint of blood. The suddenness of the report, in fact, had startled Tom Riddle into shooting a cashier, which raised the reward for his capture to fifteen hundred dollars.

There was nothing secretive in Mysterious Bob's past. Much of it was public record, and his list of criminal accomplishments filled a paragraph in his circular going back to age twelve. He just never talked about himself. Although he'd spent three years with Brixton in the service of Missouri guerrillas—an opinionated group, who punctuated their arguments with gunfire—none of the men who slept and ate and rode with him had ever been able to determine just where he stood regarding slavery and states' rights. Arch Clements, his immediate superior, thought he was a mute. When Brixton, who knew otherwise, asked Bob point blank why he never set Clements straight, the quiet man let a full minute pass, then said, "I reckon he didn't ask." He made his best remarks with his Winchester, and like his tongue he never used it until he was certain of the effect. He never missed.

Tom Riddle did enough talking for them both, and for that matter all the rest of the crew. Short and compact where Bob was tall and lanky, he'd once spent most of a week stuck in a badger tunnel in California, where he'd been sent by his prospecting partners, larger men all, to look for color. He'd survived on roots and earthworms, talked to himself the whole time to keep from going loco, and acquired a taste for his own conversation, if not for earthworms and roots, which he frequently and at length compared to the meals they were forced to eat on the trail. He also avoided going into vaults and other tight places. Tom was a good man with dynamite, and a little deaf from the explosions; his speech was loud as well as incessant. "Shut up, Tom," was a phrase repeated wherever the group bedded down, usually in chorus.

In enterprises of this nature, there is in all likelihood a man called Breed, who demonstrates the less fortunate traits of his white and Indian ancestors. They wear their hair unfettered to their shoulders, resist hats, and clothe themselves in fringed leather vests and striped cavalry trousers stripped from the carcass of some unlucky trooper like the skin of a slain animal. Ace-in-the-Hole's Breed spent his leisure hours curing the ears he'd sliced off bartenders who refused to serve him whiskey and stringing them on the buckskin thong he wore around his neck during robberies, which had a dampening effect upon individual heroism. He had *Mother* tattooed in a heart on his right bicep and *Father* encircled by serpents on his left, and prized his big Bowie knife above all other weapons. Brixton, who had balked at Bloody Bill's "spare the women and children" policy, found Breed's company distinctly unpleasant.

The Kettleman brothers, Ed and Charlie, had fled Texas one step ahead of the Rangers, who sought them for running guns to the Comanches, and of the Comanches themselves, who were eager to talk to them about the quality of their merchandise. They'd commandeered a wagonload of Springfield rifles with rusted actions and broken firing pins on its way from Fort Richardson to the Fort Worth scrap yards and traded them for a total of four thousand dollars in buffalo robes. They were businessmen who always got the best price for bonds, bullion, and other items that could not immediately be converted into cash, much of which they won back off their companions at poker. In action, they worked in perfect union, as if they shared one brain, and also at the table, where each had a sixth sense for what cards his brother held in his hand. They were the least popular members of the gang and the most indispensable. Identical twins, slack-jawed and skinny as rails, they looked in life very much as they did in a picture the Pinkertons took of them in 1875, propped on a barn door with seventeen mortal wounds between them.

These five formed the unchanging center of Black Jack Brixton's band of desperadoes; ten thousand dollars on the hoof to the bounty hunter foolhardy enough to dream of capturing them. The authorities and outraged commercial interests responsible for this reward were parsimonious, as always. Acting separately and in concert, the wanted men had looted a quarter of a million from legitimate concerns and circulated it back into the economy by way of saloons, women of casual character, and the army of camp followers who supplied them with arms, ammunition, horses, and shelter. Counting temporary help and onetime alliances with other gangs, a million dollars had passed through the hands of between twenty and thirty individuals associated with Ace-in-the-Hole. It was never at a loss for recruits, because in the bleak aftermath of the Panic of 1873, banditry was the fastest-growing cottage industry in America. Bicycle sales placed a distant second.

The bold daylight robbery of the Chicago, Rock Island & Pacific Railroad near Council Bluffs, Iowa, which we have witnessed, removed sixteen thousand dollars from the hands of its rightful owners, the robber barons of New York City and San Francisco. When word reached civilization, the sheriff of Pottawattamie County—rock-ribbed and sunburned, dumb as salt pork—assembled a posse of the usual hotheads who convened in the Boar's Neck Saloon to burp up pickled eggs and damn the Republican administration. They mounted up, milled around the town square making speeches and terrifying the horses, and rode out, whooping and waving torches and shooting up private property.

By the time they reached the stranded train, Black Jack Brixton and his companions had been gone for hours. The sheriff's men followed their tracks half the night, stopping briefly to set fire to barns and smokehouses along the way, and wound up back at the train; whereupon they straggled back to town and wired the Pinkerton office in St. Louis.

Ace-in-the-Hole, meanwhile, had scattered like so many cards.

Anticipating a hot reception to so successful a raid, they sought bolt-holes as far south as Louisiana and as far west as California. The Pinkertons, who lost no time in identifying the train robbers, were just as quick to declare the trail cold, and counseled waiting until Brixton's men struck again. The board of directors of the Chicago, Rock Island & Pacific howled at the delay, and bumped the reward up a hundred dollars per man.

Money won in the course of a few minutes' work, however intense and fraught with peril, spends quickly in sinful Barbary and the deadfalls of New Orleans. Fifteen men had taken part in the raid, and sixteen thousand divided so many ways melts like grease in a skillet. As winter broke up beneath the heavy rains of early spring, six men in shining slickers waded their horses through the muddy streets of Denver and tied them to the rail in front of Nell Dugan's Wood Palace. Inside, Brixton, Mysterious Bob, Tom Riddle, Breed, and the Kettlemans took their pleasure out of what funds they had left and blocked out a plan to rob the Overland office in Salt Lake City.

That same day, the Prairie Rose Repertory Company commenced rehearsals of *The Legend of Sleepy Hollow* at the Salt Lake Theater, directly across the street from the Overland.

8

Salt Lakers who happened to be looking out across the flats that morning saw a half dozen men on horseback, small as clothes-pegs and shimmering through ribbons of heat; a few swore they heard ghostly flute music, but that was probably just the Denver & Rio Grande blowing its whistle.

By noon the riders appeared no closer. Then suddenly they had passed Temple Square and were clattering down Main Street, using their reins as quirts and sending Mormons and Gentiles alike scrambling for the safety of the boardwalks. Elder Sterne, who'd been expecting revenge for Mountain Meadows for twenty years, dove into Browning's gun shop and had to be subdued by three employees to prevent him from running back out with a Whitney double-barrel.

They saved his life. Rounding a corner onto State Street, the riders surprised a dog into lunging at their horses' legs and pumped eleven bullets into it in a group no larger than a man's spread hand.

Daniel Oberlin, who managed the Holladay Overland Mail & Express Company office across the street from the theater, thought at first the men in dusters with bandannas over their faces were fellow members of the Zion Club come to play a trick on him; nobody in the history of the company had been robbed twice in twenty-four hours, and it was just the kind of low humor he expected from that society. He changed his mind when the man with the words, a big fellow with eyes as empty as the safe, backed him to the wall behind the counter and stuck the muzzle of his big revolver against the bridge of Oberlin's nose.

"Open the safe or I'll open your skull."

Oberlin opened the safe.

"Where the hell's the money?"

"I gave it to a fat fellow last night. He had a gun as big as yours."

"Kill the son of a bitch." This in a hissing tone from one of the other gunmen, who wore his black hair long like an Indian.

"I swear it's true! All he left was the petty cash in the box."

"Hand it over."

He gave the man the tin box he kept on the shelf beneath the counter. It contained forty-five dollars and seventeen cents.

On the way out of town, the Ace-in-the-Hole Gang registered its disappointment by shooting out windows in several establishments, including the temple, where city commissioners and church elders were meeting to discuss forming a citizens' vigilance committee to deal with outrages such as the freight office robbery the evening before. (The motion passed unanimously after the dignitaries crawled out from under the table.) Mysterious Bob Craidlaw entered the lobby of the Deseret Hotel without bothering to dismount and removed six hundred dollars from the safe at the point of his Winchester, and one of the Kettlemans separated an employee of the Salt Lake Theater from his right index finger as he was taking down a bill advertising last night's performance by the Prairie Rose Repertory Company. Breed had to be restrained from going back and slicing off Daniel Oberlin's ears.

They'd left provisions and fresh horses at a disused Butterfield stage stop ten miles east of town, where they stopped to divide their small gain.

"I got more'n this out of that badger hole in Sacramento," said Tom Riddle, fingering his shallow stack of banknotes.

Breed said, "I still want the ears off that son of a bitch. I bet he stole it himself when he heard us coming."

"He'd of said it was a dozen men," Brixton said. "You don't make up one fat man with a pistol in your face."

"It wasn't the James boys." Ed and Charlie Kettleman spoke in unison. Ed, older by two minutes, continued when his brother fell silent. "This is a piece off their range."

"The Renos neither," Riddle said. "They always work in a bunch."

"Turkey Creek," suggested Breed.

Brixton shook his head. "They always leave a dead man behind. That's how you know it's Turkey Creek."

Riddle said, "We sure as hell left a dead man behind at Council Bluffs."

"He committed suicide." Brixton threw a fistful of pennies against the wall, knocking a piece out of the adobe. "When I find out who the fat bastard is, I'll skin him and use his belly to carry away the cash."

"I bet he's local," Riddle said. "It costs them Mormons plenty to take care of all them wives. What you figure makes a man want more than one?"

"Maybe he done it to get out of the house." Once again, the Kettlemans spoke together, and fell to wrestling playfully. Breed put an end to it by sinking his Bowie up to its hilt in the rotten wood of the tabletop.

"One of us ought to go back into town and poke around."

Five pairs of alkali-reddened eyes swiveled toward Mysterious Bob. They were the first words he'd spoken since Denver.

"It's still all in one place," he said. "One man's easier to stick up than a whole freight company."

Nearing the middle of a spartan but comfortable bachelor's life, spent almost entirely within a brief streetcar ride of the house where he was born (which, like him, had stood through the fire among others that had not), Philip Rittenhouse discovered to his surprise that he quite liked traveling.

It posed its challenges. In the weeks since Allan Pinkerton had assigned him to investigate the robbery of the Wells, Fargo office in Sioux Falls, the bald man with the carrion-bird profile had put out fires in his clothes ignited by sparks from a dozen locomotives, cracked a tooth jouncing over the Bozeman Trail in a succession of stagecoaches (none of them the fabled Concord "Rocking Horse of the Plains"), been bitten by species of bedbugs unknown east of the Mississippi, and lost a valise containing his best suit to a thief in the train station in St. Louis. He was peeling from sunburn, shivering with the ague, and a suspicious fungus had begun to grow between the second and third toes of his right foot. A woman uglier than he, in a dirty satin dress, had called him "Phizzle-Face" when he'd declined her advances on the street in Kansas City, and an attack of food poisoning had forced him to crouch over a chamber pot all through the night he'd spent in Omaha. It was a splendid adventure. He intended to ask the old man to assign him more fieldwork once he'd lain this case to rest.

He'd been more bored in Chicago than he'd let on, even to himself. For years, those brief few moments of satisfaction he'd experienced upon the successful closing of an investigation had more than compensated for the hours, days, and weeks spent at his desk, clipping items out of newspapers, reading reports and telegrams, drafting responses, and maintaining stoic patience in the presence of minds slower by far than his own—turtle-brains, to be blunt; William Pinkerton, Allan's second son, was particularly chronic in this regard—but of late, as he'd come to realize that half his span was behind him, the prospect of merely repeating himself throughout the second half depressed him deeply. For the first time, he understood the motives of the men he'd brought to justice who had thrown over decades of good behavior for the lure of a dollar unstained by the sweat of honest labor. It amused him to consider that he, who turned down such harmless temptations as a free meal for his part in exposing a thieving restaurant employee, might have turned highwayman but for this opportunity.

There'd been no danger of that; he didn't even stray so far as to enter a personal expenditure of a nickel into the account-book he kept for the agency. But he entertained himself with the conviction that he'd have made a criminal of the first rank. In order to apprehend one, it was important to understand his mental processes, and in effect to think more like a thief than a thief-taker. In this he had a decade of experience. Certainly, that approach had proven most useful during his interviews thus far in his journey.

Being of an honest temperament, Rittenhouse would most likely have become a senior file clerk in some business concern but for the chance encounter that had brought him to the attention of the nation's foremost detective. He never read a newspaper without a pen and a pair of shears close to hand, to underscore and remove items of interest for closer study, and the pigeonholes in his desk in Chicago were packed with lists he'd compiled of mundane details connected with larcenous events, compiled from reporter's accounts and replies to telegrams he'd sent requesting further information: calibers of firearms, the bandits' dress and idiosyncracies of speech and behavior, the nature of the containers in which spoils were carried away; there was no end to his patience with regard to such minutia, and he had a mesmerist's skill for gleaning data from witnesses who insisted at first that they'd been too preoccupied by personal danger to notice whether the robbers were right- or left-handed or what they wore on their feet. Nothing was without interest, and no observation too unimportant to record.

He applied this same thoroughness to his daily reading of out-of-town newspapers. While other agents satisfied themselves with a cursory examination of the criminal columns, Rittenhouse made it a point to scan the inside pages containing local advertisements, notices, and items of human interest. When the announcement of a visit by a group of itinerant actors calling itself the Prairie Rose Repertory Company appeared in issues of both the *Kansas City Times* and the *Omaha Herald* reporting the robbery by a lone bandit of first the Farmers Trust Bank and then a livestock auction, he was alerted; when he learned that the Prairie Rose players had been present also at the time the Wells, Fargo office was struck (again by a man acting alone), he was committed. A close study of papers from Cheyenne, Wyoming, and Tannery, Nebraska, settled the question as far as Rittenhouse was concerned.

He was encouraged rather than put off by the variant descriptions of the robber involved in each outrage. Here he was tall and well-built, there thin and stoop-shouldered; elsewhere, he left the impression of an adolescent boy. He knew a little something about repertory players and their skill at playing one another's roles upon short notice, and from the more detailed reviews of the company's performances he was satisfied that the cast fulfilled all the body types mentioned in the criminal accounts, to wit:

> In the role of young Master Pip in Mr. Ragland's ingenious abbreviation of *Great Expectations,* Miss April Clay engagingly and convincingly reverses the Elizabethan conceit for placing young male actors in the guise of women. Had your correspondent not spoken with the lady in costume shortly before the curtain went up on last night's performance, he would have invoked Holy Scripture to maintain that the company had sneaked a boy into the cast, and unwittingly committed blasphemy.

So read the notice in the same number of the *Cheyenne Leader* that had reported the robbery of the Cattleman's Bank the previous evening. Rittenhouse wasn't put off by the robber's description, tall and rough-voiced. It would have been begging the question to present Miss Clay as a boy in both places. The company was bold, but not incautious.

Rittenhouse shared his certainty with no one, not even the old man. Pinkerton responded to his wire reports with querulous telegrams, demanding to know what in thunder he was doing wasting fares and accommodations visiting such flea specks on the map as Tannery, when his orders were clearly to begin his investigation in

Sioux Falls. The fledgling field agent replied that all would be explained in the fullness of time, knowing the tightfisted old Scot would bite through his own lip before he'd incur the expense of withdrawing him and replacing him with a more easily intimidated subordinate. However, he knew also the boundaries of Pinkerton's patience, and conducted his business posthaste, seldom staying in one place overnight before moving on to the next location.

Marshal Fletcher of Tannery, Nebraska, was a man after his heart. An unprepossessing figure, fat and lethargic, and manifestly out of favor with the town council, which allowed him to remain in office only until an adequate replacement could be appointed, he impressed Rittenhouse with how quickly he'd acted to investigate the Prairie Rose the night the Planter State Bank was robbed. Although authorities in some of the other towns had taken the same course, none had done so with such alacrity, and still others had ignored the company entirely, choosing instead the standard action of assembling a posse of amateurs to go haring all over the countryside looking for incriminating tracks among the scores leading into and out of the city limits. Moreover, Fletcher remained confident about the propriety of his decision, even as he was at a loss to explain why a thorough search of the Prairie Rose's traps and possessions failed to turn up so much as a silver dollar that couldn't be accounted for. Asked for an inventory of what had been found, he produced a sheet from his desk, transposed in his own hand from notes taken by the deputies who'd conducted the search.

"I won't trouble you to return it," said the marshal. "I won't need it clerking at Pardon's store."

Rittenhouse thanked him, and rose to leave. At the door, he turned back and retraced his steps to give Fletcher his card.

"I can't promise anything," he said. "Mr. Pinkerton prefers his men fit."

"I expect Stella Pardon'll work some of the tallow off me." Fletcher stretched an arm and tucked the card into the corner of the bulletin board next to the picture of Black Jack Brixton.

The detective reread the list frequently, riding in day coaches, hanging onto straps aboard the Butterfield, and resting his sore muscles on lumpy boardinghouse mattresses. None of the inventories he procured elsewhere was as exhaustive; Kansas City's was oral and vague, and in Cheyenne and Sioux Falls the actors had not even been questioned, let alone submitted to a search. Instinctively, he felt Fletcher's list contained the answer to the mystery that troubled him, keeping him awake even though he'd become inured to the bedbugs' torment and spoiling whatever appetite he'd developed for watery dumplings and chunks of undercooked chicken floating in curdled gravy. His quest for the solution wore the paper to pieces and continued to elude him long after he'd committed every item to memory: four large trunks; one army dispatch case; two train cases; six satchels, various sizes; one pr. duelling pistols; one Colt's revolver, .45 caliber; four fence foils; one bicycle; many, many items of clothing, each detailed within the limits of a frontier lawman's knowledge of such things; and etcetera.

Any one of the satchels could have been used to carry away the money from those robberies where satchels were reported. The company seemed to prefer oilcloth sacks, but there was no mention of one on Fletcher's list. Even if there had been, it didn't explain just how they'd gotten the notes and gold and silver out of town. Whatever plan they used, it would be in place as well in the communities where they hadn't been searched; they could never be sure they wouldn't, and this was one gang that took no unnecessary

chances. They might have buried it, but that would mean returning to the scenes of all their robberies, braving the very risk they'd
taken careful steps to avoid the first time. This wasn't a bunch of
guerrillas, shooting up the town and hollering and riding hell-for-
leather into open country, saddle pouches stuffed with cash. The
means to retrieve the spoils had to be as clever as the means they'd
used to acquire them in the first place. For the first time in his career, Philip Rittenhouse was—well, *baffled*, as the sensational press
often said of the police back East. It was an uncomfortable feeling,
and of late he'd become enough of a connoisseur to assign it a rare
vintage.

Pondering the problem again after his interview with the Wells,
Fargo manager in Sioux Falls, he stopped to buy a copy of the *De-*
seret News in a mercantile that carried several territorial newspapers. The stacked headlines had caught his eye:

DOUBLE OUTRAGE AT THE OVERLAND

FREIGHT OFFICE STRUCK TWICE IN A MATTER OF HOURS

SECOND BAND FORCED TO LEAVE EMPTY-HANDED

REIGN OF TERROR FOLLOWS

PERSONAL RECOLLECTIONS OF MANAGER OBERLIN

Sipping weak coffee—it might have been strong tea—in the window of a restaurant looking out on Main Street, Rittenhouse chuckled over the account of the hapless second gang's reaction upon
finding they'd been outflanked by a rival. He strongly suspected
they were Jack Brixton's Ace-in-the-Hole marauders. Salt Lake City
was a plausible ride from Denver, where they were known to pa-
tronize Nell Dugan's Wood Palace; much good that did, with Nell's
lips sealed as tight as her corset. He recognized Breed's description.

That was the old man's headache, with his obsession for protecting railroads, a frequent Brixton target. But he'd wire the office. There was no telling if anyone was reading the farther-flung papers in Rittenhouse's absence, and in any case Pinkerton wasn't likely to pay much attention to what happened at Overland. He'd written off stage companies as a vanishing source of income.

Turning the page, the detective was excited, but not much surprised, to read half a column about the presentation by the Prairie Rose Repertory Company of *The Legend of Sleepy Hollow* at the Salt Lake Theater.

He lifted his gaze across the street to rest his eyes from the dense print; at this rate he would soon need spectacles to read. He watched a dusty fellow in range attire lead his equally dusty mount up to a community trough, watched it plunge its muzzle into the water and suck.

Rittenhouse thought of his memorandum book then, and the notes he'd taken from newspaper accounts and eyewitness testimony concerning the robberies. He saw Marshal Fletcher's list, as clearly as if he hadn't discarded it when it had grown too tattered to read. He spilled his coffee, burning his hand. He let it blister. He knew how the thing had been done, and how it was still being done, as recently as Salt Lake City.

9

Charlie Kettleman got the job.

He was the obvious choice. Mysterious Bob's conversation skills were lacking, Tom Riddle was too loud and too deaf, Brixton's face was too well known, and Breed—apart from the fact he stuck out among all those Mormons like an ear of Indian corn in a tin of peaches—was far too likely to let his Bowie knife ask his questions. Charlie, who'd stayed outside to watch the horses, was the least likely to be recognized by the Overland manager. In addition, the Kettlemans were experienced negotiators who came away from the table with more than they brought. Charlie got a fresh mount from the corral behind the fallen-in stage stop and rode back into Salt Lake City to find out who had stolen the money that was properly theirs to steal.

He went to the Overland office first. That was the test. If the manager had happened to look out the window and could place him, he'd have to cut his losses and run. He tethered his horse in front and went inside, resting a hand on the Forehand & Wadsworth in his coat pocket.

"If you've come to rob me, you'll have to take a seat. I haven't had the chance to go to the bank."

Charlie hesitated. Then he saw the beaten look on the face of the man behind the counter, no recognition there, and knew he'd made a feeble joke. Charlie took his hand out of his pocket and drew the door shut behind him.

"I heard you had a run of bad luck. I just came to ask when the stage leaves for Ogden."

The glum-faced manager exhaled. Clearly, he was relieved to respond to a normal query from an ordinary customer.

"We canceled that route two years ago. You can take the Denver and Rio Grande straight through."

"Oh. It's been three since I was here last. My name's Cuthbert. Denver Mining Supplies." He stuck out a hand.

"Oberlin." The manager took it listlessly. "You rode here clear from Denver?"

Charlie was ready for that one. His horse could be seen through the window and there wasn't much he could do about the alkali dust on his clothes. "I rented a mount at the livery. I like to go out riding after sitting on a train."

"I didn't know Ike Gunther had horseflesh like that."

"I reckon I got all the luck intended for you." He moved on quickly. "I wonder you don't quit."

"I gave notice today. I'm only staying on to break in the new man, whoever he is. He better be Wild Bill. This country's gone to the devil."

"That's what I hear. Two gangs in one day."

"Well, the second was gang enough. The first time it was just one man."

Charlie whistled. "He must've been eight feet tall."

"He was as long as he had that big gun, as far as I'm concerned. Without it he was shorter than you, and twice as wide."

"Fat man, you say? He can't have got far on horseback."

"He doesn't have to since the railroad. Hop on in Denver or someplace, stop off in Salt Lake City, say, 'Stick 'em up,' then hop back on and ride all the way to San Francisco. Why spend money on board and feed when fares are so cheap? You're in the wrong business, Mr. Cuthbert. Mining's on its way out. Robbery's the coming thing, and you don't need riding lessons."

" 'Stick 'em up,' that's what he said? I thought folks only talked like that in the dime novels."

"Well, he never did. 'Hand over the swag,' that's what he said."

Charlie laughed. He was that surprised.

Oberlin's face darkened. "That's what he said. Like a pirate in a play."

From there, Charlie went to a barbershop and then a bathhouse, where he gave the boy a quarter to brush some of the Utah Territory off his clothes while he soaked the brine out of his skin, but all he overheard from the other customers were stories about the robbery of the Deseret Hotel and the shooting spree that had followed the unsuccessful raid on the freight office. Over a plate of fried chicken in a restaurant he heard a man had lost a finger and a dog its life, but he'd known that already. He learned Mormons were no better cooks than anyone else. That was all there was to get from the locals.

When he came out onto the boardwalk, picking pinfeathers

from between his teeth, dusk had slid in. He wondered if he should ride back in the dark or take a room. Night riding was the worst part of being a desperado, but he couldn't be sure if Oberlin wouldn't check his story about hiring his horse from the livery and alert the town; lynch mobs scared him worse than Texas Rangers and mad Indians. He'd just about decided to mount up and leave when someone came down the street pedaling a bicycle.

Bicycles interested him. Back in Fort Worth, he and Ed had seen an advertisement in a catalogue and had discussed stealing a shipment somewhere and selling them to Comanches, but had abandoned the idea because Indians were suspicious of the wheel. He still thought there was profit in it, if robbery got too various and there was a way to do it without the stigma of legitimate commerce.

Instinctively, he dropped his toothpick and backed into the shadows as the rider passed. In the light coming through the window from the restaurant, it was a tall fellow in a cloth cap, heavy sweater, tan britches, and boots that laced to his knees. Charlie figured he was a telegraph messenger.

Charlie was about to turn away toward where he'd left his horse when the rider lifted his feet off the pedals and coasted to a stop next to the boardwalk. He alighted in front of a dry goods store, shut up and dark. There was no one there to accept a telegram.

The fellow got off, and something about the way he stood looking up and down the street moved Charlie to take another step back into the dark doorway behind him. He watched as the rider leaned his bicycle against the hitching rail and bend down over the watering trough in front of the dry goods. He turned his head left and right again, then tugged up one sleeve of his sweater, stuck a hand inside the water, groped around, and pulled out something heavy. Water ran off it in a sheet, splashing back into the trough. Oilcloth glistened.

Charlie couldn't believe his luck.

As the rider slapped the bundle into the wicker basket attached to his handlebars, Charlie stepped that way, taking the revolver out of his pocket.

His luck didn't hold. The restaurant door opened and someone came out, bumping into him from behind. "Beg pardon, brother."

He stuck the revolver back into its pocket. Startled by the sudden activity, the rider threw a leg over the seat, pushed off from the hitching rail, and began pedaling like mad. Charlie pushed the clumsy fool from the restaurant out of his way and took off in the other direction, sprinting toward where his horse was tethered.

"Gentile!" The man from the restaurant stalked off down the boardwalk.

The bicyclist was nowhere in sight when Charlie came back that way aboard his mount, but he held it to a canter. The salt flats threw back moonlight like a fresh fall of snow, and that single tire track made a dark line down the center of the road leading west of town, running parallel to the railroad tracks. He had the thing put together now; the man he was after wouldn't turn aside from that route.

Outside the city limits, he broke into a gallop. The bicyclist came into view, a vertical mark with reflected light from the great lake bouncing down from a sheet of cloud, bright as Abilene on Saturday night. Charlie drew the Forehand & Wadsworth and fired a shot high. It rang clearly in the dry air.

The bicycle wobbled. The driver twisted in his seat, then turned back forward, bent over the handlebars, and made the pedals whir. Clearly, this was not the fat fellow who'd held up the freight office, but Charlie wasn't confused. He didn't believe in lone bandits; there was always a silent partner somewhere, and usually several. He let the man gain a few yards, then smacked his reins across his horse's withers, took aim, and squeezed the trigger again. He didn't expect to hit the man, and he didn't, but the bullet must have struck close enough to remind him that a bicycle can't outrun a good horse. The rider went another ten feet at top speed, then slowed to a stop and got off. He let the bicycle flop over and stood on the side of the road with his hands raised.

Charlie was hauling back on the reins when one of the hands swung down. Something gleamed, but he didn't waste time trying to bring his own weapon around. He let go of it and launched himself out of the saddle. A hot wind smacked his ribs. His momentum snatched the man off his feet, they struck ground with a *woof,* and rolled over and over. It wasn't until Charlie had the man's gun arm pinned to the earth and his body trapped beneath his own weight that he realized he'd been wrestling with a woman.

"It *looks* like snow," April said, "but it isn't. Still, I'm cold. Explain that." She'd drawn on Katrina's shawl from *The Legend of Sleepy Hollow* and paced the hardpack floor of the miner's shack hugging herself, and incidentally stealing glances at her fetching image in the window's single unbroken pane. Beyond it stretched the white flats, ending in an abrupt line where salt met black sky.

Major Davies took a pinch of snuff. "Self-mesmerization. Your brain tells your heart it's salt, but your heart is unconvinced. It's a condition of womanhood." He blocked a powerful sneeze and swept away tears with a handkerchief bearing someone else's initials.

"The other explanation is we're in a desert." Cornelius Ragland sat at the warped table, filling sheets of foolscap by coal-oil light and pausing to dip his pen. "It's a scientific fact that the grains are too loose to hold the day's heat. The result is the same whether it's sand or salt."

"Rubbish. If that were the case, I'd cool my soup by shaking salt into it rather than blowing on it. I am a man, ruled by my brain and not my heart. Therefore I'm not cold."

"You're fat," said April. "You ought to be hibernating. Look at Corny, shivering like a leaf. Does that make him a woman?"

"He's consumptive. When he isn't burning up with fever he's freezing."

"Actually, I'm neither. This is rather a stirring scene and I've let it get the better of me." He sat back, removed his spectacles, and wiped them on his sleeve.

April bent over the page before him. "What is it this time? Not Dickens, I hope. Except for old hags and insufferable little girls, all his women are simpletons. Lizzie's Miss Havisham blew my Estella clear off the stage."

"This one is an original story, based upon the tragedy of Joan of Arc."

She gasped. "Oh, Corny! I take back everything I've ever said about your acting. Will I get to bob my hair and wear a breast-plate?"

"That will be up to Johnny. However, if we simulate the flames properly while you're burning at the stake, you'll have cover and time enough to slip out and hold up the Denver Mint."

As if he'd heard his cue, Johnny came in from outside and rubbed his hands above the chimney of the lamp. "Cold out there. You'd think it was snow and not salt."

"Rubbish!" The Major took snuff.

"Oh, Johnny, I'm going to play St. Joan!"

"Good God, Corny. Why not write about the Virgin Mary and make the challenge impossible?" He caught April's wrist in midswing. "No, dear. Smite the English."

The Major blew his nose. "What news?"

"Not a sign. She ought to be back by now." Johnny took off his coat, black broadcloth with three capes and a red silk lining. He'd seen a photograph of Irving wearing one like it and had had it made to his measure in St. Louis. He looked dashing in it, and with his long flaxen hair and moustaches a bit like a buccaneer.

April said, "You don't suppose she's been arrested."

"We always knew that was a possibility. Hers is the riskiest part of our plan."

"Your plan, not mine. A posse could be on its way here at this moment." She touched her throat.

"What of it?" asked the Major. "There's nothing here to incriminate us."

Cornelius laid down his pen. "She has the money. That's incrimination enough."

"Only for her."

Everyone looked at the Major, who shrugged. "She would say the same thing, if our situations were reversed. That's the solid foundation upon which our relationship rests."

"Are you two even married?" Johnny asked.

"We exchanged the necessary vows. However, I have my doubts about the minister. He played Horatio for five weeks in Philadelphia."

"We're sitting hens if she peaches," said April, "or even if she does not. Someone is bound to recognize her, and the rest will follow. I've said all along we should include horses in our arrangements."

"I haven't been aboard a horse since Harrow."

Johnny said, "The Major's right, dear. He's too fat to ride, and Corny's too delicate. The more players we leave behind, the greater our chances of conviction and imprisonment. Even if you and I make the train, the authorities will just wire ahead. We'll be arrested at the next stop. It's our word against Lizzie's if it's just her, and something else if it's two against three."

April sighed. "A fine honorable lot of thieves we are."

Johnny laughed. "There's no honor anywhere. I've seen the other side." He unshipped his watch. "We'll give her half an hour, then start searching. Perhaps she fell and broke her leg."

Cornelius picked up his pen and dipped it. "Let us hold on to that hope."

Thirty minutes of silence followed, interrupted only by April's pacing and the scratching of Cornelius' pen. Johnny looked at his watch for the twentieth time, then snapped shut the face with finality. "Right." He threw on his coat.

The door opened then and Mme. Mort-Davies came in, pushing her bicycle. The front wheel was bent and her sweater was torn. The Major struggled to his feet. Johnny lifted the lamp, casting light on Lizzie's face. One eye was swollen almost shut and blood crusted her chin.

Johnny took the bicycle while April and the Major helped her into the Major's chair. Cornelius reached inside the picnic basket and gave Johnny the bottle of brandy they'd been saving to celebrate. Lizzie winced when she opened her lips to receive the bottle; the lower one split open afresh and trickled more blood onto her chin. She took two more sips, and between them reported what had happened on the road outside Salt Lake City.

"He got all of it?" demanded Johnny.

"He didn't offer to divide it. Search me if you like."

"Don't take offense. If you stole from us, you wouldn't stop at one day's profits. What about the Colt?"

She tugged up her sweater, pulled a small revolver from under the belt of her trousers, and gave it to him. "He took it, but I found that after he left; he lost it when he jumped off his horse. I'm afraid it wasn't much of a trade."

The Major asked if he'd assaulted her. She looked at him piteously.

"He knocked me to the ground, cut my lip, and blacked my eye."

"You know very well what I meant."

"No, Evelyn. I'm still the same unsullied girl you married."

"You were living with a fire-eater when we met."

"Don't think I don't miss that."

The Major balled his fists. "That fellow should be behind bars."

"So should we," said Johnny. "Did he say anything?"

"He said, 'Teats! Jesus Christ!' Either my disguise is better than I'd hoped or I'm not as comely as I once was."

"Is that all he said?" April asked.

" 'Hand over the swag.' "

Johnny's watch ticked loudly in the profound silence.

Lizzie smiled sourly, gasped, and touched her lip. "*Annabelle and the Pirate*. It brought down the house at the Metropolitan in Detroit in fifty-eight. They held us over ten days."

"Twelve," murmured the Major.

Johnny glared at him. "Just what did you say in the Overland office?"

"I don't remember."

"If you say anything at all, you say, 'Reach for the sky.' We rehearsed it."

"It's hackneyed."

"It's intended to be. Swag! By God! You might as well have appeared in full costume and handed the fellow a programme. You might have autographed it."

"What's the point in directing him now?" April said. "This is terrible, Johnny, terrible. If the manager told this—this bandit what the Major said, he's told everyone. We're found out."

"Quite likely." He walked over to the table and lifted one of the sheets Cornelius had written on, read for a moment. "This is good. I'm sorry we won't be able to use it this season."

"It needs work in any case. My French is rusty."

A whistle blew, drawn thin by distance. Lizzie pawed at her attendants and got up to help put the bicycle in its trunk. Cornelius found his wrench.

"We have a few minutes," Johnny said. "Major, the lantern."

A railroad lantern with a red lens was produced. Johnny lit it from the table lamp. "So much more convenient than waiting at the station," he said. "Ladies and gentlemen, it's been a successful tour. We're long past due for a holiday."

The Major blew out his moustaches. "There are no holidays in the theater. Except Sundays, of course. Lizzie and I haven't had Christmas off since the Coliseum burned down in Baltimore."

"I'm declaring one. I'd intended to, anyway, after Boise. We're carrying too much gold and paper to distribute among ourselves and in the strongbox and claim it as box office receipts much longer. The time has come to place it in a bank in Denver. Since we've demonstrated that none of us can be trusted to do it alone, we shall all go. I see no reason why we shouldn't spend some of it while we're there and entertain ourselves for a change."

April buttoned her traveling cloak. "Does this mean the end of the Prairie Rose?"

"Just for a season, while we cede the headlines to a more conventional breed of blackguard and brigand." He put on his soft black hat and smoothed the brim. "And then—"

"The show must go on," said the Major.

Johnny smiled. "If only you remembered all your lines as accurately."

10

We glide down Pike's Peak, bluer than the ocean beneath its white coronet, into a hurdy-gurdy metropolis of macadam and brick, teeming with surreys, streetcars, beer wagons, top hats, and spinning parasols, "O Susannah!" fiddling on the soundtrack, white letters with square serifs on the scrim: DENVER. Crowding in for a tight shot of the scripted legend on a sign, swinging crazily from chains attached to a porch roof trimmed in gingerbread, we remove our hats, pat down our hair, and prepare to enter the Wood Palace. We step back a moment to allow a burly party in shirtsleeves and handlebars to hurl a drunken saddle tramp out through the swinging doors, then join the customers inside.

The main room, two stories high and hung with a chandelier that doubles as a trapeze, features green baize gaming tables, a mahogany bar as long as the *Mayflower* and more cunningly carved, a stage, and a high ballustraded hallway with stairs cantilevering up to it; nymphs and satyrs randy about in oil on canvas at the top, bordered by bronze cherubim. All the tables are in use and none of the six bartenders is idle. The usual chubby quartette gallops in sparkling leotards onstage; if we strain our ears, we may detect the anachronistic notes of a can-can. This is an entertainment after all, and not a historical tale.

We're just in time to see that high railing collapse and a pair of battlers fall ten feet to the table beneath, demolishing it and interrupting a lively game of faro. Once again the burly fellow goes to work.

We suspect, of course, that all this is staging. The Wood Palace's real business is conducted behind the numbered doors lining that second-story hallway. From one of them, if our fortune continues (and this is the same as catching a glimpse of Victoria passing through the Buckingham gate in her coach), Nell Dugan may make an appearance before the last drunk is swept out.

Late in life, when the laws of time and nature had packed off with those physical charms that had made her a doubtful subject for serious journalism, Nell told a reporter from the *Post* that she'd come to America at fourteen with just a dollar and forty cents in her pocket. Matronly vanity gave her license to pare six years off her age, and social discretion to leave out mention of the letter of introduction she'd sewn inside the lining of her shabby coat, addressed by the mayor of Limerick to Michael McFee, president and principal stockholder of the Denver Topical Mining Company.

It was an arrangement of convenience for all three parties. The mayor's wife had become suspicious to the point of certainty, and Nell had placed in safekeeping a number of letters of an indiscreet character written to her in his hand. McFee, a confederate of the mayor's before emigrating ten years before, lived like Vanderbilt so far as the scale of life in the Colorado Territory could support, and desired both a mistress and a taste of the companionship of old Erin; Nell chafed at the restraints placed upon her by a puritanical father and a farmer husband who stank perennially of sod. "It was like going to bed in me own grave," she told the reporter, who recorded the remark in his notes but forebore to publish it. The mayor stood her passage to New York, McFee her train fare to Denver, where the question of her accommodations pivoted upon the impression she made. It was a gamble; but like any good gambler, she was well aware of the odds, and that they were in her favor. A photograph made at the time the article appeared in the *Post* suggests, beneath the folds of fat of a prosperous middle age, something of the stake she brought to the table at twenty. Forty years of good Irish whisky, half-dollar cheroots, and carnal calisthentics may thicken the waist and coarsen the skin, but can neither alter the impudent tilt of the nose nor dim the devil in the eye.

McFee was a gambler as well, and knew a good hand when it was dealt. He set Nell up as titular owner of a former boarding-house on Holladay Street that had been converted first into a hotel for prospectors weary of canvas and thrice-boiled coffee, then into a saloon, and finally into a "melodeon"; a designation made popular by San Francisco, promising all the entertainments of a debauched civilization adrift in the wilderness. Opium could be consumed there, as well as liquor in the original bottles, women who did not smell like bacon fat and their last customer, keno and cards, and music by the best third-rate orchestras west of the Gaiety in Kansas City. It was a profitable enterprise, reducing the strain on McFee's pocketbook, and ran smoothly enough on its own to place Nell's charms at his disposal whenever his business affairs got the better of his nervous system. Seen in this light, his situation makes it difficult to look upon his untimely death as a tragedy.

"The Wood Palace" was a misnomer with a legitimate pedigree. Built of brick to comply with the new city ordinance requiring all new construction to be of sturdy, noncombustible material, it occupied the site of its original namesake, which had been swept away by a flood in 1864, rebuilt, and consumed by fire in 1870. It was one of the city's more enduring institutions, respected for its tradition of survival, if not for the nature of its business.

The Panic of '73—brought on by greed fueled by the economic boom following the Union victory in 1865—brought thousands of investors from private Pullmans down to shank's mare, without a penny for a streetcar, while the speculators who had precipitated it found themselves forced to order champagne of a less fashionable vintage. It was in this climate that Michael McFee paused to confer with his attorney before the offices of the *Denver Times,* which had libeled him, and interrupted his consultation to greet a pedestrian who recognized him from the most recent stockholders meeting at the Denver Topical Mining Company. Following an exchange of pleasantries, the stockholder produced a pistol and shot him twice in the stomach. McFee died six weeks later, raving for ice water and oysters; his assailant, who turned out to be a former clerk fired by McFee's company, took a short drop through a trapdoor and broke his neck.

Nell was saddened, but alert. Through a lawyer, she purchased the Wood Palace outright from McFee's estate, and continued as she had, only now with full access to the profits, which she reinvested in the business, securing its reputation as the finest establishment of its kind on Holladay, a wide-open street in a wide-open town.

Among the improvements she added was a suite of rooms in the basement, accessible only by a trapdoor hidden beneath a heavy Persian rug in the back parlor, where tenants were accommodated in absolute secrecy, at rates that rivaled those of the Astor House in Manhattan. Although none of the legendary Astor luxuries was in evidence, highwaymen could rest there in relative comfort while heavily armed men combed caves and barns the countryside over looking for them. Nell did not keep a guest book, but had she done so, the signatures of the outlaw luminaries who had taken advantage of her hospitality would have crowned the collection of any autograph hunter of sinister bent.

As a result of her double income, Nell Dugan was the wealthiest unattached woman in Denver. Her dresses were cut to her petite frame from organdy of a quality that came dear after the collapse of the cotton industry in the defeated South—deep purple was her color of choice at night, lavender during the day—and she wore peacock feathers in her thick auburn hair, her best feature, for public appearances at her establishment. She kept her creamy skin pale beneath a vast collection of parasols, and her carriage-and-pair were the envy of Denver's newly rich. She made it a point to take them out often, and to drop as much as a thousand dollars on a dubious hand at poker, her only addiction, by way of inspiring confidence in her clandestine guests; a woman of such conspicuous means was far less likely to turn them in for the reward than the storied prostitute with a heart of gold. It was a reality of frontier economics that internal organs assayed out at considerably less than twelve dollars per Troy ounce.

While the spring runoff was floating miners' tents on the eastern face of the Rockies, the entire Ace-in-the-Hole Gang stayed dry snoring and playing poker (for stakes much lower than Nell's notorious "thousand-burners") in the hidden rooms beneath the Wood Palace. The money Charlie Kettleman had reclaimed from Mme. Mort-Davies made the stop affordable, and the fuss the gang had created in Salt Lake City made it imperative. The Pinkertons had never stopped looking for them in response to the robbery of the Chicago, Rock Island & Pacific, and the wire Philip Rittenhouse had sent Allan Pinkerton after reading of the Overland fiasco in the *Deseret News* had announced their recent whereabouts to the national press. That very day, agents of the Denver branch had searched the upper and lower stories and the basement storage rooms on the other side of four feet of solid masonry.

"You should of put a round in her." Black Jack Brixton threw in his cards.

Charlie raked in the pot. "What's the point? We got the money."

"It would of put her fat friend in some other line of work. Next time we open an empty safe I'll shut you up in it."

"That's my job," Ed Kettleman said. "He ain't your brother."

"If he was I'd dig up my mother and punch her in the mouth."

Tom Riddle listened to the conversation with a hand cupping one ear. "You told me your mother's alive."

"I'd shoot her and bury her first."

Charlie said, "I never busted a cap on a woman or a child."

"You never busted a cap on a bottle of Old Gideon," Ed said. "You couldn't hit a three-hundred-pound Chinaman with a scattergun."

"Amateurs got to be discouraged," said Brixton. "You kill a man's woman, it takes the fight right out of him."

Ed shuffled the deck. "You ought at least to put the boots to her before you let her go, or brung her back for the rest of us. I do like to shinny up a tall woman."

"She had a face like Tom's bay mare."

"What's that? It was dark, weren't it?"

Breed said, "We going to jabber or play cards?" He was down a hundred and fifty.

"That bay mare's a good ride," said Tom, who'd only half heard what Ed said. "I ate the best horse I ever had in California. One time—"

"Jacks or better." Ed dealt. "You know, there's a mint right here in town. I don't reckon them James-Youngers ever bought into a pot that big."

Brixton said, "That's because the federals got the whole army guarding it. This bunch can't even stick up Mormons."

"We got the money," Charlie reiterated.

"I don't appreciate being made to look the fool. You should of at least found out who the fat man was that got there first. We could of rendered him down and ate him with onions."

"I ate an injun once," Tom said. "He might've been a half-breed, meaning no offense to the breed present. California, it was. We'd been out prospecting—"

"Shut up, Tom," said the others in unison.

Ed said, "You could leave out California and make your stories shorter. Everything you done was in California before you joined up with us. What made you leave in the first place?"

A chorus of oaths followed this injudicious query. A hail of red chips bounced off Ed's slack-jawed face.

"There's a story behind that," Tom said. "It was up around Eureka; coldest place I ever been. Don't let no one ever tell you California don't get—"

"Why *not* the mint?"

Even Tom fell silent, waiting for Mysterious Bob's next remark. Bob, who disliked poker for the conversation required, sat on one end of a brocaded settee, most of whose springs were at odds with one another, lubricating an unidentifiable component of his Winchester with an oily rag. All the other parts were spread out on the cushions.

"I been fighting the army a dozen years, same as you," Brixton said. "They don't beat."

"New gold, that's all they care about." Bob traded the odd-shaped part for the barrel and peered inside. "I always wondered how those boys got paid, the workers and soldiers and such. You reckon they just scoop it out of the bin?"

Charlie said, "That'd make too much sense. The government don't work that way. They send it out from Washington, same as at Fort Lincoln."

"How do you know how the government works?" Ed asked. "You voted for Greeley."

Bob ignored Ed. "How you reckon they send it?"

"How's anybody send anything?" Charlie's face changed. "Holy Christ."

Breed looked up, frozen in the act of stealing a card from Tom's deadwood. "Goddamn."

"By train," said Brixton, who'd forgotten whose bet it was.

Bob began swabbing the inside of the barrel. He'd used up his conversation for the week.

We who are privileged to sources not available to historians and the makers of legend can enjoy the frisson of knowing that while the Ace-in-the-Hole Gang was planning what scholars argue might have been the most spectacular train robbery in American history, two-fifths of the Prairie Rose Repertory Company were enjoying the more celebrated diversions on the second story of the Wood Palace, two floors above their heads. Johnny Vermillion, looking more Byronic than usual with his shirt unbuttoned halfway down his smooth, hairless chest, greeted Cornelius Ragland from the depths of a tufted velvet chair in the sitting room of his temporary suite over a glass of Napoleon from Nell Dugan's cellar, which had recently been swept clear of Pinkertons. "Congratulations," he said. "I was afraid you'd succumbed."

Cornelius blushed and filled a glass from the decanter. "Only to conversation, which is quite as expensive as the other. Not that I'm consumptive; just weak. My father was a butterfly and my mother a wisp of smoke."

"You ought to write that down."

"It seems to me I did. Do you know I've submitted poetry and stories to every periodical in North America without a single acceptance? That requires talent." He slumped onto a divan with part of the Bayeaux Tapestry wrought in the maple frame. "You're the only man on God's fertile earth who hasn't tried to convince me I was born to be a secretary."

"You're a born thief. It's a natural mistake."

"I'm serious, Johnny. You're the first person in my life to look at me and not through me. If you told me to assassinate the Czar of Russia, all I'd ask is what method you preferred."

"A bomb, naturally. The only socially acceptable way of destroying an emperor is to blow him to smithereens. I often wonder where the Smithereens may be. In the Scottish Highlands, I suspect."

"You're drunk, Johnny. I've never seen you this way."

"You should have known me in Chicago."

The hall door opened and Major Davies tottered in. He wore his morning coat and his necktie was in disarray. Without preamble he plunked himself down beside Cornelius.

"You're as red as a radish," Johnny observed. "I thought you were back at the hotel with Lizzie."

"She's gone shopping with April. I left a note that I was going for a walk."

Cornelius said, "She'll see through that. You haven't walked more than ten feet from one chair to another since you joined the troupe."

"What you young single fellows don't understand is the stability of a seasoned marriage. She'll forgive me. Is that sherry?"

"Brandy. Pour him one, will you, Corny? I haven't any smelling salts."

The Major accepted a glass and drained it. "Mother's milk. I have a grand constitution, never fear. I shall be ready to rejoin the battle in thirty minutes."

"I only have this room for another fifteen. At this rate you'll be impoverished in a week."

"I doubt that. Lizzie keeps the books. Have you seen today's *Post?*" The Major patted his pockets, withdrew a fold of newsprint, and sailed it into Johnny's lap.

He unfolded it. It was torn from the front page and contained an account of that day's Pinkerton raid on the Wood Palace. A paragraph described the Ace-in-the-Hole Gang's reign of terror in Salt Lake City. Johnny finished reading and held it out for Cornelius to take. "I'd wondered what those fellows were about. I confess it gave me pause until I realized they had no interest in me or Corny."

Cornelius returned the scrap to the Major. "Lizzie had a near thing. Brixton's men are rough customers."

"Next time, one of you can ride the bicycle, or April. She's more accustomed to carrying a firearm than my dear Lizzie."

"We'll discuss it," Johnny said. "At least we can rest assured Black Jack and his gang aren't here."

Brixton dreamed he was back at Lone Jack, facing the entire Yankee cavalry with two empty pistols and no cartridges on his belt. He awoke with a yell and staggered out of his room to find Breed and the Kettlemans playing three-handed stud and Bob putting his carbine back together. "Where's Tom?"

Breed said, "He went upstairs for a drink. He said that badger hole in California ruined him for tight places."

"Why in hell didn't nobody stop him?"

"It's just so damn peaceful with him gone," Charlie said.

"Go fetch him. Anyone recognizes him, we'll ride our next train in irons."

"Deal me out." Charlie threw in his hand and rose.

"Don't *you* get recognized," Brixton called after him.

Charlie found Tom leaning against the wall just inside the batwing doors to the street, smoking a cigar. "Jack says come back. He got up on the wrong side."

"He went to bed on the wrong side. Let me finish my smoke first."

"Me, too, then. Nell's scared we'll set the place on fire we light up down there." Charlie got out his makings and rolled a cigarette. "What's the fight about?"

On the boardwalk in front of the building, a tall woman in a flat straw hat and a big bustle stood with her back to them, waggling a finger in Clyde Canebreak's big polished black face. Clyde, in his bright red Zouave tunic, greeted customers at the door and threw out undesirables, often two at a time.

"The old lady says her husband's inside, wants to talk to him. Clyde ain't having any."

"She ought to be happy he's still got lead in his pencil."

"I reckon she likes to have him do all his scribbling at home."

Clyde laid one of his coal-scuttle hands on the woman's shoulder and turned her gently aside from the door, toward the carriage she had waiting. Charlie recognized the gold device of the Coronet Hotel on the door.

He saw her face then. The match he'd lit stung his hand. He cried out and dropped it.

She started at the noise and looked his way. The blood slid from her face in a sheet.

11

"Really, Lizzie," Johnny said, "this is a domestic matter between you and the Major. There was no reason to pull us all out here. Miss Dugan doesn't approve of messages from outside. I'm surprised you were able to talk Clyde into it."

"It cost me a double eagle. It was the first thing that came into my hand when I reached inside my bag."

They were seated in a private room at the Auraria Restaurant, the entire troupe gathered around a table cloaked in crisp linen and shimmering with silver. A heap of freshly opened mussels steamed in an enormous tureen in the center. April, fetching in a powder-blue suit she'd bought that afternoon, fretted. "*My* message was waiting for me at the hotel desk. None of us even had time to change for dinner."

"I wouldn't care if you were naked." Lizzie was in an agitated state. "I saw him."

The Major said, "My dear, you've drawn the wrong conclusion.

I went to that place merely for male cameraderie. You have always been more than woman enough for me."

"Forget about yourself for once, you old goat. I don't care where you drop your seed or with whom. It was the lying I came to protest. You haven't gone out for a walk since the war with Mexico. The man I saw today was the man who knocked me down in Salt Lake City and stole our money."

Johnny put down his mussel shell still containing its prize and wiped off his fingers with his napkin. "Where?"

"At the Wood Palace. Why did you think I sent you that note?"

"I thought perhaps you were hungry. You're certain it was him? The description you gave that night was quite general."

"I haven't Corny's talent for word pictures. But I trust my eyes. Moreover, he recognized me. I saw it in his face."

Johnny said, "You mean to say he just stood there, a wanted man, knowing you could identify him to the nearest police officer?"

"I mean to say he darted away like a sparrow, taking his companion with him, a short fellow with a wizened face. I'm sure they went to report to their accomplices. That's why I sent that note and hurried here. My driver carried April's message back to the Coronet."

"Nell must have a priest's hole of some kind to conceal their like," said Cornelius. "But Denver is a big place, and they haven't the freedom to mount a search. They wouldn't know where to begin looking."

"I had the carriage from the hotel," Lizzie said. "I'm sure he saw it."

"Johnny!"

He patted April's hand. "There is every reason for optimism, and none for panic. These road agents are more frightened of us than we are of them. That's why they fled at the sight of Lizzie. They *have* the money. What else could they want from us?"

Lizzie said, "He knows I can identify him. You said so yourself. They'll murder me to prevent me from turning them in for the reward."

The Major sucked out a shell and daubed at his moustaches. "We've been overlooking an opportunity, and Lizzie has placed her finger square upon it. We should notify the authorities immediately and collect the reward for the whole gang."

Johnny said, "I question the wisdom of making ourselves too familiar with law enforcement. We're fugitives ourselves, don't forget. In any case those bounties are seldom paid in full, and we'll have made ourselves notorious for something less than we might remove from a safe in some fat mining town or cattle camp with a servicable theater."

"Guerrillas are territorial," Cornelius pointed out. "We pricked their pride in Utah. If they haven't forgotten the war in nine years, I doubt they'll have forgotten us in a few weeks. Lizzie isn't the only one who's in danger of their revenge."

The party fell into a grim silence while a waiter entered, removed the course, and glided out of the room.

"This changes nothing about our plan for a holiday, apart from the venue," said Johnny then. "We'll draw what we need from the bank for living expenses and separate. We'll meet again in Wichita and launch the fall season."

"Absolutely not." April set down her wineglass with a thump. "Cowboys pinch and grope and belch whiskey. They do everything but bathe."

"They also spend money as if it were grass," Johnny said. "Other rowdies, when they see something they approve of onstage, throw pennies; cowboys throw silver dollars. Sometimes more. In Amarillo, Lotta Crabtree fished a poker chip out of her bodice after a performance and redeemed it for a hundred dollars."

"I've seen Crabtree," said April. "She could fit the table stakes and the dealer in there as well."

"Do I detect a shade of green?" asked Lizzie.

"We can't all be cows."

Madame's cheeks colored. The Major choked, coughed, and spat a stuffed mushroom into his napkin.

"Dear me," said Cornelius, who preferred writing scenes to experiencing them.

"Yes. Separate holidays are best." Johnny sipped from his glass. "Shall we order dessert?"

Someone tapped three times at the door to the underground suite, paused, and tapped again.

"That's Charlie and Bob." Ed Kettleman got up to unlock the door.

His brother came in first, unhooking the wire-rimmed spectacles he believed provided an impenetrable disguise. An old photograph he and Ed had unwisely posed for in a studio in El Paso was floating around Texas, and although it had yet to appear on wanted posters circulated nationally, the spectacles came out whenever he separated from the gang, in case he ran into a lawman visiting from the Lone Star State. Mysterious Bob, known principally by his description, merely bent his legs to dissemble his height and put on a dirty bowler hat he'd shot a carpetbagger out from under in Dodge City. Together they looked like a pair of drummers no one wanted to buy anything from.

There was a general rattle of firearms being taken off cock and returned to their holsters; Ace-in-the-Hole hadn't much faith in such things as passwords and secret knocks.

"Put one in her this time?" Brixton was sawing at a longhorn steak with Breed's big Bowie and angry energy. The bill of fare at the Wood Palace posed no threat to Delmonico's, despite charging two dollars for a bowl of oxtail soup (twenty-five cents extra for evidence of an oxtail).

"She checked out," Charlie said; and yelled when the Bowie stuck in the lath-and-plaster six inches to the right of his head.

Ed said, "There ain't no call for that, Jack. He went soon as you told him."

"He's lucky Breed didn't throw it. I'm out of practice. He should of shot her when she was in range."

Breed put down his bottle of Old Pepper and got up to jerk his knife out of the wall. "You probably bent it cutting up that steak." He examined the blade.

"I couldn't shoot the old bat in the street," whined Charlie. "We'd be up to our ass in law."

"Nell's rules," Tom Riddle reminded Brixton, over a game of patience. "No trouble in the Palace."

"She didn't say nothing about out front."

Bob spoke up. "She weren't checked out yet when we got to the hotel. We talked to the carriage man, he said he dropped her at the Auraria Restaurant. We missed her there, and when we went back to the hotel, she'd checked out."

Brixton hauled out his big American revolver. Ed and Charlie scrambled for cover. Mysterious Bob scooped up his Winchester and levered a round into the chamber. "Hold on, Jack."

"If you two didn't have pig shit for brains, you'd of split up and covered both places."

"I needed Charlie along to point her out. If I went around shooting every tall old ugly woman I seen in hotels and train stations, I'd run out of shells."

"He's right, Jack." Charlie crouched behind the settee, covering Brixton with the Colt he'd taken from the old woman. His hand shook.

Tom Riddle said, "Let's all put up our irons now." He'd drawn his Remington.

When every muzzle was lowered, Brixton returned to his meal. "You at least get her name?"

"Elizabeth Mort-Davies," Bob said. "One of them two-part names, like that Englishman we strung up in Dry Gulch. You want to know who she checked in with?"

"If it was Ulysses S. Grant, I hope to hell you shot *him*." But Brixton put down the bone he'd been gnawing like a gaunt old wolf. Bob had never talked so long nor with anything close to enjoyment.

"Man named Davies. I reckon he's her husband. He's fat, the clerk said."

"Fat like the man stuck up the Overland office in Salt Lake City?" Breed wiped his knife on his pants, smearing them with grease and plaster.

Bob ignored him; the only man in Breed's experience to do so.

"They weren't alone, neither," Charlie said.

He was the center of attention then. He was standing now, the

Colt dangling at his side. You never knew when Black Jack would flare up again, like a heap of ashes in a campfire.

He said, "They're running with a bunch of actors. They all checked out at the same time. Waiter at the restaurant said they ate there together."

"Horseshit," said Brixton. "No bunch of actors ever stuck up no place. Whores and pansies."

"Shut up, Jack," Tom said.

A terrible quiet followed, like the space between a flash of lightning and the roar of thunder; but there was no thunder. Of all the members of Ace-in-the-Hole (except, perhaps, Mysterious Bob), Tom Riddle was the least likely to be shot by any of the others, even Brixton. It would have been like stopping a church bell. The awful empty silence that came after would have driven them all mad.

Tom alone appeared unmoved by his breach of outlaw etiquette. "Let's hear the rest, Charlie."

"They call themselves the Prairie Rose," Charlie said. "I wasn't sure I heard it right, so I made the clerk say it again. I remembered, on account of I heard folks talking about them that day in Salt Lake City. They pulled out right after the Overland was hit."

Brixton swallowed a piece of gristle and chased it down with Old Pepper. "They hit other places too, to be staying at the Coronet and eating at Auraria. They won't be hard to track. Those outfits cover the country with shinplasters telling folks they're coming and the papers write about them after they leave."

Tom said, "They're spooked now. They'll scatter to cover and stay there."

"They'll herd up again, just like we done. Gold don't go so far since the war."

Ed Kettleman said, "What good's tracking them? I never saw where they're wanted no place. They're probably selling us to the marshal right now. That rug won't keep the Pinkertons out of that trapdoor twice. We're the ones on the run."

"That's part of it," said Brixton. "They owe us for what we didn't get from that payroll train we didn't rob."

Breed scowled, looking exactly like the woodcut on his poster. "I want their hides as bad as you, but there ain't no market. They can't carry what they stole around with them any more'n we can. They've buried or banked it, or spent it same as us."

"Who said anything about taking it out of their hides? We'll just follow them around like we do trains and hit them next time they take on a big load. We don't have to worry about the Pinkertons or the law." He laughed. "Hell, it might not even be illegal. Just like milking a cow."

"Then we butcher it for the side meat," Breed said.

"Well, sure. I'm surprised you had to say it."

They arranged to take three separate trains spaced out over two hours and avoid gathering in a group at the station. Farewells were brief, with April and Lizzie embracing swiftly to indicate that all rancor was past and the men shaking hands. No personal plans were discussed, again by mutual consent, in order to prevent anyone from betraying the others' movements under duress.

"*The Merry Wives of Windsor,* I think, in the fall," Johnny said to Cornelius at parting. "We must acquiesce to the Major's superstitions, and you have to agree that *Twelfth Night* started us off splendidly last season. Do you think you can winnow it down without inviting the Bard's vengeful ghost?"

"The merry *Wife*, perhaps?" The playwright's smile was sad; and then he was gone.

Somewhat to his surprise, Johnny realized he'd miss him most of all. The former secretary's awkward expressions of gratitude and loyalty at the Wood Palace, however inspired by the pleasure of conversing with whores, had moved him to an emotion he'd thought had died on Blue Island.

The Major and the Madame departed with all the pomp and fustian of exiled royalty, he popping his silk hat and directing the cabman with his stick like a concert conductor, she fretting aloud about the fate of the bags they'd sent on from the hotel. "San Francisco would be my guess," April told Johnny, waving as they rattled off. "*The Diplomat Deposes* and petty larceny the whole way."

"Just so long as the old ham doesn't try to hold anyone up at gunpoint," said Johnny.

To confuse pursuers, Johnny and April were traveling together to Colorado Springs as Mr. and Mrs. John McNear of Chicago. There, they would separate and proceed to their chosen destinations.

On their way to the station, Johnny had their driver stop twice to let him out on errands. The first stop lasted just long enough for him to hand a cash deposit to the clerk at the storage facility where they'd sent their theatrical costumes and properties on from Boise when their plans to play that city had changed. The second was longer, and he did not confide its purpose to April, who sat twirling her parasol irritably, then in alarm at the thought that he might have been waylaid. She started when he leapt back in beside her, and would have set her sharp tongue to work had he not held out a small square parcel wrapped in cloth-of-gold with a scarlet ribbon.

"The shade's a bit off," he said. "I asked for vermilion."

"If it's a key to your sleeping compartment, I shan't accept."

"It might have been in St. Louis. Those chivalrous buffoons I've been playing have had their effect upon my deportment in general."

"A few more, perhaps. There's still a bit of shanty Irish in your *g*'s."

"I hope to correct that over these next few months." He waggled the parcel.

She took it then and twitched loose the bow. Inside the pasteboard box was a container shaped like a miniature humpback trunk, covered in green velvet. "Oh, Johnny," Her tone was dubious.

"Opening it does not imply commitment."

She tipped back the hinged top. The garnet inside was the deep red of pigeon's blood, set in a band of twenty-four-karat gold (she knew her precious metals) with a delicate filigree.

"I had my mind set on a ruby," he said, "but they paled in comparison."

She snapped the lid shut with a smile. "I cannot, of course. Please take this advice for the future, as you might from a sister. Proposals are made with diamonds. This is for the wedding ceremony."

Johnny laughed. "Good God, woman! Don't confuse me with the parts I play. If we're to carry off the act of man and wife, we'll need a convincing prop."

She exhaled, relieved. "Take no offense," she said. "I'm fond of you. I loathed casting you in the role of disappointed suitor. Such a wasteful extravagance to fool a ticket clerk and a conductor."

Their driver cleared his throat loudly.

"One more moment, my good man." Johnny lowered his voice. "I'd be inclined to agree, if it were them only. The concierges of London and Paris are far more sophisticated."

She stared at him with eyes like hazel planets.

"I don't know your plans," Johnny said. "If you could postpone them without serious inconvenience, I thought perhaps we might discover for ourselves whether the capitals of the Old World are as corrupt as the ones we know. Allow me." He unbuttoned her left glove and slipped it off.

She hesitated, then slid the ring onto the third finger. It was a snug fit, most flattering. "When you put it that way, I don't see how a lady can refuse."

As this pretty scene was playing itself out in Denver, rapid fingers were tapping on copper keys, sending messages streaking back and forth in high-pitched staccato surges along wires strung across fifteen hundred miles of desert, prairie, and crowded metropolis:

ALLAN PINKERTON

PINKERTON NATIONAL DETECTIVE AGENCY

CHICAGO ILL

WELLS FARGO TRAIL ENDS HERE STOP AM SATISFIED IDENTITY PERSONS REPEAT PERSONS RESPONSIBLE STOP REPORT ON WAY U S MAIL STOP FOR REASONS EXPLAINED THERE THINK UNLIKELY APPREHEND BEFORE FALL EARLIEST STOP SUGGEST RETURN CHICAGO UNTIL THEN STOP PLEASE ADVISE RITTENHOUSE

PHILIP RITTENHOUSE

DESERET HOTEL

SALT LAKE CITY U T

RETURN NEXT TRAIN STOP TRUST REPORT EXPLAINS NO

BOARDINGHOUSES AVAILABLE THERE

PINKERTON

The detective took one last look at Salt Lake City through the window before the train began rolling, after that first curious backward lurch, as if it were as reluctant as he to be heading back the way he'd come. He thought it unlikely he would ever be that far west again. His adventure had ended. Wherever his investigations led from there, genuine field agents would follow.

He swung down the patented Pullman footrest and settled in to read. He'd bought a copy of that day's *Deseret News,* and seldom ventured anywhere without his pocket edition of Tennyson bound in soft calfskin, but he left them on the vacant seat next to his and slid the folded programme out of his inside breast pocket. A woodcut of an obstreperous-looking rose decorated the front. He opened it to read the one-line descriptions of the acts and scenes of *The Legend of Sleepy Hollow,* adapted by Cornelius Ragland from the story by Washington Irving, and the names of the characters and cast. Once again, he drew out his memorandum book and compared the names to the list he'd made in his own hand. Next to each name was penciled the initials of a city where the Prairie Rose had played, based upon the description of the thief in the armed robbery that had taken place there. Now he uncapped his pencil and wrote SLC next to Major Evelyn Davies. Then he put everything away and closed his eyes to sleep.

· III ·

The
Grand Tour

12

The 1875 London social season began splendidly for the pilgrims from America, with more invitations than they could possibly accept during their six-week stop, and ended on a sour note, with a challenge to a duel.

The *S.S. Columbian* docked at Gravesend in calm weather, at the end of three days of rough seas that left Johnny Vermillion grateful for the support of the fine alderwood stick he'd bought in New York City and April Clay powdered more artfully than usual to conceal a gray pallor. She had, nevertheless, been a popular dancing partner for many of the male passengers during balls, and Johnny had charmed the ladies over games of whist. They went directly from the boat train to the Langham Hotel in London and registered as Mr. and Mrs. John McNear of Chicago, U.S.A. The suite included gas fixtures, a bath with running water, a magnificent Regency four-poster bed, and a divan in the sitting room for Johnny to take his rest while April slept behind lock and key with her little Remington beneath her pillow.

This last was the only condition she'd imposed, and since her arm in his improved his social opportunities every time they appeared in public, he honored it without protest. Their arrangement had already furnished him with one shipboard liaison while the woman's husband was engaged at poker in the main salon; the absence of a romantic commitment spared Johnny chagrin at April's own conquest of a commander of the British Empire that same night. At breakfast the next morning they celebrated each other's success with champagne cups.

To those who'd heard it before, the name McNear was vaguely associated with power in the great Midwestern city whose beef graced many an English sideboard. Because politics and trade were forbidden topics of discussion in a class whose estates had benefited from investments made during the American Civil War, neither Johnny nor April had been required to utter a single untruth about their livelihood. This was a relief, since to confess to a background in the theater would hardly be more disastrous than to account for their activities in banks, express offices, and pursers' cabins over the past year. Whatever small gaucheries they committed in their new company were applied to their Yankee pedigree: "Quite charming, don't you know, and neither of them appears to chew tobacco."

In private, the couple made sport of their late acquaintances as they had their victims in the cities and hamlets out West.

"They're as witless as bullwhackers beneath the accents," Johnny had confided over that congratulatory breakfast. "One wonders if their cashiers and clerks are as ripe to pluck."

"Shopkeepers and clarks, dear." April pouted. "Don't forget, we're on holiday. And Scotland Yard is not a citizens' posse."

"You're right, of course. How old Scipio Africanus would chuckle to learn I've become a slave to my profession."

"It's time you emerged from his shadow. You're a better thief than ever he was."

"A successful run depends upon a talented cast; the leading lady above all."

They clinked glasses.

The connections they'd made at sea had provided them with introductions to West End society, and also created the necessity to drape themselves properly for garden parties, shootings on weekends, and evenings at the opera. They learned quickly that what was considered the zenith of fashion in St. Louis and Denver had had its season when Gladstone was at Downing, and that high collars, round lapels, and prominent bustles had become inexpressibly provincial under Disraeli. Standards (such as those that governed adultery) were relaxed during the transition of an ocean voyage and reinstated rigidly in Westminster. Johnny spent his first full day in London on Praed Street, being measured for morning dress and tails and wardrobes for both city and country, while April consulted a Regent Street seamstress among yards of taffeta and bolts of Chinese and Italian silk. Parcels and hatboxes piled up in their suite and their memorandum books filled with appointments for additional fittings.

The days sped past. April, striking in a new scarlet habit, took riding lessons in Hyde Park; Johnny shot at grouse at Fulham and clipped the elbow off a marble statue of Hermes; April saw a Russian grand duchess in a portrait in the British Museum whom she insisted was her fabled grandmother; Johnny lost his watch at darts in a public house on Northumberland; April dined at Simpson's with the third son of a baron and returned to the hotel the following morning to find the suite filled with carnations; Johnny sprained an ankle jumping from a balcony adjoining a married lady's boudoir in Kensington. They toasted and commiserated over kippers and tea, laced with cognac from a hammered silver flask Johnny had bought from a peddler in the Tottenham Court Road.

"What did you *say* to him?" She leaned forward eagerly.

" 'Well, which is it? Irving or Henry?' "

She laughed, turning heads at the restaurant as toward a fresh breeze through crystal pendants.

He looked rueful. "I'd overimbibed a bit. I daresay I won't be invited back to the Garrick, and I may strike Irving's name off my list of professional contacts."

"Poor dear. I'm afraid you've had the short end of things."

"Not a bit of it. I came to Europe for adventure and the old girl hasn't let me down."

His next encounter with Old World customs dampened his taste for exploits.

Johnny and April attended *Lohengrin* at Covent Garden; and more than a few pairs of opera glasses turned their way when they entered their box. Her fuschia gown was a flicker of rose flame and his black cutaway and snow-white waistcoat called attention to his broad shoulders and narrow waist. At intermission, he excused himself to seek lemonade for them both, but did not return until the lights were lowering for the second act. His face was nearly as pale as his collar and he was empty-handed.

"What's happened?" she whispered.

He looked at her in silence for a moment, then gave a short hollow cough of a laugh. "I saw a woman of my acquaintance in the foyer—and her husband, whom I did not know. It seems we're to meet with pistols tomorrow at dawn."

"Oh, Johnny!"

"Where the devil is Hampstead Heath, anyway?"

April said, "I don't understand why we don't simply cut short our visit and sail to France."

They were riding in a hired brougham through the predawn damp. He wore his caped overcoat, she an embroidered shawl over a white dress. A cold mist condensed into drops on her opened parasol, white also.

"The husband is something in shipping," said Johnny. "He'd have me pulled down the gangplank and shot under the blasted rules of chivalry."

"Next time you seduce a married woman, make sure you're not on an island."

"You're in awfully good spirits considering you're about to become a widow."

"Perhaps you'll win."

"The only way that could happen is if I shot at something else and hit him by accident. No statue is safe when I take aim at a bird just released from a trap." He tapped the driver's seat with his stick. "Stop here. I'll walk the rest of the way."

"Go on, driver. You know very well I can't walk far in these heels."

"Stop, I said. I'm doing the walking. You're riding back to the hotel. I don't know why I let you talk me into bringing you this far. Women don't attend duelling matches."

"I don't see why not. We're the cause of most of them."

The driver slowed the horses to a walk and twisted in his seat. "Which is it?"

"Stop."

"Go. I won't get out, Johnny, and you'll be late for your appointment. What do the blasted rules of chivalry say about that?"

"Oh, drive on. The least you could have done was put on something less conspicuous. When the sun comes up you'll stand out like a field of lillies."

"I should hope so. It's such a dour day. Where do you want to lunch?"

"Buckingham Palace. Or on top of the Albert dome, if you prefer. I'll have wings by then."

"Perhaps we'll dine in the suite. Ah! Here we are. Good luck, Johnny." She presented her cheek.

He took her face between his palms and kissed her on the lips. "Good-bye."

As he struck off through the wet grass toward where the party awaited him, she opened her reticule and repaired the damage to her makeup. Then she swung open the door.

"You'd best stay here, missus," said the driver. "You never know which way them balls will fly."

"Isn't that the truth?" She stepped down and lifted her hem clear of the mud. As she approached the slight rise where the men stood—Johnny, the aggrieved husband, his second, the man who'd volunteered to attend Johnny, and a tall, sallow-faced fellow carrying a doctor's bag—the sun broke over St. Pancras and the rain stopped. She folded her parasol.

The movement caught the attention of the men on the rise, who turned their heads her way and began gesturing animatedly.

". . . absolutely irregular . . ."

". . . rules . . ."

". . . no restrictions . . ."

"Yellow cad."

This last, from the husband, reached her ears all in one piece, unbroken by the open distance. Johnny made no response, but as no one approached her she assumed the controversy of her presence was settled.

Johnny selected a long-barreled pistol from a box in the hands of the husband's second and made a show of testing its balance and accuracy, raising it to shoulder level and holding it at arm's length, sighting along it; bits of business straight out of the third act of *The Count of Monte Cristo*. The husband, obviously unfamiliar with the production, seemed hesitant at this display of expert knowledge, but then Johnny spoiled the effect by dropping the pistol at his feet. A delay followed during which the second extracted the ball and wadding and damp powder, cleaned and oiled the weapon, and reloaded it. The sun by this time was clear of the distant roofs, and April adjusted her position.

At last the curtain rose on the action. Johnny and the husband, a burly brute with the erect bearing of an experienced campaigner, stood back to back with pistols elevated and started pacing.

"One . . . two . . . three . . ." Johnny's second called the count.

April loosened the drawstring of her reticule, dangling from her right wrist.

". . . seven . . . eight . . ."

A cloud crept in front of the sun. April took her lower lip between her teeth and held it until it passed.

". . . ten."

The duellists turned and leveled their pistols. April jerked open her parasol. The white lace caught the sun like a sudden puff of smoke. The husband, startled, jerked his trigger. Smoke shot out the end of the barrel. A yew three twenty feet behind Johnny stirred its branches.

A brief silence followed, ending when Johnny's second cleared his throat. "You may take your shot, sir."

Johnny swayed, and April worried he'd been hit after all. Then he stiffened his stance, pivoted wide to the right, and fired at an uninhabited section of the heath.

April exhaled and tied up the reticule with her little Remington inside.

Johnny stood with arms akimbo among their packed trunks and valises. "Why don't we extend our stay a few days? Paris has waited for us this long. It will still be there at the beginning of next week."

"You're saying that only because you're the social lion this week." April, seated at the secretary, circled an item in the *Times*. "As if surviving a ridiculous stunt carries any sort of merit."

"It was gallantry. I could have struck the fellow down but chose mercy instead."

"That was luck—and my parasol. You said yourself the only way you could hit him was if you aimed elsewhere."

"The parasol may have been unnecessary. Anyone so easily distracted is no kind of marksman."

"He's wounded three men in four years. And you're forgetting duelling is outlawed in England. We should have left yesterday."

Someone knocked at the door. Johnny said, "It's too early for the porter."

She directed him to step into the bedroom and went to the door to inquire who it was.

"New Scotland Yard, Madam."

The door to the bedroom drew shut with a thump. She undid the latch.

The little man in the hall removed his bowler and introduced himself as Inspector Gargan. He was accompanied by a constable in uniform. "We're here to ask your husband to come with us," he said. "He must answer for what took place at Hampstead yesterday morning."

"My husband has left for America. He took the boat train to Gravesend two hours ago."

His moustaches twitched, increasing his unfortunate resemblance to a rodent. "What ship, please?"

"The *Dolley Madison,* bound for Boston. Here, he's circled it." She turned briefly, picked up the *Times* from the secretary, and handed it to him. It was folded to the shipping column.

He glanced at the mark she'd made. "Why did you not accompany him?"

"We've separated. He was unfaithful to me, and nearly killed another man for his transgression." Her lower lip quivered.

"Are all those traps yours?" He peered past her.

"Yes. I'm going on to Paris. Search the suite if you like." She stepped aside from the doorway.

The constable tugged at his helmet and took a step forward. Gargan stopped him with a gesture. "That won't be necessary. I'll wire Gravesend. Perhaps they've delayed departure. Thank you very kindly, madam. I'm sorry for your trouble."

Johnny came out after they'd left. His face was flushed. "That was taking a chance."

"Not really. They'd have searched the place on their own if I hadn't offered."

"What if they took you up on it?"

She smiled. "Then you'd have had your chance to play Sidney Carton. A 'far, far better thing,' and all that."

"You've bought us nothing but time, and little of that. They'll be watching the hotel and the boat train and the dock."

"True." She sighed. "Well, we smuggled banknotes and double eagles out of half a dozen towns out West. I'm sure we can smuggle you across the Channel."

The *S.S. Dover Castle* sailed with the tide for France. Inspector Gargan, his constable, and others were on hand to watch the passengers ascending the gangplank. The inspector lifted his bowler as April passed, her hat secured with a scarf tied beneath her chin to protect her hair from cinders drifting from the stacks. She nodded in response.

Her luggage arrived at her stateroom once the ship was in motion. She tipped the porter, twisted the latch on the door, and unstrapped the largest of the two trunks she'd held out from the hold. Johnny, in shirtsleeves and wrinkled trousers, unfolded himself from inside and stretched, cracking his joints. "I thought for certain they'd mixed up the instructions. I paid for first class, not baggage."

"Listen to you complain. *You* didn't leave half your London wardrobe for the chambermaid to find in the hamper. I'll need to start all over again in Paris, and I expect you to pay for it." April took a skirt from the other trunk and hung it in the closet.

"In that case, we shan't afford more than a few days in Rome."

"What of it? All anyone ever goes to see is the Coliseum and the Parthenon."

"Pantheon, dear. The Parthenon's in Athens. Really, you should read something besides the plays of Cornelius Ragland."

"Be grateful I read the *Times*."

13

While Johnny and April were taking in the wonders of the Old World and the authorities of Europe, Cornelius Ragland was taking the waters in Hot Springs, Arkansas, and writing *The Tragedy of Joan of Arc,* for which he hoped to be remembered. He spent an hour each morning parboiling himself in mineral water with steam pouring off it, then returned to his hotel room for a light breakfast in bed and spent the day filling sheets of foolscap, using his tray for a desk and stopping frequently to consult the thick research books stacked on the nightstand, all of them bloated with narrow rectangles of paper marking particular passages for review. In the afternoon he took tea only, saving his delicate appetite for supper in the hotel's excellent restaurant. He had a preference for poached salmon or boiled beef with steamed vegetables and bread pudding for dessert. Then to sleep. It was a most virtuous existence among surroundings sinfully decadent.

Cornelius was the son of a postmaster in Baltimore and had passed a civil service examination to clerk in the same post office before his health forced him to seek a position in the gentler climate of Missouri. He was asthmatic and suffered from chronic exhaustion, which a Baltimore physician had misdiagnosed as consumption, which had exempted him from the draft. A more cosmopolitan practitioner in St. Louis had corrected the record and recommended Hot Springs. However, accommodations were dear in that popular place for recuperation and recreation, and at the rate he'd managed to put money aside from his salary as private secretary to Peter Argyle, manager of the St. Louis branch of the Gateway Bank & Trust of St. Louis, Kansas City, and Denver, he'd calculated that it would take him five years to afford to stay there one week. Thanks to his association with the Prairie Rose Repertory Company, he had a suite for the season in the best hotel in town.

He was, he confessed to himself, a naïf, and still a bit shocked at how easily he'd been corrupted; but a perceptive observer of his companions and especially himself. He assigned whatever skills he had as a writer to that source. Johnny Vermillion held him in thrall. The disgracefully immoral young man from Chicago possessed many of the qualities Cornelius admired, and which he incorporated into the heroes of the plays he cribbed from the work of superior writers: charm, comeliness, audacity, athletic grace, elegant manners, and the sort of personality that drew men to him as well as women. These things gave him confidence Cornelius would never have, and the modicum of arrogance that was shared by most leaders of men. There was no telling how high he might have risen in politics had he followed his father's example.

A conscience he had not; and this, too, was a source of envy for a young man who was burdened with rather more than his share. He had witnessed far too much perfidy in banking to feel any sympathy toward the institutions from which the Prairie Rose stole, but that wisdom did nothing more than modify his own feelings of guilt. In the world that had come into being since the War of the Rebellion, he considered it more of an affliction than a virtue, and cursed himself as a weakling.

Much of Johnny had made its way into Cornelius' villains as well, although he doubted the man who had inspired them recognized himself there. It was a revelation how many traits knights and brigands had in common, at least when they were practicing their chivalry and treachery in front of painted canvas.

Cornelius could not be Johnny, as much as he tried to be, through the characters he employed in his plays. Failing that, he found it enough to be near him, and to consider him his friend. He had no others. The head of the company treated him with more warmth and regard than any man he'd known before, beginning with his stern, disappointed father. He praised Cornelius' writing, gave him courage and patient advice when his turn came to commit robbery—*armed robbery,* more terrible and exhilarating than his one experiment in the pleasures of the flesh, with a prostitute who'd accosted him on the levee in St. Louis—and in all things celebrated him as an equal.

Cornelius Ragland loved Johnny Vermillion.

His feelings toward the others were more ambivalent.

Mme. Elizabeth Mort-Davies intimidated him with her mannish height, large hands, and top-lofty ways, but on stage was a versatile character actress whose range permitted him to embroider heavily upon Dickens' grim dowagers, Shakespeare's dithering nurses, Dumas *père's* fawning duchesses, and the long chain of sculls, dames, palm readers, hags, fishwives, nannies, landladies, daubs, frumps, flounces, and queen mothers who rattled and clanked through the distaff side of the British and American theater, to say nothing of the hordes of androgynous sailors, footmen, grave diggers, friars, churls, and sergeants at arms for which her statuesque build and husky contralto suited her. She could also, in a pinch, as when April Clay's less celebrated talents were wanted elsewhere (in seldom-traveled towns where a female of any description might pass as the Jersey Lily), play the heroine for one brief scene staged artfully; or more convincingly, the romantic lead. Still, he preferred to keep his distance, and to channel whatever suggestions he felt appropriate during rehearsals through Johnny, who proved a patient and per-suasive director. The man's abilities appeared to be without limit.

Cornelius held Major Evelyn Davies in genial contempt, but found him the perfect blithering foil for Johnny's urbane swash-bucklers, as clever at parlor banter as they were at swordplay and fisticuffs. When the time came to announce the ambassador from the Court of St. James, or the father of the bride, or the bishop who'd made one trip too many to the chamber where the sacra-mental wine was stored, the fat fellow with the preposterous white handlebars knew no peer. He was also an unscrupulous part-padder and stealer of scenes, and without Lizzie close at hand to still his unpredictable impulses, tended to boast about things best kept in-side the company, at a level intended for the back row of the bal-cony. He made Cornelius exceedingly nervous, both as a playwright and as an accomplice to numerous felonies, each punishable by many years at hard labor. He enjoyed the Major's outlandish sto-ries about the London stage (which he may or may not have expe-rienced at firsthand), but was contented to leave his keeping to Johnny and the inestimable Madame.

April Clay was not so easily summed up by language; and lan-guage was all he had.

In the lexicon of melodrama, she seemed to be equal parts guileless maiden and scheming harpy—although a more passive and sweet-natured she-beast would have been difficult to find in the history of theater. She seldom raised her voice, never uttered so much as a mild oath, and apart from that tense hour outside Salt Lake City when Lizzie was thought to have been captured and their own freedom was in question, the playwright had never seen her more than mildly upset. She did not insist, she did not assert, yet there were times when she appeared to be leading the Prairie Rose, and not Johnny. Sex, of course, was the instrument, but there were no secrets in the close society of a company touring the primitive reaches of the frontier, with its shared dressing rooms and tight hotel quarters often separated by no more than two thicknesses of wallpaper, and Cornelius was certain the two were not intimate. But a woman whose merry glance could make a man's heart miss a step, and whose touch on his arm when he reached up to retrieve her train case from an overhead rack could turn his knees to water, could enslave him without unpinning her hat.

He was writing St. Joan with her in mind, and it would be one like no other. He could picture her neither listening to any voice outside her own nor succumbing to any flames not of her kindling. In Philadelphia, the authorities would shut down the opening-night performance before the end of the first act; in Wichita, where such Joans were Saturday-night staples in every saloon and bawdy house, the play might run six weeks.

It wouldn't, of course. With a sigh, Cornelius Ragland remembered that his was no ordinary repertory company, and that its concept of theater was more sophisticated than most county sheriffs and committees of public vigilance were prepared to embrace.

He sipped his tea, which had grown cold, and trimmed his pen, which had caked. Just thinking about Johnny, the Davieses, and April made one feel as if he'd been creating vivid characters for hours, when in fact he hadn't touched nib to paper.

The editor of the *Eureka Daily News* had a talent for caricature, and had enlivened his column on last night's presentation of *The Diplomat Deposes* with an amusing and accurate pen-and-ink sketch of the fictive elder statesman, resembling a tulip bulb wearing a silk hat, and the erect and somewhat equine object of his passion. At the moment, copies of the sketch torn from the paper were clutched in the hands of Wendell Zick, city marshal, and three of his deputies as they watched passengers board the Northern Pacific bound for San Francisco. They were eager to interview Major and Mme. Mort-Davies in connection with a number of silver snuff-boxes, gold toothpicks, and a fine buffalo coat reported missing from the theater cloakroom, and the matter of an unpaid hotel bill.

Traffic was heavy, with the loggers down from the hills to shake off the effects of the long winter hibernation in the hellholes of Barbary with their accumulated pay, and the Russians remaining from old Fort Ross hurrying to meet relatives for Easter services in the Orthodox church, and all of them impatient to get away from the mud and one another. Several times, Zick and his men had had to lunge to pull likely candidates out of the stream and compare their faces to the features in the illustration. None of those thus delayed took the inconvenience with good grace, and the press of those coming up behind led to collisions, harsh words in a number of languages, and the intervention of officers to prevent fistfights and possibly a knifing or gunplay. Zick himself swore a

German oath when a tall Russian in a fur hat and full beard ran over the marshal's instep with a wicker bath-chair bearing an old woman piled with rugs and wound to her white hair with scarves, a carpetbag in her lap. The couple continued on its way without pausing until a pair of porters stepped down from a car to help hoist woman and wheelchair aboard. Eureka, a rough place when Zick first came to it, but open and friendly, had since the completion of the spur to San Francisco turned as sullen as any of the Gomorrahs in the East.

As the train pulled out, the marshal sought his men, only to find them with empty hands and shaking heads, and stepped back to study the passenger windows fluttering past, but none of the profiles he glimpsed there drew a close enough resemblance to the sketch to warrant sending a wire to the next stop. He tore up the scrap of newsprint and walked off the platform, trailing the pieces like Hansel and Gretel in the wicked forest.

The Northern picked up speed coming down the coast and leveled out at forty with a long blast on its whistle, a catcall to those left behind in Eureka. The Russian couple sat in facing seats; the porters had removed the bath-chair to the baggage car on the assurance that the old woman could manage the trip to and from the water closet with a cane and the assistance of her companion. Major Evelyn Davies snatched off his white wig and scratched his bald head with a furious, motoring movement like a dog.

Elizabeth Mort-Davies blew exasperatedly through the mass of llama hair covering her face and leaned forward to take the wig and tug it back down to the Major's ears. "Wells, Fargo pays porters for information. If they suspect anything they'll have us held in Frisco and wire back to Eureka if nothing comes of it, and something might. Don't forget Sioux Falls."

"You might at least have given me one without fleas."

"You might have foregone oysters in garlic sauce the last time you wore these whiskers."

At about the time Johnny Vermillion and April Clay were crossing to France and Major and Mme. Mort-Davies were riding the rails in disguise to San Francisco, the Ace-in-the-Hole Gang was in the middle of its worst run of luck since three of its more colorfully named members died under violent and ignominious circumstances, clearing Black Jack Brixton's path toward its leadership.

In a vainglorious moment during the robbery of the Pioneers Bank in Table Rock, Wyoming Territory, the president of that in-stitution scooped a Schofield revolver from the belly drawer of his rolltop desk and shot Tom Riddle high in the chest. The rest of the gang responded characteristically, perforating the president with lead, but Tom did not benefit. Shock and loss of blood tipped him out of his saddle a mile outside town and they were forced to retreat to a cave to patch his wound and give him rest. By morning he was feverish and jabbering more than usual; it was clear he needed med-ical attention to survive. Brixton and Breed were in favor of finish-ing him off and skedaddling, but Ed and Charlie Kettleman voted to fetch a doctor, and Mysterious Bob broke the tie by throwing in with the brothers, possibly because he suspected his own habitual silence would become oppressive without Tom's garrulity to bal-ance it. Internal tension had broken up more successful criminal as-sociations than the Pinkertons and the U.S. marshals combined.

They sent Charlie. He'd proven himself capable of recovering the money from the Salt Lake City debacle, even if he'd lacked the foresight to drive home the lesson by killing the woman he'd found in possession. He went without protest. Brixton was still simmering over Charlie's failure to secure the woman's silence in Denver, and when it came to insubordination he'd been known to override the will of the majority with a bullet.

Leading his horse down Table Rock's main street to avoid spooking the recently robbed residents, squinting at signs in search of "M.D.," Charlie caught a bit of luck when a pudgy, gray-haired man in a rumpled suit stepped out the front door of a private house carrying a small satchel just as the bandit was passing. The man paused to touch his hat to a woman standing just inside the doorway, who addressed him as "Dr. Edwin."

Charlie waited while the man set his satchel on the seat of a worn buggy in front of the house, then when he turned to untie the equally worn-looking horse that was hitched to it, tethered his own mount to the back of the buggy, stepped up behind him, and stuck the muzzle of his captured Colt against the man's ribs.

"You drive, Doc. I got a new one for your rounds."

Edwin put up a squawk, said he wasn't the doctor for him, to which Charlie replied it wasn't for him, and put an end to the palaver by thumbing back the Colt's hammer. Edwin climbed onto the driver's seat without another word and they rode out of town with the big revolver in Charlie's lap pointing at the driver.

In the cave, where the atmosphere was thick thanks to Ed having mistakenly tossed a Douglas fir branch onto the fire and filling the place with noxious smoke (and his companions with homicidal intent), Dr. Edwin goggled at the sight of Tom stretched on his bedroll, babbling in his stained bandages torn from a canvas bank sack. "What is it you wish me to do?"

"Do? Dig out the slug, for chrissake!" Brixton looked more disconcerting than usual with his bandanna tied over his nose and mouth to prevent asphyxiation. He'd taken the precaution of soaking it in Old Gideon and was inebriating himself further with each breath he drew. Needless to say, he was an unpleasant drunk.

When Edwin remained hesitant, Breed tore the satchel from his hand and dumped it out onto the cave floor to facilitate. Instead of instruments and bottles, books spilled into a pile, with Volume Five of Gibbon perched on top.

During interrogation, it developed that Edwin was a doctor of philosophy, retained by the woman of the house Charlie had seen him leaving to tutor her fourteen-year-old son in the history of Western civilization. More smoke ensued of the burnt-powder variety, and Erastus Edwin, professor emeritus of the University of Maryland, claimed his own footnote in history as the only Roman scholar to lose his life at the hands of frontier bandits.

Brixton's fury having spent itself on the unfortunate pedant, Charlie took his punishment in the form of a fresh horse and a third trip to Table Rock to correct his error. This time, he broke into the office of Benjamin Ruddock, M.D., at the top of a flight of stairs slanting up the outside wall of a harness shop, and finding it unoccupied spent his time while waiting for the proprietor's return satisfying himself as to the medical nature of the equipment and spelling out the script on a framed diploma on the wall above the examining table. When after forty-five minutes the door opened, he threw down on the rat-faced individual who came in carrying a cylindrical case and explained his errand. Dr. Ruddock shrugged and turned to precede him out the door.

"Hold on! Let's have a look in that there bag first. If it's full of books I'll plug you right here and save the trip."

Ruddock unlatched the case, spread it open, and held it out for Charlie's inspection. While the desperado peered at the probes, forceps, rolls of gauze, and corked containers arranged neatly inside, the doctor swept a two-pound medical dictionary off a shelf, knocked him senseless, tied him with bandages, and went for the county sheriff, whose office stood next door to the harness shop. Ruddock, as it happened, had just returned from an identical abduction to tend to a member of the Turkey Creek Outfit, who'd lost three fingers blasting open a safe in the mail car of the Santa Fe Railroad outside Bitter Creek two days before; he'd been hot, tired, trail-sore, and in no humor for another enforced house call so soon after the first.

Ironically, Tom Riddle survived. Breed, impatient over the delay, used his big Bowie to extract the bullet, not caring overmuch whether the surgery was fatal so long as it freed them to ride, and Tom's miner's constitution did the rest. When he was strong enough to sit a horse, Ed and Mysterious Bob took him to his sister's pig farm in Nebraska to complete his recovery and returned to help Brixton and Breed separate Charlie from the jail in Table Rock. This they managed to do while the sheriff was at supper, leaving an inexperienced deputy in charge. So pleased was the gang by this unaccustomed stroke of good fortune that it satisfied itself with binding and gagging the deputy and locking him in Tom's former cell instead of shooting him. (Ungratefully, the Table Rock Merchants Association added a hundred dollars a head to the reward for Ace-in-the-Hole's capture or destruction. The late president of the Pioneers Bank was a popular member of its poker circle.)

When Tom rejoined the gang, he had an anthology of new stories to tell, including a fanciful version of how he'd come by his wound despite the evidence of his listeners' own eyes, and an involved anecdote about his efforts to teach simple arithmetic to one of his sister's hogs. The others were grateful for the fresh material, and happy to be hearing something other than Bob's deadly quiet and their own stale thoughts. For a solid week, their "Shut up, Tom" lacked conviction.

But Charlie Kettleman was never the same after Table Rock. The blow from the medical dictionary had addled him, and during his occasional lucid moments he insisted that a bunch of those long words had leaked into his brain through the crack in his skull, tangling with his thoughts and making them come out incomprehensible and impossible to pronounce. This ruined him for horse trading; brother Ed was forced to increase his own skills twofold to keep the others from dwelling on the wisdom that Charlie had lost his usefulness and ought to be expelled.

Black Jack Brixton's theory about this latest setback was simpler than Charlie's. He was superstitious, it must be remembered, and had formed the conclusion that Ace-in-the-Hole's sour string had begun with its first encounter with the Prairie Rose Repertory Company, and would continue until they closed the curtain on its final performance.

14

In Paris, although they shared a suite in the century-old Hotel d'Hall-
wyl, Johnny and April were kept so busy by their respective sched-
ules they rarely saw each other except to say good night on their
way to their rooms. Each missed the other's company and perspective, and at length they decided to revive their St. Louis tradition
and meet every day at a restaurant they both found pleasing, to re-
new their acquaintance and compare the details of their day.

Their choice was the Maison Cador, next to the church of Saint-
Germain-l'Auxerrois and across from the east end of the Louvre,
where Claude Monet had stood on a balcony to paint that Gothic
pile eight years before. There in a cream-and-gold room decorated
in relief and hung with crystal chandeliers, they sat in cane chairs
at a pink marble table, sampling the patisserie's sweets and omelets
and correcting each other's French.

"Another new frock?" said he one day, admiring her pearl-colored
suit and gray silk shirtwaist. Her straw hat wore an abundance of

intricately tied ribbons. "Shall we rob the *Banque de France,* or stow away in a lifeboat during the voyage home?"

"The *Banque* is impregnable to our method. I made a point of checking it out last week. In any case, you have our return tickets stitched inside the lining of that hideous caped overcoat. You oughtn't to leave it lying about."

"I don't consider hanging it in the wardrobe in my room leaving it lying about. You sewed it back up with admirable skill. I didn't detect it."

"I took it to a seamstress, and supervised her work."

He nibbled at a cream-filled pastry. "Did you think I was hoarding love letters? I'm beginning to think you're living your role. Repertory players are especially susceptible when they don't trade off."

"That's poppycock, and you know it. I wanted to make sure you weren't selling forged American railroad stock to gullible Europeans. You might end up in the Chateau D'If for real, and then where would I be, a woman alone in wicked Paree?"

"A bit less emphasis on the second syllable. I distinctly heard the double *e.*"

"It's pronunciation now, is it? Have you been taking French lessons behind my back?" She took a forkful of egg poached in white wine, made a little face, and sipped water to dilute the effect. Parisian food did not agree with her, much to her dismay; she felt it betrayed her American palate to the natives. In consequence, she ordered Parisian only, and bought peppermints by the half pound to put her stomach to rest afterward.

"Only indirectly. My fencing instructor has taken it upon himself to turn me into a *boulevardier.* He makes his vocabulary points quite literally." He touched a tiny scratch on his left cheek.

"I'd wondered about that. I thought you'd run afoul of a married marquis. Precautionary measures?"

"I think and hope I've fought my last duel. If challenged again, I'll choose parasols at dawn. I merely wish to improve my form the next time I cross swords with Corny onstage. He's gotten more graceful, have you noticed? It wouldn't do for Hamlet to lose to Laertes."

"Your poor beautiful face. Haven't those foils little round beads on the ends?"

"Buttons. Monsieur Anatole doesn't believe in them, nor in protective headgear. He considers fear of serious injury a useful learning device."

"*Un gros sauvage.* He'll put your eye out, and you'll play nothing but beggars and pirates the rest of your days."

"*Sauvage, oui. Gros, non.* He's scarcely your height, and I rather think you have the advantage of a pound or two. In all the most charming places, I hasten to add. He's damnably fast, and I think he has it in for men of greater stature."

"He'll kill you. Or give you one of those horrible white scars that look like tapeworms."

"I wonder which will distress you most," he mused. "You needn't be concerned about the former. I pay him only after each session, and then by cheque. He's an officer retired on half pay, with little more coming in thanks to his temperament." He sipped his coffee. "And what athletics have you attempted? Waltzing with counts?"

"I tired of the nobility the first week. The men all wear corsets and the women smell like mortuaries. My interests have taken a Bohemian turn. I've met the most interesting painter."

"Not one of those ragged Impressionists, I hope."

"He isn't that kind of painter. He specializes in houses and bridges, which in this city should keep him employed for life. He has muscles in places I didn't know they could be grown."

"You always fascinate me when you blush," he said. "It's a characteristic I've tried to develop, but in vain."

"For that, you have to have been raised in the Catholic faith."

"Oh, but I was. Every Sunday my father and I shared a pew with the governor, where Father delivered his graft by way of the collection plate. So will you surrender your citizenship and rear Anglo-French bastards on the Left Bank?"

"If I made that choice, they'd not be bastards."

There was no banter in this; her tone was cold and metallic. She attacked her eggs.

They finished the meal in silence. She was gone before he could rise, her skirts swishing over her curt good-bye.

Johnny finished his coffee in deep thought. He'd never known April to take serious insult to anything he'd said. He wondered if perhaps they shouldn't leave Rome to the philosophers and return home. Britain and the Continent had begun to corrupt them with its centuries of respectability.

Gilbert Anatole was a former colonel of the Second Empire, who claimed to have lost his right hand to Prussian grapeshot at Sedan, converted to Marxism under the Commune, and dedicated himself to the overthrow of the Third Republic in favor of a government run by the proletariat, of which as a humble soldier he considered himself a member in good standing. He was an ugly little man with a dark complexion who parted his scant hair in the center and wore a singlet and old-fashioned silk breeches that

accentuated his womanly hips and a set of genitals all out of pro-
portion to his small body. Johnny could not help looking at his
crotch, to his own intense shame and near disaster to his person
when they fenced. Fortunately, although he was convinced Anatole was a pederast, he himself was not the man's romantic preference. Valèry, the shaggy, paunchy gnome who showed up at the
end of each session to drive him home, displayed proprietary interest, and his unwashed body left a tang in the air of the grubby
little gymnasium in the Rue de la Glacière several minutes after
their departure.

Preposterous as he appeared when at rest, Anatole was a demon
on the mat; a whirling, lunging, unstoppable engine of destruction, lethal at every angle, as if he'd sprouted razor-sharp quills on
all sides in addition to the single foil (épée, properly, since the tip
was neither blunted nor rendered harmless by a button) in his remaining hand. In place of the other he wore a curious hook that
ended not in a point but in an elongated loop shaped like a narrow
spoon with a slot an inch and a half wide in the center. On the
rare occasions Johnny defended himself sufficiently to lock blades
in a tight clinch, the little colonel inserted Johnny's nose in the slot
and gave it a savage twist that brought tears to the victim's eyes—
and once a deviated septum, which Anatole later corrected by repeating the operation in the opposite direction, wrenching it back
into place with a heart-stopping crack and nearly as much pain as
the original injury.

"Damn your eyes!" Johnny sprang back with his hands to his
face. Blood seeped between his fingers.

"*Devene un homme, Americain.* Be a man. I have left a piece of
myself on every battlefield in Europe, and not a single tear. Did
you not fight the rebel and conquer the red Indian?"

"Not personally. If Lee had armed his troops with contraptions like that, they'd be eating grits in Washington. Sometimes I think you forget we're only practicing. You confuse me with Bismarck."

"Ha. If you were Bismarck, they'd be eating crepes in Berlin. You poke when you should pounce. That is a sword, not a knitting needle. We go again. *En garde!*" He leveled his weapon, hook akimbo.

"On your own guard, you Gallic Attila. I'm through for the day." Johnny racked his épée and fished out a handkerchief.

Still, he progressed. He lost fat, although he had little surplus at the start, gained muscle, and straightened his posture; April commented on it at the end of his first week, before she learned what he'd been about. His reflexes improved rapidly, as they had to if he were to avoid decorating his face and torso with sticking plaster after each session, as he had after the inaugural. He was sore and sprained throughout that opening week, but ten days in he'd begun to acquire the kind of agility and economy of movement he'd only been able to affect onstage, naturally and without thought. Oddly enough, he first became aware of this not while fencing with Anatole, but on the ballroom floor, where a turn with the pretty daughter of a wealthy importer led quickly to her boudoir upstairs, where he could hear the violins still simpering below, and smell the smoke from her father's cigar in the sitting room of his chamber down the hall, where (she said) he was busy writing an eloquent letter to President Grant on the subject of tariffs. Johnny had never closed a seduction so promptly nor with so little conversation. Throughout that hour, he wondered at England's obsession with pugilism, when fencing was so much more rewarding. Monsieur Anatole was puzzled, and awkwardly pleased, when at the end of the course his student presented him with a splendid gold Swiss watch engraved with the master's initials; Valèry scowled.

Much later, in another hemisphere, Johnny Vermillion would ponder whether he ought to have given him much more. A watch, however beautiful and well-crafted, seemed poor payment for a life even so discreditable as his.

Allan Pinkerton loved to walk. The wiry fifty-six-year-old's morning constitutional was the delight of those visitors to Chicago who refused to leave the city until they had caught a glimpse of the internationally famous detective, and the bane of those subordinates who preferred to meet with the chief in the library of a gentlemen's club downtown, in leather chairs with snifters at their elbows. He conducted these conferences on the trot, swinging his stick and covering several miles of park and macadam without loss of breath. Nine years hence, that walk would end his life, when he would trip, bite through his tongue, and owing to careless treatment develop a fatal infection, making his the only documented case in history of a man having bitten himself to death.

But in the late spring of 1875, the rugged Scot was in the glory of good health, and Philip Rittenhouse, who had balked at neither the misery of three days aboard the stage aptly christened the Bozeman Bonebreaker nor a week of dysentery brought on by the chicken and dumplings served at Ma Smalley's boardinghouse in Omaha, found himself hard-pressed to keep up with his superior. The trek lacked the adventure of life on the border, with a subtext of sadism on the part of its instigator; for the man who coined the phrase "We never sleep" secretly loved to torture those in his employ, including the two who shared his blood. His sons, William and Robert, longed for his decline and their opportunity to remake the agency in their image, with due public obeisance to the old-world individualism of its illustrious founder.

Rittenhouse lifted his bowler to mop his bald head with a scarlet handkerchief, his only ostentation, and new since his Western sojourn—a sort of personal Order of the Garter for services rendered unto the goddess Justice. Those who called him the Reptile would gawk at the spectacle of his perspiring under any circumstances, including the old man's dreaded constitutional.

"I fail to see why you called me out of the office," said he, "unless the prospect of deadly apoplexy looks better to you than paying my pension."

"I ought to dismiss you for that. No one speaks to me so, including my sons. I sometimes wish they would."

"They're in a precarious position. You might decide to leave the agency to the boy who cleans the water closets, and they'll have to go to work."

"That is unjust. William at least is a top-notch detective. I know you've had your problems with him, but for my sake you might try to be insincere. I called you out here because I don't want to embar-r-rass you in the hearing of your colleagues. Jim Hume has been after me over Sioux Falls. That was your assignment."

"It still is, unless you've decided to take it out of my hands. Some cases take time to resolve, in spite of the lesson of those dime novels you write."

"Those are case histories. There is a great deal more to the detective business than apprehending criminals. The good will of the public is an invaluable source of unpaid information, and fear of retribution is a deter-r-rent to crime."

"Forgive me if I speak outside my station, but if we deter crime, do we not risk putting ourselves out to pasture?"

"I'm not hosting a debate," Pinkerton snarled. "Where does the investigation stand at present?"

"All over. I know from newspaper advertisements that Evelyn and Elizabeth Mort-Davies are performing in California, but if they're breaking the law, it's in too small a way to appear in the news columns. Cornelius Ragland seems to have fallen off the face of the earth, but then he was barely here to begin with. John Vermillion and April Clay have vanished also. I suspect they're in South America, or abroad. They attract attention wherever they go, but the effect is delayed here by the separation of culture and distance. It's possible the Prairie Rose has disbanded permanently."

"If that's the case, I advise you to swear out a complaint with the authorities in California against the Davieses and have them taken into custody. A rigid fare of bread and water ought to loosen the Major's tongue at least, if he's as fat as you say."

"He may know nothing of the others' whereabouts; in which case the publicity of the arrest will drive the rest deeper underground. I said it's possible they've split up for good. Such a move upon our part would make it a certainty."

"Suggest an alternative."

"The theatrical season begins again in the fall. We have crimes enough to occupy us until then. Ace-in-the-Hole and Turkey Creek struck within a few miles of each other in Wyoming Territory just last month."

"Each sustained a casualty, our confidential informants told me. Their luck has turned."

Rittenhouse was surprised. "I wasn't aware we had informants there."

"If I reported them to everyone in the agency, they wouldn't be confidential for long. We'll have ever-ry last man rounded up in a matter of weeks. Meanwhile the Davieses may slip through our fingers. Swear out that complaint."

They'd stopped to let a streetcar pass. Rittenhouse wiped off his scalp again and used the handkerchief on the sweatband inside the crown of his hat. Then he put it back on, reveling in the cool touch of the leather against his skin.

"Suppose we leave the authorities out of it for now and I investigate them in person," he said.

"Your last foray into the field was not a resounding success."

"I disagree. Before I made it, we thought a lone bandit had stuck up the Wells, Fargo office in Sioux Falls. Now we know the names of all the accomplices and have connected them with at least five other robberies, including one we didn't know about in St. Louis, which I suspect was their first. Thanks to reviews and advertising and my interviews, we know a good deal more about them than we do about Ace and Turkey Creek, not counting what you've heard from your phantom informants. Theirs may be the first criminal enterprise in history to employ the techniques of a press agent."

The streetcar had moved on, but the strollers had not. Pinkerton turned to study him. "What could you learn from the Davieses that sworn law enforcement could not?"

"Nothing, perhaps. Everything, possibly; but only if I went inside."

"Undercover?" The old man made an explosive noise, which for him was laughter. "Will you juggle, or sing opera, or teach a bear to dance?"

"Now would be an opportune time to inform you that my father was a theatrical booking agent on the vaudeville circuit.

He represented people who did all those things and more, and I ran his errands until age fifteen. If you'll stake me to an office in Portsmouth Square and a couple of hundred for advertising and promotion, I'll manage the rest."

The voyage home was gentler than the one out. The sun was strong on the top deck, the motion of the waves soporific. In adjoining deck chairs, April half dozed over a book while Johnny sipped gin and bitters, a taste he'd acquired in London. A gull perched on the railing looking for crumbs and, detecting none, took its leave, flapping indignantly. The sound awakened April, who sighed and found her place on the page. Johnny peeped at the title stamped in gold leaf on the spine: *La Vie de Jeanne D'Arc*. "Research?"

She started a little and looked at him as if she'd forgotten he was aboard. "Mm-hm." She resumed reading.

"If the ship's library has Shakespeare, you might want to give Anne Page a look. Remember, we're opening with *The Merry Wives*."

"Mm-hm." She turned a page.

"The Major will quite enjoy playing Falstaff, don't you agree?"

"Mm-hm."

He drained his glass and caught the eye of a steward, who came over for it. Johnny ordered another. The steward asked Mrs. Mc-Near if she cared for anything.

"No, thank you."

When they were alone again, Johnny turned onto his hip. "If you're disappointed about Rome, I'll make it up to you in New York: a suite at the Astor, dinner at Delmonico's. I understand Verdi has a new opera opening on Broadway. That's at least a taste of Italy."

She said nothing, reading.

He reached over and tipped her book forward. "Your French isn't that good, dear. You've said more to the steward than you have to me. Is it Rome?"

She placed the attached ribbon between the pages and closed the book. "I don't give two snaps for Rome. That was your idea. Johnny, have you never thought of retiring?"

"From the theater? I'm only thirty-one."

"You're barely *in* the theater, but you could be in it a great deal more. Denver is not so snobbish as St. Louis. If we played there three weeks, we could make as much as we took from any safe, and we'd not have to worry about arrest, or such horrible creatures as that fellow who assaulted Lizzie and ran us out of the country."

"Perhaps. And where then? Someplace like Tannery, at fifty cents a head and all the hump steak we can stomach? You're letting a few complimentary notices turn your head. We're far more successful desperadoes than thespians."

"We could be better if we kept to it. If we spent as much time rehearsing Corny's plays as we do preparing to commit felonies, we could put the Booths to shame. As it is we have some talent and only adequate skill."

"Bravado, certainly, and most of that onstage. You mustn't be discouraged by a couple of minor setbacks. Look at those guerrillas the Jameses and Youngers, hunted in every corner of the land. The Pinkertons and the railroad detectives don't even know we exist. Anyway, you knew the risks when you threw in with me."

She turned upon him the full force of her eyes. "We could be Mr. and Mrs. John McNear in truth. That's your real name, after all. You must have realized by now how fond I am of you."

"My father had a buggy horse he was fond of. That didn't stop him from having it shot when it broke a leg."

"Why must you bring your father into every serious conversation? He's dead, dead, dead!"

It was only the second time in their acquaintance he'd known her to display so much emotion without an audience looking on.

"Well?" she demanded.

"I wish——" He broke off.

"What do you wish?" she whispered, touching his arm. He felt an electric crackle: St. Elmo's Fire, not uncommon in open seas.

"I wish I were actor enough to know when you were performing."

Her expression did not change so much as congeal into something he could not hope to penetrate. She withdrew her hand.

"Well, we don't dock for a week. We'll discuss this again." She opened her book and returned to Joan of Arc.

The steward cleared his throat. It was Johnny's first intimation he'd returned from the bar. He turned back and accepted his drink.

"Lifeboat drill in fifteen minutes, sir. Will you be participating?"

Johnny squinted up at him. The sun was at his back. "Do they actually lower the boats into the water during the drill?"

"No, sir."

"In that case, the answer is no."

"Very good, sir." The steward bowed and left.

· IV ·

The
Final Season

15

In June 1875, the nation—or at least that part of it not engrossed by the scandals of the Grant Administration, or preparations for the American Centennial celebration to take place in Philadelphia a year later, or the surrender to U.S. forces by the Comanches at Fort Sill, or in converting to Christian Science after reading Mary Baker Eddy's *Science and Health,* or following *The Adventures of Tom Sawyer*—thrilled to sensational accounts in the press of the destruction of one of the West's most notorious outlaw bands in the sleepy hamlet of Spanish Trot, Colorado Territory.

The James and Younger brothers were still at large, and would continue to commit depredations to the entertainment of Eastern readers weary of the dismantlement of the Tweed Ring in New York City for another year, when a similarly spectacular end awaited them in Minnesota. It was not them, then, who completed their bloody cycle in Spanish Trot, nor the Ace-in-the-Hole Gang; but the Turkey Creek Outfit, who would fade from history in the shade of Northfield, Little Big Horn, and the assassination of Wild Bill

Hickok, all in 1876. ("I see no mystery in that," Bernard DeVoto would comment, two generations later. "Spanish Ridge, yes; perhaps even Spanish Fly. But Spanish *Trot*? I think I had a touch of it in Juarez.") There is no accounting for the choices made by posterity, as witness the inexplicably enduring legend of Billy the Kid, who in his only surviving photograph looks like the offspring of an incestuous relationship in the Appalachins, wearing a silly hat.

For a season, however, Turkey Creek in extremis offered all the active ingredients necessary to create an American myth: a daring daylight raid on a bank, the murder of an employee who in confusion transposed two digits in the combination of the vault, and a headlong plunge by the gang out the front door into a maelstrom of lead supplied by a determined citizens' committee that had been anticipating the visit for weeks. Interestingly, the information had come courtesy of the same gang member who had lost three fingers to a premature explosion of dynamite during the assault on the Santa Fe Railroad near Bitter Creek, Wyoming Territory, one month before, and who at the time of the bank disaster was recovering from his injury in Cheyenne. George Adam Cedarcrest, normally a fair hand with a powder charge, was an operative in the employ of the Pinkerton National Detective Agency. According to conventional wisdom, his conflict of interest had played an important part in his carelessness on that occasion. It also spared him his life, as Allan Pinkerton had turned over his intelligence to the local authorities to avoid tying up his agents for an indefinite period, and citizens' committees were not known to discriminate between friend and felon in the heat of fire.

Cedarcrest, whose maimed hand, together with his brief fame, had rendered him unsuitable for undercover work, was assigned to the file room in the San Francisco office, where he stayed until his retirement in 1891. Twenty-five years later, he died in the midst of negotiations with Famous Players-Lasky to adapt his self-published memoirs to the screen. The film was never made, and thousands of unsold copies of the book went back to the pulp mill. The rest of Turkey Creek found longer lasting recognition of a sort in 1974, when Time-Life Books published a picture of their corpses, arranged on planks for purposes of identification in Chicago, in its series on the Old West. The caption referred to them merely as a "bandit gang, ambushed by vigilantes in Colorado." (Black Jack Brixton, who saw the shot displayed in the window of a photographer's studio in New Mexico sometime after the disaster, noted a dirty toe poking out of a torn stocking, and laid in a supply of socks. He determined never to embark on another robbery without putting on a fresh pair.)

The other big story of that quarter, although it failed to inspire exclamatory headlines in the first column, proved more nourishing over the long run, in the form of journalistic speculation on slow news days. The disappearance of the Ace-in-the-Hole Gang, after a busy decade, puzzled authorities and was said to have created tension between Allan Pinkerton and the heads of all his Western field offices, who reported with palms spread that none of the sporadic episodes of rapacity that had taken place since the removal of one of their members from the jail in Table Rock bore their signature, and that nothing useful had been heard from any of the confidential informants they depended upon to keep track of itinerant marauders. A staple of frontier outlawry seemed simply to have floated off into outer space; a most unsatisfying end to an investigation that had claimed years and dollars far in excess of the amount Brixton and his followers had removed from banks, railroads, and express companies going back to the sack of

Yale, Kansas, on April 10, 1865, twenty-four hours after the surrender of the Confederacy.

Pinkerton ordered a relentless search of all the gang's known haunts, beginning with Denver. An army of grim-faced men in bowlers invaded Nell Dugan's Wood Palace with mauls and axes, punching holes in suspicious-looking walls, splintering locked doors, and demolishing a pump organ large enough to conceal a man behind its front panels, which it did not. Nell and her ladies of easy reputation followed the agents from room to room, slashing at their cigar smoke with Chinese fans, derogating their efforts in language colorful and cutting, and energetically attempting to seduce them away from their mission, with some success; three of the searchers did not report back to the Denver office until the next day, when they were summarily suspended for a month without pay.

Eventually the trapdoor in the back parlor was discovered, and laying down their tools in favor of pistols, the Pinkertons descended into the basement quarters, where they found all of the beds stripped except one, their mattresses rolled, and no one in residence except a vagrant known and loved by the citizens of Denver, all of whom were aware of his sad story of impoverishment after the vein of gold he'd been mining had thinned to nothing and his first flush of prosperity had been squandered at the Palace and its competitors. He explained, at gunpoint, that Nell had employed him to conduct odd repairs and given him shelter. In the six weeks of his stay, he insisted, none but he had appeared below ground except the Negro maid who came to change the sheets once a week. After some difficulty over a heavy chest of drawers that had been inadvertantly pushed over the trapdoor, sealing them in the basement, the agents departed empty-handed except for the tools they'd brought with them.

Altogether the damage to private property came to fifteen hundred dollars and change, which a judge of the First District Court of Denver County ordered the Pinkerton National Detective Agency to reimburse to Nell Dugan. The *Colorado Rocky Mountain News* denounced the decision in a fiery editorial that quoted liberally from Revelations and the Reverend Doctor Eccles Monsoon's multiple-volume history of the white slave trade in North America. The *Denver Post,* with whom Nell advertised the more wholesome entertainments of her establishment, celebrated it in half a column, pointing out that the Pinkertons had spent more money in the Wood Palace in one day than all its other customers combined spent in a week. The wires acquired this item and enlivened the telegraph columns of the Eastern press for weeks.

"Do we not do business with the *Post?*" demanded Allan Pinkerton, crumpling the copy of the Denver paper that had come by rail under Philip Rittenhouse's subscription.

William Pinkerton, seated in his father's office, recrossed his legs and tugged down the points of his waistcoat. Unlike the old man, he was inclined to be stout, as was his younger brother Robert, and to bring dignity to his jowls wore coarse whiskers that twisted like rusted wire. "We have a standing order of two columns, three days a week. The Wood Palace buys half a page every Saturday. Miss Dugan may have the edge."

"Cancel the order. What in thunder has become of Ace-in-the-Hole?"

"Possibly they were frightened by what happened at Spanish Trot. Were I in their place, I'd consider it an object lesson."

"You're making the mistake of thinking like a detective and not like a criminal. Lessons are lost on them. They'll see it as a blow to the competition, and redouble their efforts to fill the vacancy."

"Evidently not, or we'd have heard from them before this. Outlaws have been known to return to the straight and true in the past."

"Not these outlaws. In Brixton's case, it would be no return. He killed his first man at the age of twelve."

"Ten, according to Ned Buntline. If this keeps up, he'll have been too young to stand up to the recoil."

"This isn't a subject for jest. If you spent more time studying case files and less time reading rubbish, you'd be a greater asset to this agency."

William pressed his lips tight.

"It's a conclusion with no payoff," said the old man. "If it *is* a conclusion, which I choose to doubt. They must be planning something hor-r-rendous."

"Perhaps your confidential informant has gone over to the other side."

"His silence explains nothing. These fellows have a way of calling attention to themselves." He picked his cigar out of the tray on his desk and puffed, apparently unaware it had gone cold. "I'm tempted to call in Rittenhouse from San Francisco. He knows more about what's afoot in the Gr-reat Desert without stepping outside his office than all the men we have on the spot. Certainly his talents are wasted in the field. I should not have let him talk me into letting him go."

"You indulge him. One would think he was your own blood."

In this, William echoed the whispers of all who hated and feared the Reptile, a society which included the heir apparent. It was a transparent canard. While it is possible to father a bastard at thirteen, at that age the old man was still in Glasgow, working day and night to support his mother and younger brother; he had not had time for a liaison of that kind. In any case, there was nothing of the Scot about Rittenhouse, who was Prussian in his meticulous method and disconcertingly American in the way he spoke out. But William never missed an opportunity to undermine his authority with Allan.

For his part, the old man gave no indication that he knew anything of the rumors. He was the world's foremost detective when it came to crime and the densest of men when it came to the office intrigue all about him. "If that were the case," he said, "I'd never have given him leave. I treat you and Robert no differ-rent from anyone else in my employ."

"Excluding the Rep—Rittenhouse," William corrected himself. He lit a cigarette to conceal his agitation.

Alerted by this gesture to the status of his cigar, the old man struck a match and reignited it, drawing smoke deep into his lungs. He blew a ring without thinking, and scowled at it. He disliked ostentation. "Who do we have in Mexico?"

"On the payroll, or under the vest?"

"Both."

"Well, Horton's the field man in Mexico City. We've a *federale* captain in Nogales and some informants masquerading as bandits or vice versa in Chihuahua. I can get their names."

"When you do, wire them descriptions of Brixton and his men, and have Denver and San Francisco send photographs and sketches. It's been my observation that whenever a band of brigands vanishes, it's to Mexico they've gone."

"Not Canada? It's a closer ride to where they were reported last."

"They're smart, or they'd not have lasted this long. They won't flee the Eye to risk the Mounties. I dislike dealing with the arrogant redcoats myself, but there's no denying they're effective. Perhaps if we had a queen in this country we'd have the same free hand."

"We're too close to Independence Day for that kind of talk." William scowled. "While I'm about it, do you want me to recall Rittenhouse?"

The old man smoked, shook his head. "No. We'll let him have the bit a while longer. I've a hunch the apprehension of the Prairie Rose would make a fine subject for a case history. It may even tell better than Ace-in-the-Hole."

16

Philip Rittenhouse, who unlike most detectives never laid claim to any sense beyond the five God had given him at birth, was oblivious to the discussion of his subject in Chicago. As it was taking place, he sat in the squeaky captain's chair in his furnished office above a Chinese laundry on Washington Street, with a view through the streaked windows of three of San Francisco's best-known shops of iniquity: Gilbert's Melodeon, Bert's New Idea, and the Adelphi. The Bella Union, more famous than all the rest, stood on the side of Portsmouth Square to which he had no window, only a patchwork quilt of playbills advertising extinct entertainments pasted over cracks in the yellow plaster.

He was conscious of it nevertheless, as a farmer in Nebraska was conscious of the Department of Agriculture in Washington and an architect in Buffalo was conscious of the Taj Mahal at Agra. But then they hadn't the thud of brass instruments in the soles of their feet to remind them, nor the *baroom* of a remote kettledrum in their ears whenever a dancer in pink tights executed a split. As Peter Ruskin, proprietor of the Ruskin Dramatic Arts Agency (est. 1875), he thrilled to the proximity of that splendid showcase of theatrical talent, and as Philip Rittenhouse, an operative with the Pinkerton National Detective Agency, he had the comfortable sensation of knowing that as long as places like the Bella Union existed, his work would always be in demand; for it drew thieves and murderers the way an abandoned carcass drew vermin, and the prices it charged for admission, as well as for the diversions inside, discouraged its clientele from honest occupations and the spare living most of them offered.

He'd been there, of course, as he had to its competitors. For three weeks he'd divided the rest of his time between the wormy cylinder desk, its pigeonholes stuffed with decaying programmes, telegraphic pleas for money from stranded artists, and bottles of whiskey that smelled like the sinister brown wax women used to remove unwanted hair—items left by the previous tenant—and his sweaty little quarters next to the coal furnace in a rooming house on Kearney Street built of old packing cases and green timber. For authenticity's sake, he'd traded his usual nondescript dress for a flowered waistcoat, green glass stickpin, tan bowler, and yellow garters, and chewed licorice to cover the scent of alcohol on his breath, of which actually there was none; he was a confirmed teetotaler, and there were only so many things a man would do to support his disguise. All these things he kept track of in his expense book in his personal code, as well as the cost of the advertisement that ran twice weekly on an inside page of the *San Francisco Call,* which we here insert, in its proscenium-arch border:

THE RUSKIN DRAMATIC ARTS AGENCY
Peter Ruskin, *Esq.*
Representing Artists
Specialising in
All Acts of Elocution,
Spiritual Uplift,
Poetical Recitation,
Melodrama,
Tragedy and Farce
No fees charged except for services rendered
Single rates for husband-and-wife acts
Inquire at
504B Washington Street
(Across from the Bella Union)

He was particularly pleased with the European spelling of "spe-cialising," which he thought would appeal to the tastes of his in-tended target, and the bit about husband-and-wife teams sharing a single rate. The list of specialties had been selected with that same purpose in mind. Originally, he'd included acrobatic acts, but the parade of tumblers, high-wire artists, and human pyra-mids that had tramped through his office the first week had wea-ried him and he'd had the line removed. In any case, Mme. Elizabeth Mort-Davies, who his research told him had been no mean physical performer in her younger days, was past the age where limbs and sinew began to rebel at anything more ambi-tious than a short sprint (or a bicycle ride), and Major Evelyn Davies was too fat. The stream of applicants slowed to a trickle, and Peter Ruskin, *Esq.* (a real name from among his father's contemporaries, which happened to contain his own initials), turned them all down with professional brusqueness while possessing his soul in patience.

With one exception: He promised himself that if he heard "O, Captain! My Captain!" one more time, he'd strike *Poetical Recitation* from the list.

Saturday nights, he bought drinks for the bartenders in all four major houses of pleasure and left stacks of his business cards, with instructions as to the kind of husband-and-wife act he sought, promising a finder's fee for every one he booked. He refrained from asking for the Davieses by name. No agent in the show business did that, as the whole point of the enterprise was to discover obscure talent and exploit it. Bartenders were suspicious by nature, and the history of vigilante activity in Barbary kept the proprietor of every den of dissipation on his guard; one false step, and Allan Pinkerton would never know what had become of his most reliable man in Chicago.

On his way back to his room each evening, he stopped to purchase an armload of local newspapers, and sat up on his cornshuck mattress scanning the reviews and theatrical advertisements in the *Bulletin, Call, Chronicle,* and *Star* for some sign that the Davieses were playing locally. The fact that their names did not appear failed to deter him, as he thought it possible they sometimes worked pseudonymously, either to obfuscate their identities or in response to an old thespial superstition about changing one's luck with one's billing. He circled promising acts in pencil, turned out his lamp at ten o'clock in obedience to his landlord's curfew, and spent part of the next day visiting matinees, but so far had not spotted a performing couple who matched the descriptions he'd memorized.

At the end of these three weeks, his emotions were tangled. Pinkerton was impatient and a skinflint, and could not be ex-

pected to subsidize his subordinate's experiment in theater indefi-
nitely. At the same time, the old man had caught the best-selling
author's bug, and could not fail to grasp the entertainment potential in the apprehension of a company of actors who supple-
mented their box-office receipts with armed robbery. He might
be contented with a looser grip on the reins this one time. The
newspaper trail—Rittenhouse's answer to the great Chisholm—
led solidly toward a Davies appearance in San Francisco, the pleasure capital of the American frontier. On the other hand, stage
players were not often creatures of logic, and the Major and the
Madame might have detoured into the interior after Eureka, for
no other reason than that their train had struck and killed a white
heifer, souring their luck. Artists were far less predictable than
the common run of road agent. That was how John Vermillion's
troupe had survived this long without having to flee a single posse.

There was also the possibility that he had waited too long to
set his trap. He'd never questioned his assumption that the company would reconvene, and he did not do so now. He'd based his
timetable on the conventional theatrical season, which began during the first frost of autumn and ended before the hammering
heat of summer turned auditoriums into ovens, but upon reflec-
tion there was no defensible reason to expect this particular association to behave according to convention. Perhaps *The Diplomat
Deposes* had returned to its trunk and its champions were even then
steaming east to meet the others for a brand-new season of stirring
oratory, thrilling swordplay, and thievery on the grand scale.

Such were the doubts and ruminations that befell the man who
staked himself out as a goat in lion country.

There was one more: the likelihood, if his quarry did not surface soon, that Peter Ruskin would be forced to sign one of the

acts that passed through his office. Agents, while discriminating, had to live, and if word got around that the representative was refusing to represent anyone, he stood the risk of discovery, or what passed for it in lieu of evidence to the contrary. There was no more certain route to a death sentence on the part of the shadowy hordes than to be exposed as a "crusher" working undercover for established law and order, no matter who was the object. Merely to be suspected invited tarring and feathering at the least. Rittenhouse made up his mind to offer his services to the next glimmer of talent that crossed his threshold.

Fortunately—for he was far less confident of his abilities as a booker of exhibitions than as a detective—that glimmer happened to belong to a middle-aged woman of preposterous height and her companion, who was as fat as a rolled armadillo and dressed like the Prince of Wales. He had made contact with the Prairie Rose at last.

The fogs of San Francisco harbor vanish, burned off as by a magnesium flash by a Panavision shot directly into the sun, with its chain of reflective circles: Welcome to the Chihuahua desert, where it's always 105 in the shade, and the nearest shade is in El Paso. The state bird is dead. Even the gila monsters have migrated north to the relative comfort of Caliente Infierno, which translates roughly as Hot as Hell.

But heat is of small consequence in the little village of San Diablo, where a fiesta is always in progress. Careering down from the Sierra Madres, we hear first the drunken tinny blatting of trumpets and the out-of-synch crash of tambourines, then swerve around a pie-faced peasant in a tattered sombrero fancy-stitching his way down the broad main street with a bottle in one hand, and pause with a pleasant sigh to regard the girl dancing barefoot on a plane table in the middle of the square. She is all flying black ringlets, bare brown shoulders, whirling skirts, slender feet, and the regulation dagger strapped by a garter to one thigh, to the accompaniment of guttural cheers from the guitar players and that climbing, tongue-fluttering squeal ending in a high-pitched cackle that no *Norteamericano* can imitate. In six years, the girl will resemble the gourd-shaped women in weeds grinding corn in stoneware bowls on the front porch of the mayor's hacienda nearby, slit-eyed, contagiously vilipendent, but just now she is a welcome sight after all those rocks and cactus. Her name is Fiona, but it may as well be Dolores, Conchita, Rosario, or Mirabelle. There is one in every community of its size in old Mexico; but one only.

Our pause is regrettably brief, as we are not here to take in the local fauna. From there we move on to a small pavilion constructed of four cypress trunks supporting a roof of woven fronds topped with black Spanish moss. Beneath its screen, Jack Brixton, Tom Riddle, Mysterious Bob Craidlaw, Breed, and the Kettlemans sit on cane chairs in a semicircle facing a man who is fat even by the standards of a generation that would elect Grover Cleveland to the presidency; the yards of white cotton in his simple shirt and trousers alone would furnish dust covers for a parlor full of furniture, and his hips are stuck fast between the arms of his fan-backed chair. Bandoliers of large-caliber shells cross his ringed torso. With one hand he fans his huge streaming moustachioed face while the other cups a convenient breast belonging to the fat *señorita* seated astraddle his enormous left thigh. His name is Matagordo.

Mexico's blood-flecked history has not been kind to Matagordo; even his first name has been lost. He was a general in the revolutionary army of Benito Juarez, which he joined after the government of Maximilian refused to promote him beyond the rank of lieutenant colonel. Had he accepted a peacetime post in Mexico City and helped to oversee the return of the country to its citizens, his fame might have survived that of his successors, Francisco Villa and Emiliano Zapata, but he chose instead to return to rural banditry. In June 1875, he'd settled into semiretirement in San Diablo, where the mayor was his creature, and Ace-in-the-Hole his guest.

"My friends, your stubborn sobriety pains me. In this pueblo, we nurse our children with tequila and wean them from their virginity after Communion. We produce bastards the way other pueblos produce apricots; therefore we depend upon visiting seed to prevent our women from bearing idiots. *Por favor,* help yourself to our hospitality. Business without pleasure violates our charter." His English was impeccable, if somewhat prosy, as he'd learned it from crumpled pages torn from American dime novels used as packing material for the weapons he ordered from New Mexico and Texas. Owing to the fragmented nature of his reading, he thought Buffalo Bill was a figure of mythology, part animal and part man.

"There'll be time later," Brixton said. "Will you loan us the men we need?"

This brought a grunt from Charlie Kettleman, who'd risen to comply with Matagordo's appeal. He slumped back into his chair and crossed his arms. The general's *señorita* wore no underthings, and the occasional glimpse he received when she shifted her weight on the fat man's thigh made him restless. Since his encounter with Dr. Ruddock's dictionary in Table Rock, the only time his brains weren't snarled with medical Latin was when he was in a woman's arms. Brother Ed gave his knee a sympathetic pat.

Their host fanned himself, looking troubled. "You have not yet confided the purpose of your appeal. A train, yes; but you do not say *which* train, nor why you cannot manage to rob it with your own fearsome band. I must know the risks."

"What's it to you?" Breed cut in. "No horse could carry you across the Rio Grande."

"I would not ask it to, as I am kind to animals and small children. However, my men trust me not to send them into danger I would not myself face. There is also the matter of an enterprise I have planned in Hermosillo at the end of summer, which will be quite impossible if they do not return to me in the condition in which they left."

Brixton said, "It's a military operation, right up their alley. That's all I'll say if you don't give me your word it don't go beyond this here tent."

"You have it, as a gentleman and a soldier of fortune."

"That and a squirt of mercury'd cure a dose of clap."

The general aimed a scowl at Charlie Kettleman, saw where his gaze was fixed, and put on his sombrero to free his hand to adjust the fat girl's skirt. "The details, please, *Señor* Brixton. I won't ask again, and you may put aside any thought you have about trading me for my men. A dozen guns are trained upon you at this moment."

"Only a dozen?" But Brixton's face was gray beneath the sunburn.

"I took El Paso del Norte with less. All of those are present."

Brixton shrugged. "Custer and Terry's fixing to give the injuns what-for in the High Plains next year. Army train's on its way to Fort Abraham Lincoln with the payroll for the whole campaign.

Fort Dodge is the first stop, up in Kansas; we'll hit it on its way there. Right around seventy thousand in greenbacks and double eagles, and under armed guard from the caboose to the cowcatcher."

Matagordo fondled the girl's breast, meditating. "What is your source?"

"I got friends. Just because they turned coat and swore to the Stars and Stripes don't mean it stuck."

"Seventy thousand?"

"Maybe more, maybe less. That's seven thousand to you, and you don't need to get up out of that there chair to earn it."

"He couldn't if it was ten," Tom Riddle said. "I knew a man fat as you died in a Pullman outside Sacramento. He was so stiff they couldn't get him out the door. They cut a hole through the roof and pulled him up with ropes and pulleys. You ought to go for a walk once in a while."

Brixton said, "Shut up, Tom. What about them men, General? That there dozen ought to do it."

Matagordo summoned over a little barefoot boy, possibly an illegitimate grandson, and spoke to him in rapid Spanish. The boy sprinted away. "In San Diablo, we seal all our transactions with tequila." The host looked at Tom. "We shall see which of us can walk at the end of the day."

The celebration stretched into three, at the close of which even Charlie Kettleman was content. It was time to go. Breed, who insisted it was his white half that couldn't tolerate liquor, slumped over his horse's neck, Tom was too drunk to prattle, and Ed dismounted often to vomit on the way out of town. Bob showed no effect, but then no one knew how much or how little he had drunk. They all avoided conversation with Brixton, who was exactly three times as mean when hung over as when he hadn't had a drop. The twelve men Matagordo had lent them for reinforcement, each a traveling arsenal with bandoliers, two Colt revolvers, and a Mexican carbine, were still drinking, and singing all the old songs of the glorious revolution at once. They had no idea where they were headed or what they were expected to do when they got there, but they loved and venerated Matagordo, and were sorry only that *El Tigre del Norte* had grown too fat in his retirement to accompany them. There wasn't a full set of natural teeth in the entire band, but they had enough gold in their mouths to charter a train to Kansas instead of riding their gaunt, grass-fed mongrel mounts.

When they had left, the general prised himself out of his chair and waddled to his spare soldier's quarters on the side of the square opposite the mayor's residence. With difficulty he pulled himself up the stout ladder to the stuffy attic, where twenty or thirty pigeons in wooden cages cooed and plucked lice from their feathers. He dipped a pen in the ink pot on a little writing table, scribbled on a sheet he tore off a tiny block, removed a fat bird from one of the cages—Benito, his favorite—and clipped the rolled sheet securely to one of its thin legs. It had made the trip to the El Paso office of the Pinkerton National Detective Agency twice as many times as any of the others and knew the way even in the dark.

Matagordo tugged on the rope that lifted the hatch away from the square opening in the roof, tied it off, kissed Benito on the head, and released him with an underhand scoop to help him in his flight. The bird took to the air, flapping furiously.

A shot crashed. Benito dropped straight to the ground and lay as still as if staked to the spot. The general stared, openmouthed, at the little carcass, then slid his gaze to the man seated on horse-back in the square with the Winchester still raised to his shoulder. Mysterious Bob levered in another round and kneed his sorrel in a half circle to throw down on Matagordo.

17

"Do not mistake professional curiosity for desperation, Mr. Ruskin," announced Mme. Mort-Davies, stirring her chilled cucumber soup, a specialty of the Parker House dining room. "As a matter of fact, we've done quite well representing ourselves. However, one always wishes to know whether someone else might improve upon the status quo."

Rittenhouse touched his linen napkin to his lips. He was enjoying himself thoroughly, both with the company and with the superb fare at the hotel and gambling hall so convenient to his office, and whose prices he could not afford out of his day-to-day expenses. The old man would grumble, but he understood better than anyone that confidences came more quickly over good wine served in crystal than over a cup of rotgut with silverfish floating on top. Rittenhouse had lost no time in changing the venue after the initial introductions.

"No one would argue the regularity of your appearance on the middle of the bill," he said, with just a touch of Yiddish throat in his *r*'s. "But you were right to come to me. You should be nearer the top."

Major Davies stopped slurping his soup. "Not *at* the top?" He'd tucked his napkin under his guillotine collar and hung his silk hat and opera cloak on a hook on the pillar near their table. The hour was two o'clock, and ridiculously early for evening wear. His wife was attired more appropriately, but the ruffles in her shirtwaist accentuated her pigeon breast; even in jaded San Francisco, the couple attracted attention like a brass band that had turned down the wrong street.

Rittenhouse shook his head, smiling sadly. "I won't delude you with the impossible. That spot belongs to the empty-headed ingenue and her pompous beau: people who have outward beauty, but no character and, let us be frank, undetectable talent. Much has changed since the war. Theatergoers want their nosegays to look at and sniff."

"The war." The Madame's nod was grim. "Politicians speak of the loss of men, and poets write of it, but who will stand up and announce the death of culture?"

"It is not dead so long as such as the Davieses continue to perform."

"You've seen us? I say, waiter, this soup is cold."

The waiter who'd appeared regarded the Major. "It's intended to be served that way, sir."

"Then it's pudding, isn't it? Bring me chicken broth, and have the chef test it with his elbow."

The waiter bowed and departed with his bowl, which was nearly empty.

"I had the good fortune to admire you twice in St. Louis last fall," Rittenhouse said. "Once in *The Diplomat Deposes,* and again in *Twelfth Night*. I scarcely knew I was watching the same couple. You contain many parts."

He pretended interest in his salad, but watched their expressions closely from under half-lowered lids. His oblique reference to the Prairie Rose did not seem to have placed them on their guard.

The Major belched into a pudgy fist. "That was a lark. Not real Shakespeare, of course; you need a full-scale production to do the Bard justice. But a respectable sampler, if Bowdler's your cup of tea. Personally I prefer my Elizabethans full-bodied and bawdy."

"And your soup warm," said the Madame, not without amusement. Rittenhouse suspected she was fond of her husband. He would make no progress pitting them against each other.

"An admirably shaded performance nonetheless," he said. "The reviewers overlooked the nuances."

"Frogs, the lot of them! Had we done Molière, they'd have hailed us as Lafayette. I nearly called one of them out. Lizzie restrained me."

"For his sake, Evie, not yours." She touched his wrist. "If you admired us, why did you not speak with us there?"

"I felt I'd missed my opportunity. Actors are inclined to be contented just after they've joined a troupe. The time to approach you would have been after you left the company you were with and before you signed with another. In any case, I was with a large agency then, and was in town to persuade a Swedish soprano to let us represent her. She declined, straining my relationship with my superiors. It was after that I decided to open my own agency here in California. You cannot imagine how pleased I was to see you of all people enter my office."

The Madame said, "The bartender at the Adelphi gave Evelyn your card. He said you were looking for a married act."

"I began my search with you in mind. Not you, precisely; I'd hardly hoped that opportunity would come my way again. I thought I might perhaps find a pair of potential Davieses—in the bud, as it were—and bring them along. Have you left that company you were with? What was the name?" He sensed a stiffening in her attitude, if not that of the Major, who was watching the waiter setting his broth before him, and backed off. "Well, the name doesn't matter, if you're free of all ties. Waiter, if the chef hasn't started on my crepes, I believe I'll ask for a bowl of that broth instead. It looks quite hearty."

"It is," said the Major, using the corner of his napkin to mop off his moustaches.

"Very good, sir." The waiter collected his salad and the Madame's cucumber soup and left.

"The Prairie Rose Repertory Company," furnished the Madame. "We expect to rejoin them this fall. They have no ties upon us. We are free to leave whenever we wish, although of course we'd not leave them shorthanded once we're in rehearsal. What are you proposing?"

Rittenhouse rearranged his silver just so. He was walking on hen's eggs now.

"My agency is new, as I said, but my experience is not. At the moment, I'm a trainer with many contacts, but no stable. You have a history with this Prairie Rose, and if I'm any judge of human nature, it appears to be a happy one. I'd betray my principles if I tried to steal you out from under them and leave bad feelings all around. If you would grant me permission to speak to the head of the company—"

"Out of the question." The Major blew on his broth; steam rolled off it in a visible manifestation of chef's pique. "You could not speak for us on a contingency basis. Only an agent of record could undertake such a conversation."

The detective sipped water from his goblet. He hadn't expected integrity, particularly on the part of this elderly voluptuary, his face flushed on 1845 Bordeaux. He abandoned the flank for a frontal assault.

"Certainly not. I was hoping for an understanding before I made so bold. Jim Nixon, the proprietor of Nixon's Amphitheater in Chicago, is a personal friend, and he's in a bind. He requires a Ferdinand and Isabella for a grand pageant about the discovery of America this fall and his leads have separated. He'll pay one hundred dollars apiece per performance, six nights a week with a matinee on Saturday, and he'll guarantee seven months out of his own pocket. The only condition is that no legal complications are involved. It seems he had problems with Ned Buntline over *Scouts of the Plains*— an old felony warrant—and he wants assurance his profits won't go toward some lawyer, and possibly a fine, in case of litigation. In order to provide that assurance, I'll need to meet with the head of your company and obtain his signature on a release. It would be convenient if your intended reunion took place here, but if it's to be somewhere else, I must have time to adjust my schedule to include travel."

Again he watched them closely, this time without pretending disinterest; but they were actors, and he found their expressions unenlightening. They *were* actors, however, and therefore theatrical creatures. He decided to risk overplaying his hand.

"It's the opportunity of a lifetime."

"One lifetime, perhaps," said the Major. "Artists have so many."

"Shut up, Evie."

The Major shrugged and returned to his broth. Rittenhouse was alert. Without straining visibly, the woman seated across from him seemed to have grown taller, until she was peering down at him from a great height. She was a bigger talent than he'd realized.

"Your Mr. Nixon will have to be satisfied with your assurances based upon ours," she said. "We are not, as you made clear, headline performers. What you earned representing us the first month would not pay for the distance you'd have to travel to speak with the head of our company. It wouldn't be sound business."

"That would depend upon the distance."

She gazed at him with a considering eye. He felt like a small rodent trapped in the open by an owl, and thought he'd been seen through. She parted her lips; but it was her husband who spoke, confining himself for once to a single word.

"Wichita!" bellowed the conductor, crimson-faced with an accurate chart of the Kansas Pacific's route traced in purple on his nose. He carried his announcement to the next car, walking on shattered arches.

"They certainly named the place well." April spoke through a scented handkerchief. "Macbeth's crones never brewed anything that smelled more foul."

"Tut-tut, dear. The Major would have your tongue if he heard you mention the Scottish tragedy at the very start of the season. Think of the curse." Johnny watched the parade of clapboard slow to a crawl as they slid into the station. Lanky boys dressed in flannel shirts and faded dungarees leaned against porch posts, rolling cigarettes, and a face painted like a ship's figurehead peered between lace curtains in an upstairs window. Over everything lay the stench of cattle, rich and brown and shot through with sweaty greenbacks.

"What curse could be worse than this? Look, the undertaker's sign is shaped like a coffin. I shudder to think what's above the door of the bustle shop."

He hopped up to haul down their bags, as light of heart as he was on his feet. At last, April was complaining of old familiar things, assaults on her comforts and proprieties, and not their domestic situation. Women went through the most frightening phases, only to revert to normal once they were past. He'd vexed himself over nothing less transient than a case of sniffles.

"Is there a church, I wonder?" She took one last sniff at the crumpled linen and returned it to her reticule.

"Most of the Christian denominations seem to be represented, judging by the steeples I saw. Has the Continent converted you?"

"Only to the extent that I require a minister to sanctify our union. Don't forget my train case, darling. You nearly left it behind in New York."

He reached for it, feeling clammy cold at the center.

By the time they stepped down onto the platform, he'd recovered sufficiently to clasp the hand of Tim Saunders, who stepped up to introduce himself as the proprietor of the local variety theater. He was a spare fellow with a sly face and untenable black whiskers in an Eastern-style suit. Johnny thought instantly of the ward bosses who'd lined up outside Scipio Africanus McNear's office in Chicago with their hats off and their hands out. Saunders bowed deeply to April.

"I withheld your arrival from the newspapers, as you requested," he told Johnny. "I hope they don't take it badly. They've run out of novel ways to announce the comings and goings of Texas herds."

Johnny said, "We'll make it up to them at the reception. At the moment, the Prairie Rose is spread across five states. We shan't steal the thunder from our other players."

"I think you'll find your accommodations at the Occidental Hotel quite comfortable. The rooms at the Texas House are larger, but they're undergoing renovation. Shanghai Pierce chased a stray through the front window last month and roped it in the pantry."

"Johnny! It's worse than Tannery."

"Patience, dear. I'm sure the good people of Wichita pass weeks at a time without a cow in the kitchen."

"We're young, miss, and I don't argue some of our transients couldn't do with a good spanking. But we value our entertainers. The night we opened, Eddie Foy took eight curtain calls and scooped ninety dollars in double eagles and silver off the stage floor."

"I'd prefer it if you'd hand us a bank draught," she said. "I left my shovel in Kansas City when we changed trains."

"Haw-haw! I heard you'd a hand for light comedy. The ninety was in the way of appreciation from the house, over and above Mr. Foy's percentage of the box office. You'll break his record, or I'm a horse thief. When do you expect the rest of your company?"

"Mr. Ragland is on his way," said Johnny, "with the costumes and properties we stored in Denver at the end of last season. I expect to hear from Major and Madame Mort-Davies any day."

Before leaving New York City, Johnny had placed the following notice in the classified sections of the *St. Louis Enquirer,* the *Denver Post,* and the *San Francisco Call*:

SIR JOHN, DR. CAIUS, MRS. FORD:
Come home. All is forgiven. Wire
Fenton, Breevort Hotel, NYC.

The names addressed belonged to three of the principal characters in *The Merry Wives of Windsor*; Fenton was the leading man.

Johnny selected the three major newspapers as those most likely to be obtained wherever the cast had scattered.

"Why so formal?" April had asked, when he showed her the text. "One would think you met them in a drawing room. What could they possibly have done that would require your forgiveness?"

"The gentleman from Avon saw fit to give only one of them a Christian name. I told them to expect something on this order. If they're smart enough to rob banks, they're smart enough to respond."

"Peace officers read Shakespeare, too. Some of them must. You could be arrested the first time you inquired for a message for Mr. Fenton at the desk."

"Am I to stand trial for placing a counterfeit notice? I rather think three wars were fought to preserve that right."

"Two, perhaps. Mr. Frederick Douglass might present you with an argument as to the third."

"I thought you were reading about Joan of Arc. When did you switch to Harriett Beecher Stowe?"

"You're always throwing up your education to me. One would think you studied at Oxford instead of the trash bin behind the city library." She returned to *La Vie de Jeanne D'Arc,* in which she'd made scant progress.

Johnny had then wired out the notices with payment.

Lizzie saw the advertisement in the *Call* and pointed it out to the Major, who'd seen the paper first but seldom ventured beyond the theatrical columns. They dispatched a telegram to New York saying they were under way, sent a message round to Peter Ruskin to inform him they would be unavailable to meet with him again in the forseeable future, and set about packing their bags and trunk with the tent-show efficiency of experienced troupers. For once they settled their hotel bill; the guarantee of another successful season had made them expansive.

"Falstaff, by thunder!" said the Major on their way out of the lobby. "I've always wanted to play the old rogue."

"You do, Evie; you do."

After reading their message, Philip Rittenhouse lost no time. He closed his office, wired Chicago that he was on the move, hurried to the station with his bag, and upon learning that no couple of the Davieses' description had bought tickets that day, waited in an unobtrusive corner of the depot for them to arrive. He'd traded his bowler and loud waistcoat for a soft hat and linen duster and now looked very little like either a booking agent or a detective. When the Madame and the Major swept in with all the furor and feathers of comic-opera royalty, he waited until they'd checked their trunk and boarded before buying his ticket. They rode in separate coaches. He knew their destination, thanks to the loquacity of the Major, and that there was small danger of losing them at some stop along the route. He avoided the dining car and the possibility of a chance meeting there; it had been important to convince them Wichita was too far for him to travel just to ensure their availability.

"Pleasure trip, sir?" The conductor handed back his punched ticket.

Rittenhouse smiled. "Yes. As a matter of fact, I suppose it is."

"One can always tell." He turned toward the next passenger.

Cornelius Ragland, who in keeping with a lifelong habit of caution had formed the custom of purchasing all three of the above-named newspapers daily, as well as the *Kansas City Times,* the *New Mexican* of Santa Fe, and the *Portland Oregonian* (although he admitted to himself he took the last mainly for the variety of patent medicines whose manufacturers advertised in its inside pages), read the notice in the *Denver Post* and sent his immediate reply, volunteering to make arrangements to transport their costumes and stage equipment from Denver to Wichita. Johnny's response came by return wire:

BREAK A LEG

FENTON

The young man treated himself to one last, luxurious soak in steaming sulphur water, returned to his room, read and made corrections on the last pages of *The Tragedy of Joan of Arc,* and put the draft in his old leather portfolio along with a copy of *The Merry Wives of Windsor* bound in scuffed green boards and his notes for the adaptation. He'd intended to polish his original play first, then organize his notes on the comedy into a script, but now he would have to embrace Shakespeare on the train. He packed his valise, paid his bill, and took the hotel carriage to the station. He didn't regret saying good-bye to Hot Springs. His stay there had been rewarding personally and professionally; his health was stronger than it had ever been, and he had written the best thing of his young career, which he did not delude himself would ever be an old one. But it was a deadly dull place, and his adventures with the Prairie Rose had spoiled him for the life prosaic. Thus, his patience was strained when the conductor announced that the train's departure had been delayed to make room for an express train headed West; he had no details to add.

Five minutes later, Cornelius spotted the conductor on the platform outside his window, in conversation with the clerk who'd sold him his ticket. He lowered the window and strained to overhear what they were saying.

". . . make it up on the other end if they'll just come on ahead," said the conductor, frowning at his turnip watch.

The clerk set fire to a stubby pipe, broke the match, and ground it underfoot. "When's the last time you ever knew the army to hurry up and do anything?"

"Well, it ain't like Fort Dodge has needed 'em since the injuns went west."

18

When Tom Riddle was lying on his saddle blanket in a dank cave half a day's ride from Table Rock, burning with fever on one side, shivering with cold on the other (a living campfire steak), he changed.

He wasn't proud of it, never spoke of it, but a fact was a fact; color of one kind meant you'd tapped into the mother lode and color of another meant you'd tapped out, and no matter how hard or soft you swung your pick, you couldn't change it. If he could, he'd be soaking his saddle sores in champagne up on Nob Hill right now and not contributing to them on the board seat of a day coach rattling its way north to Kansas.

Normally he liked to talk, and if it had been anyone else who'd survived a .44 slug fired into his chest at close range and Breed's indifferent efforts to carve it out with his big Bowie, he'd have gone on about it in all its detail until Ace-in-the-Hole's voices rose in chorus telling him to shut up. Instead he'd contented himself with a stretcher he'd concocted during his convalescence on his sister's pig farm about teaching a hog to do sums. Tom saw himself as a pioneer on the road less traveled, both in his choices of professions—prospecting, then robbery—and in his ability to tell tall stories he made up as he went along. But being a changed man was a commonplace on the frontier, where every third man had fled to escape illness, creditors, and past mistakes, and where every third one of that third had changed his name in a ceremony of self-baptismal gratification. If he'd *wanted* change, goddamn it, he'd have gone through it when he pulled himself out of that badger hole in California where his friends had left him to starve. He hadn't (although he'd lost his enthusiasm for digging in any kind of dirt), and *that* had been something to brag on. It was a rare man who was satisfied with himself no matter what; but the business in Wyoming had put paid to that.

Whiskey tasted better, for one thing, and the glow lasted longer. His first time with a whore after his recovery had been as good as anything he'd conjured up lying on his back under the stars thinking of the pen-and-ink sketches of the corset models in Sears &Roebuck, and a bowl of beans and a slice of cornbread in Guacho's Cantina in San Diablo after the long hungry ride down had nearly taken off the top of his head. He slept longer and deeper, his dreams were drenched in rich color, and he awoke as alert and ready for the new day as a child. It was a pain in the ass.

The core problem was he had to keep it all from his companions. Life on the scout was just a little bit better than hell, if you listened to the padres and believed what they said about the contorted chains of mortal souls and the lake of fire. You got piles from riding day and night, you entered every town through the asshole-ugly back section to avoid passing the post office and jail where your description was posted for all to see and compare, you shelled out money like Vanderbilt to live in rooms a dog wouldn't shit in just to keep your name off the registration, and when you were flush you couldn't spend a nickel because you were hiding out in a cave or a cornrick or the hole under an outhouse because of the way you got it and how many people were looking for you to get it back. Bitching about the life was your badge of brotherhood, and if for some jackass reason—say, you're alive when you should be dead—you found yourself whistling in the saddle for the pure joy of hearing the notes, you were just asking the fellow riding next to you to blow your skull through the back of your hat.

"Tom, you look like you just pissed a porcupine. What're you so mad about?" Ed Kettleman plunked himself down into the seat beside him.

Tom straightened his spine. He hadn't heard him coming up the aisle. "I never did take to trains. Somebody else is in charge and you never know when you're going to get robbed."

Ed hooted. "That'd be a sight to see. I'd admire to know how Jack would take to it."

"I reckon he wouldn't, if Salt Lake City means anything." That whole episode made him think of Ed's brother. "How's Charlie?"

"Nutty as pecan pie. Now he's talking about hanging out his shingle. He says getting hit with that doctor's book ought to qualify him for a country practice. I sure hope he snaps out of it."

"Maybe if you clobbered him with a Jesse James dime novel."

"It'd take a stack. That book left a dent big as Fort Worth. What you fixing to do with your part of that seventy thousand?"

The car was half empty, and no one was seated near them. Still, Tom lowered his voice a notch. "Go to Venezuela, I reckon."

"What's in Africa?"

"Venezuela's in South America, you dumb Texican. They just got through fighting a civil war; now they're building railroads, just like it was here ten years ago. I could start all over again with my own crew, and there ain't a Pinkerton in a thousand miles."

This was the first he'd let anyone in on the idea that had been teasing and plaguing him since before he left Nebraska. In order to occupy his mind while he was healing, his sister had handed him a stereoscope and a box of glass plates, among which was a series about Venezuela: the Andes, as tall and jagged as the Rockies; the *llanos,* indistinguishable from the Great Plains; and Lake Maracaibo, which made the one in Utah Territory look like a glass of tequila with salt floating on the surface. There stood Caracas, the capital, which was San Francisco and Denver and St. Louis all rolled into one huge sprawl, with mansions on the hills and (he'd bet his cut of the payroll train job) cute little mud huts down on the flat where a man could have fun for a fraction of what it would cost him in any of those other places.

When he was strong enough to drive a buckboard, he'd gone into Lincoln on the pretext of bringing back supplies and spent a couple of hours in the county library reading up on South America. Venezuela had gold and copper mines and tobacco plantations to rival the vast cattle ranches in Texas, and the only law worthy of the name rode on the backs of mules in the persons of loose bands of federal officers, which if they were anything like the ones in Mexico could be bought with a sack of gold dust. Tom Riddle had decided that if there was a heaven for highwaymen, Venezuela was that place.

"What do they talk down there?" Ed asked.

"Mexican, I reckon."

"I didn't hear you talk much Mexican when we was in Mexico."

"What do I got to know except 'Stick 'em up?' "

"Well, you can have your South America, and I'll raise you

China. Me 'n' Charlie are taking our cut and opening a saloon in Tijuana. Even the greasers there talk American, and we can have prizefights every Saturday night, and take a cut off the top of every bet for the house. It's legal down there."

"When did anything not being legal ever stop you and Charlie?"

"We been running from one kind of law or another since we was kids. It'll be good to find out what it's like sleeping on the right side of the sheet. Also Charlie can jabber all he wants and no one'll pay him any more attention than a burro with a bellyful of loco weed."

"You can always put a burro down."

Ed rubbed his slack unshaven jaw. "I'll warrant you don't have any brothers."

"I got a brother-in-law on that pig farm I wouldn't mind putting down. He'd of charged me rent for that ticky bed if Aggie'd let him."

"It ain't the same thing. I'd take it a favor if you didn't bring it up again."

Tom was enjoying the conversation, that was the hell of it. He wondered just how long it took being happy to be still alive to wear off. It was worse than mescal, which made you drunk all over again every time you took a drink of water for a week. He changed the subject. "Where's the Mexicans?"

"Boxcar. The conductor didn't like their look, even without their bandoleros on. I expect they think it's a Pullman. They ain't rid inside since before the revolution." Ed produced a plug and offered it to him.

Tom shook his head, and looked out the window while the other cut himself a cud and went to work on it. For some reason, chaw was one thing Tom had lost his taste for; just watching someone chewing revolted him, and the smell made him ill. "What are the others fixing to do, you reckon?"

"I figure Jack to bury his part and go on sticking up banks and trains and shooting folks till they put a slug in him or string him up. I don't figure he got into this for the money as much as raising the devil. Breed, he'll just keep getting worse and worse till they elect him governor of hell. I don't calculate Old Scratch will put up much of a contest."

"What about Mysterious Bob?"

"Shit, I know better how that locomotive up front thinks than I do Bob. I seen him reading a book once written in Greek."

"How'd you know it was Greek?"

"I asked him what that book was he was reading. He said it was Greek."

"You believe him?"

"I don't see why not. It was just about the longest conversation we had since I knew him."

"What was the book about?"

"I didn't ask. I figured why push my luck. Anyway, the print looked like a mess of squashed bugs."

"Huh."

Ed nodded. "That about sums up Bob."

"When's the next stop?"

"About an hour. I asked the porter. We change to the Kansas Pacific in Wichita."

Johnny Vermillion had smoked a cigar on a balcony overlooking the Champs Elysées, with the gas lamps glowing saffron at twilight and stately coaches rumbling along the broad avenue with the Arc de Triomphe at their backs; drunk fifty-year-old port on a barge gliding down the Thames past Big Ben, the Albert, and the Houses of Parliament; wagered the last of his father's allowance on a single hand of poker in the bridal suite of the Palmer House, hung with cloth-of-gold and decorated further with Chicago's most beautiful ladies of the evening clad in nothing but their beauty patches; attended a reception for Lillie Langtry at the Academy of Music in New York City, where she'd sung selections from *Faust*; yet none of these places had granted him so fine a view as the window of his room in the Occidental Hotel in Wichita, Kansas, looking out on Douglas Avenue and the homely two stories of the Longhorn Bank.

He knew its history, as he was a serious student of his profession who learned all his lines as well as those of the other members of his cast, and was moreover a quick study. Open only two years, and christened strategically to attract both the cattle barons of Texas and the meatpacking moguls from Chicago, the institution advertised more than a million in assets, and at the height of the season (which it was approaching) stored as much as fifty thousand in its vault; in gold and silver, since neither the unlettered ranchers nor the swollen-bellied businessmen who had survived the Panic of '73 trusted securities or greenbacks. He wondered just how much that came to in pounds and ounces, and whether he might have to make arrangements involving some form of transportation other than Lizzie's bicycle.

He knew the bank's present as well, or as much of it as five days of casual observation could provide. At half-past nine every weekday the guard, middle-aged and limping slightly in a tight blue uniform and forage cap from which all the military insignia had been removed, arrived and let himself in the front door with a key attached to a ring the size of a duck's egg; he wore what appeared to be a big Navy revolver in a scabbard on his left hip. ("Left-handed," the observer noted.) The manager, a comfortable-looking fat man in a clawhammer coat, appeared fifteen minutes later, followed in close order by three cashiers, young men dressed respectably but more simply—a diplomatic decision, no doubt. Almost invariably, customers were waiting when the CLOSED sign on the door was reversed and the door opened to the public. The routine never varied more than a minute either way, and traffic coming and going was steady until nearly closing, when it increased noticeably as the hands crept around the clock toward four.

Johnny pondered briefly the wisdom of liberating the early-bird customers of their parcels, but rejected that plan on the theory that they would contain no more than one day's receipts on the part of Wichita's other businesses, or possibly documents of no value to the Prairie Rose. It would be like leaving a laden banquet table with only crumbs from the floor. In addition, he had developed a keen interest in the fat manager.

The spring roundups and brandings were over. The drives had begun. Very soon, thirsty cowboys would descend upon Wichita at the heads and flanks of thousands of bawling beeves. The street would become a river of swaying horns and twitching tails, and the Longhorn vault would fill with Eastern money to buy them and the profits from the saloons and bawdy houses, stuffed to bursting with the drovers' wages. Johnny threw up the sash and breathed in the stench of herds past; that which offended April's delicate nostrils smelled to him like early retirement, and after only two seasons in the theater.

Then something happened that caused the image of money on the hoof and gold in his pockets to evaporate.

It started as a shudder, as of a thunderhead forming far out on the plain, or coal sliding down a chute on Michigan Boulevard. Then the sound separated into a rhythmic tramping. It was too regular for cattle, and too measured for hoofbeats. Then the first column of infantry rounded the corner from Second Street onto Douglas: blouses buttoned, caps tilted forward, a Springfield rifle on every shoulder. A master sergeant marched alongside them, chevrons blazing, bellowing cadence. Pedestrians and loafers gathered on the corner to watch them pass, merchants stood in the doorways of their shops, hands in their pockets. Two minutes passed, and half a hundred soldiers, before Johnny realized that his own heart was thumping in rhythm with their booted feet. A great deal more time seemed to have gone by before the end of the column passed beyond his view. A dog trotted behind, pausing to sniff for promising jetsam, then lost interest and scampered down the alley next to the bank to lift a leg next to a rain barrel. The pedestrians resumed walking, the loafers loafing. The merchants retreated behind their counters.

"Shut the window, Johnny. Isn't it bad enough the whole town smells like a stockyard, without the reek getting into the linens?"

He slid down the sash and turned from the window. He hadn't heard April entering. She wore one of the plainer outfits she'd bought in Paris, a blue cotton suit with gray suede patches on the shoulders and a hat of the same blue material. The inevitable parasol hung from one wrist by a thong.

"Knocking is a sound idea here in the provinces," he said. "You forget we're no longer Mr. and Mrs. McNear."

"Not at present. Anyway, I'm an actress. My morals are already in question. You must know everything there is to know about that bank from the outside by now. Isn't it time you paid a visit in person?"

"That time may have eluded us. Did you not encounter the Grand Army of the Republic on your way back to the hotel?"

"I've been back for an hour. I saw them through the cafe window: Boys. I doubt the entire company would offer a razor much challenge." She unpinned her hat and gave her hair a push.

"It's closer to a regiment. Do you suppose Corny or the Davieses got careless and tipped their mitts?"

"Don't talk like a Spitalfields ruffian. You never got closer to the East End then Waterloo Station. The army doesn't care what we're about. How conceited you are!"

"Who have you been lunching with, Phil Sheridan?"

"I had tea downstairs with the mayor. The dear old fellow manages DeMoose's Saloon, where I suspect he learns more from gossip than he does in his official capacity. The troops are here to reinforce an express coming through tomorrow. They're departing for the territories and some sort of campaign."

"Indian fight?"

"Oh, I suppose. We're not at war with anyone else, are we? It's so hard to keep up."

"I wonder if there's anything valuable aboard."

"Now, don't go off chasing butterflies. The mayor says the Longhorn does more business in Kansas than Wells, Fargo. He was trying to impress me, poor dear. He's a stockholder."

"Well, *I'm* impressed. Why have I been wasting time standing at this window with you in my arsenal?"

"Why, indeed?" She smiled. "Oh, Johnny, we're such a good team. Can't you see we must seal the partnership?"

But he was facing the window again, and the path of the infantry. "Still, a train would be a refreshing change of pace."

19

"Don't just stand around like a bunch of Denver whores. Get your god-damn horses before the train pulls out."

Tom Riddle, who'd paused on the busy platform with Ed and Charlie Kettleman waiting for the crowd to thin out, watched Jack Brixton's retreating back, headed toward the livestock car where they'd loaded their mounts in Texas. "Who the hell stepped on his tail?"

"Jack don't sit still good," Ed said. "It puts him off his general sociability."

Charlie muttered something that may or may not have been a medical term.

Brixton and Mysterious Bob had their horses off the car when the three got there. The Mexicans they'd borrowed from Matagordo, looking more rumpled than usual after their trip in the freight car, stood in a knot waiting their turn. They conversed in volleys of bastard Spanish broken by high-pitched cackles and kept passing around the same hand-rolled cigarette. Tom wondered if tobacco was so hard to come by down there. Breed had some trouble with his gelding, but a swipe alongside its head with the bridle crossed its eyes and brought it into line. The bridle in place, it fixed a baleful brown eye on its master as it came down the ramp. It had never really come to terms with its surgery.

Nobody at the station seemed to pay much attention to this strange new band that had come to town. Cowboys black and white had gathered to see who was arriving and departing, harlots dressed in all the bright colors of tonics and restoratives in a barbershop patrolled the yard scouting up business, drummers in tight waistcoats and dandies in piped lapels bustled about swinging their sample cases and sticks. A tame Indian in a plug hat and a dirty blanket wandered around asking strangers for tobacco until the station agent came out from behind his window and sent him on his way with a kick in the seat. Tom guessed the man would have his hands full of derelict savages in a year or so; for a Yankee, Custer could fight.

While Ace-in-the-Hole was leading its horses off the right-of-way, the train blew its whistle and backed onto a siding to make way for another coming in from the West under a distant plume of smoke. Half the Mexican mounts, runty and earth-colored and scrawny as coyotes, had no saddles, just blankets, and hackamores instead of proper bits and bridles. They all looked like biters to Tom, who had not failed to note that most of the men who led them had pronounced limps. He bet they'd each left a piece of a haunch somewhere in the Chihuahua desert. They were the sorriest-looking bunch of road agents he'd ever seen: sallow-skinned, underweight, and bowlegged, dressed as beggars with holes in their sombreros you could pitch a jackrabbit through without touching the sides. It was no wonder the *federales* hadn't been able to run them to ground in ten years of trying; they'd galloped right past them, looking for guerrillas.

He had to ask himself how they spent the gold they'd stolen in the past. He doubted cute little Fiona could handle them all, and none of the other women he'd seen in San Diablo seemed to be worth it.

While he was pondering, a hesitation in his bay mare's gait distracted him. He knelt to examine a hoof and discovered the shoe missing. Ed agreed to take the reins, and Tom went back to see if he could find it on the cinderbed. He carried a hammer and a sack of nails in a saddlepouch for such emergencies, but spare shoes added too much weight. Black Jack would call him sixteen kinds of a son of a bitch if he had to go into town to find a farrier.

He was about to give up the search when he spotted one iron leg sticking out from under the railroad platform. Bending to pick it up, he found his eyes on a level with a slim ankle in a black patent-leather pump. Tom was a connoisseur of ankles. He steered away from thick ones, no matter how pretty the face or narrow the waist that went with it; they always meant a coarse temper, and if you forgot yourself and put the band on, a fat middle age. It was as if God had provided them with a foundation firm enough to build on later.

From there, his gaze went up a tall frame, past a bosom that reminded him of a prairie hen, to a disappointingly mannish profile, just before its owner turned away to instruct a porter who approached pushing a big trunk stood up on end on a handcart. Tom stood, forgetting the horseshoe. He'd recognized the face.

He watched her step inside the station on the arm of a fat old goat in cinderproof clothing, wearing yellow gaiters and carrying a stick with a gold knob the size of a cue ball. She didn't seem to have seen Tom, but if she had he was pretty sure she wouldn't place him. During their one encounter in Denver, she'd been more interested in Charlie Kettleman, who'd knocked her off her bicycle just outside Salt Lake City and stolen back the money she and her companions had stolen from the Overland office there.

Philip Rittenhouse, who seldom missed anything, did not notice the reaction of the man who rose suddenly from a crouch off the edge of the platform just as Major and Mme. Mort-Davies were leaving it; nor did he connect the wizened features with the spare description that appeared on circulars offering a reward for his capture or death, although he'd read it often. He did note in passing that the fellow was an experienced horseman, more comfortable in the saddle than on the ground, and was gratified, when at length the man turned toward the open prairie, to see him turn back and stoop to pick up a horseshoe lying loose beside the track. A drifter, from his clothes and sunburn, but not a cowboy. One of those tramps he'd seen so often during his two visits to the frontier, living on odd jobs and handouts and whatever he could steal.

Such was the train of his thoughts, and had he been able to follow it down its track he might have come very close to the truth—indeed he would have, if Ace-in-the-Hole were his responsibility and all his instincts pointed in that direction. But his concern was the Davieses and the man they had come all the way from San Francisco to meet, and whom he had crossed the country three times to see in the flesh. Tugging down his soft hat to conceal his bald head, and flipping up the collar of his duster to dissemble his reptilian features, Pinkerton's man in Wichita turned away from the worst gang in the West and toward the Prairie Rose.

Within five minutes of his arrival, he got that first look and nearly destroyed his mission in the process.

Stepping into the dimness of the depot from the dazzling sunshine on the platform, he was blinded momentarily and banged shoulders with a man striding the opposite direction. The man was tall and well built and his momentum spun Rittenhouse halfway around, almost toppling him. Instantly the stranger caught his upper arms in two strong hands and steadied his balance.

"I beg your pardon, sir. I didn't intend to derail you."

When Rittenhouse's pupils adjusted to the light, he found his face six inches from the regular features of a young man with fair moustaches and a well-trimmed triangle of beard in the hollow of his chin. He wore a black hat with a dramatic brim, almost Restoration in its width, and a caped overcoat too heavy for late spring, but which contributed to the dash of his appearance as naturally as the fine stick he had tucked beneath one arm. His reassuring smile was even and white. The detective, familiar only with descriptions in theatrical reviews and a crude engraving in the *Deseret News* of the actor who had portrayed Brom Bones in *The Legend of Sleepy Hollow,* knew nevertheless that he was in the presence of John Vermillion.

He muttered that it was his own fault and turned quickly away out of the young man's grasp; but he knew his face had been committed to memory and that his undercover status had been compromised.

Alarm flashed through him. He darted a glance around the inside of the narrow building and was relieved to find neither of the Davieses among the pilgrims and greeters trickling toward the street and the waiting carriages. He'd managed to make a spectacle of himself at the very outset, and had they witnessed it, they'd undoubtedly have recognized him. Even the Major was not so self-besotted as to accept an explanation that Peter Ruskin had traveled all this way merely to secure their release from the company. They would report their suspicions to Vermillion, who would abandon whatever was planned for Wichita, and possibly dissolve the association. As the old man himself was fond of saying, it was not the responsibility of the Pinkerton National Detective Agency to prevent crime or put an end to it, but to apprehend the criminals and bring them to justice, preferably in full view of an admiring press. They were in business to attract clients, and whatever personal satisfaction they might derive from running a band of brigands to cover could hardly be recorded on the black side of the ledger.

Hanging back from the street door, which stood open to give egress to those assembled inside, he spotted the Major smoking a cigar on the boardwalk, and next to him his wife, brushing nervously at creases in her costume. Plainly they awaited the return of their companion, who passed Rittenhouse a moment later carrying a carpetbag that one of them evidently had left behind on the platform. In a moment they had all boarded a handsome phaeton with the couple's oversize trunk strapped to the back and rattled off.

Rittenhouse waited a beat, then stepped outside and caught the attention of a cabman, who stepped down from his seat to take his valise.

"Never mind that. My friends left before I could find out where they were stopping. Please follow them until they alight." He described the phaeton.

When that vehicle turned down Second Street and drew up before a hotel on the corner, he directed his driver toward a plain-faced structure that faced it at an angle, identified by a sign as the

Douglas Avenue Hotel. He did not fail to note, as he paid the fare and turned toward the entrance, that his hotel stood next to a bank, and that that institution stood directly across from the other hotel and a few doors down from the elaborate facade of a variety theater. The Prairie Rose was a most transparent enterprise—an important factor in its success so far. It was a veritable Purloined Letter, boldly concealed in plain sight.

He asked for a room facing the street, and was given one on the second floor. After unpacking and placing his things in a maple bureau, the revolver tucked between two folded shirts, he went to the window, drew down the shade, and slid it aside an inch to study the side of the Occidental Hotel across the way. He'd hardly hoped to catch Vermillion or any of his crew at a window, but instinct and experience told him the room occupied by the head of the company would face the bank.

He did not, in fact, see anyone standing at a window, nor any shades drawn with no bright sunlight striking that side to justify it, but he was contented his theory was correct. He'd been in town barely half an hour, and had spotted both his quarry and its target, leaping far ahead of where he'd been in six months of hard work. It nearly made up for his blunder at the station and the likelihood that he would have to wire Chicago and request a replacement unknown to the repertory players.

Rittenhouse sighed. Unpacking had been a waste of time as well as an exercise in foolish optimism. Common sense—and Pinkerton policy—required him to turn over his information to another agent, and with it the opportunity to trip the snare personally. He would not even get to see it happen, as the old man would undoubtedly recall him rather than take the chance of his being spotted. He'd already risked a great deal in trailing the Davieses halfway across the continent and failing to report the action to headquarters, knowing what steps the old man would take if he knew. Now the choice had been taken out of his hands.

He was about to let the shade slip back when his eyes were drawn toward a movement in a doorway, where a common loafer—that fixture in every frontier settlement—removed his shoulder from the frame to touch his hat to a woman passing his perch along the boardwalk that ran past the Occidental.

Instantly the loafer was forgotten. Notwithstanding the fact that the detective was a confirmed bachelor, and an ugly man who had surrendered all thought of unrecompensed feminine companionship late in his adolescence, he appreciated a small waist and a dainty profile as well as any male creature. The appearance of both in a comely pearl-pink dress and clever hat under a matching parasol was compensation enough for hundreds of hours spent watching buildings and strangers and conveyances passing to and fro. His angle gave him a view of the front of the hotel as well, on Second Street, and when the apparition stepped briskly around the corner and lifted an abundance of skirts and petticoats to climb the steps to the entrance, he was certain he'd identified the member of the company who'd commanded more column inches on the part of masculine journalists than all the rest combined.

He found himself (he was loath to use a word that connoted personal weakness, but no other signified) enchanted. In the romance of newspaper work, every victorious general was handsome and distinguished, every visiting dignitary a gentleman, every actress older than twelve and younger than forty a vision, virginal and touched with stardust; the facts, that Custer looked like a basset hound, Grand Duke Alexis was a drunk, and Sarah Bernhardt had the morals of an alley cat and rather resembled one, were things the mature subscriber assigned to harsh reality. But no hyperbole did justice to April Clay in the flesh. Even from a distance, Philip Rittenhouse understood immediately that it didn't matter how well or poorly the young lady acted as long as one could say that he had seen her. And he knew then that no other employee of the Pinkerton National Detective Agency would be the one to put her in shackles.

20

As long as he could remember, Jack Brixton loved to blow things up.

He'd conducted his first experiment in detonation at the age of five, removing a tablespoonful of black powder from the keg his father used to charge his squirrel rifle and mixing it with the tobacco in his pouch. When that rugged old farmer touched a match to his tightly packed corncob pipe, the powder went up with a sharp crack and a blue flash, singeing his whiskers and eyebrows and puncturing his right eardrum, leaving him deaf on that side for life. It was all very satisfying, and worth the razor-strop beating that followed, even though it made thick welts on his backside that many a woman of lewd reputation would remark upon in later years.

From there he'd gone on to blasting outhouses, rain barrels, and a bobcat that had scratched him something fierce as he held it down and slipped a collar over its spitting head attached to a snuff tin filled with powder, touched off a fuse made from packing cord soaked in coal oil, and let it go. It was his bad luck that the cat had doubled back his way.

He recovered more quickly from the burns than from the scratches, which became infected, contributing to his general disagreeability; but the memory of the close call led him to the decision to leave such technical things as timing fuses to someone more qualified like Tom Riddle, who'd blasted holes through solid rock in California looking for color. But Brixton never lost his fascination with the destructive power of a well-placed charge. He'd been known to blow up railroad tracks that could just as well have been barricaded by chopping down a convenient lodgepole pine, and to burst open safes in spite of the presence of a cooperative bank manager with the combination, just for the pleasure of the spectacle. When dynamite came to the frontier in the late 1860s, he'd celebrated by having Tom dump three tons of Rocky Mountain onto a train carrying nothing more valuable than what was in the passengers' pockets. The account of the atrocity that ran in the *Territorial Enterprise* marked the first appearance in print of the nickname Black Jack.

Train robberies were his favorite, because of the amount of explosives required to bring a charging locomotive to a halt and open the doors of strongcars with guards forted up inside. A satisfying blast, with boards and bodies and lengths of tangled rail flying and reverberations that shattered windows in towns a mile away, was often all the compensation that was needed for a disappointing haul. Breed, alone among the members of Ace-in-the-Hole when it came to speaking his mind, had once told Brixton he'd have blown up General Jackson just to see if he was really made of stone. (Brixton, in a mellow mood at the time with bits of brakeman on his shirt, had merely smiled in response.)

Now, three days' ride from Wichita, Brixton clung to the timbers of a tall trestle spanning the Arkansas River outside Fort Dodge, watching enviously as Tom bound a bundle of dynamite to a diagonal support and smeared the twine with tar to prevent it from soaking up water in the event of a sudden rainstorm and coming loose. Tom unwound several yards of cord from a spool hitched to his belt and threw the spool underhand to Ed Kettleman, standing atop the trestle where it rested on the high bank. He waited until Ed caught it, then wet the end of the cord between his lips like a bit of sewing thread and tied it to a blasting cap. He then inserted the cap in the bundle with the delicate touch of a surgeon. Tom had fine hands for a former pick-and-shovel man, slender and spatulated at the ends like a piano player's.

"Whyn't you just tie it off and pay it out yourself when you climb back up?" Brixton asked. "If Ed missed, you'd have to climb all the way down to the river to fetch it back."

Tom drew a sleeve across his glistening forehead. "You know much about blasting caps?"

"Not a thing. I got out of the blowing-up business myself before dynamite."

"I used to prospect with a fellow name of Spangler. He came up with the same plan. He retired all over northern California."

Brixton scowled at the bundle of sticks. "It don't look like it would blow up much more than a man. You reckon it's enough?"

"It ain't how much you use, it's where you put it. You could tie it to that there strut and just impress the fish, but if you put it in the right place you can blow up Ulysses S. Grant and most of the Republican Party."

"I'd admire to do that. I would for a fact."

"That's where you and me choose up sides. I'm a common thief, not no anarchist."

Brixton narrowed his eyes, which never much opened wider than bullet creases to begin with. "What's got in you, Tom, apart from that Yankee banker's slug? Sometimes I think you got your brains all scrambled like Charlie's."

Tom thought, not for the first time, of telling him about the woman he'd seen at the Wichita station. But Brixton was unreasonable when it came to that Prairie Rose crowd. His fixation seemed to run counter to Ace-in-the-Hole's best interests. Once again Tom censored himself. Above all he had to keep secret the euphoria he felt each time he drew a breath. Black Jack wouldn't understand it, and what he didn't understand he extinguished.

"War's over, Jack. General Lee's writing his memoirs and the niggers got the vote. We got to stick with what we know best: robbing folks and blowing things up."

Brixton grinned, surprising him almost off his perch into the river thirty feet below. Black Jack just never showed his teeth except when he was gnawing on a chicken leg. "You ever blow up a bobcat?"

"You mean on purpose?"

"Well, sure."

"No, Jack, I can't say I ever did. I blew up a cinnamon bear once, but it just happened to come along when the fuse ran out."

"Bobcat's a mangy critter, sucks eggs and licks its privates right out there in front of God and Jefferson Davis."

"That may be so, but I don't see the percentage in blowing one up."

"You might try it once, I mean when you're testing a cap or somesuch. But you want to make sure and jump clear when you let go of it. You never know which way a bobcat's going to run once you got your charge in place."

Tom chewed on that. For the first time since he was shot he wished he had a plug between his teeth, just to cover up how much thinking he was doing. There weren't any rules at Ace-in-the-Hole about thinking as such, but there wasn't any evidence of it either, beyond the engineering. Weasels put their intellectual activity on hold once they'd found a hole in the henhouse.

"Well, Jack, I consider that smart advice. If I ever do take it into my head to blow up a bobcat, I'll be sure and jump clear."

But Brixton didn't appear to be listening. He was watching the Arkansas gurgling far below, carrying away twigs and muskrat huts and clumps of Kansas. "You ever blow up a building?"

"You mean like a bank? All you got to blow up's the vault or safe. You can pop open a Smith and Waddell with half a stick if you know where to put it, but a Foreman Choirmaster's made mostly of iron. Half a stick would just bend it out of shape. Two'd blow off the door and turn all the greenbacks into rat's nests. I wouldn't go beyond a stick and a half with no Choirmaster."

"I don't mean like a bank. I mean like a theater."

Something about the way Brixton drew out the word—"thee-ay-ter"—filled Tom with icy dread. The drawl had a drooling quality. The whole conversation had been a bubble off true, but this was hydrophobic.

He decided to play it out. "Six sticks might do it, if there's a second story. Maybe one more for luck. Depends on whether it's board or brick."

"Tell you when I know."

Brixton seemed ready to continue, but Breed's harsh twang cut across the noise of the river. He stood on the bank with his fists on his hips.

"If you two hens are through squawking, that train's due in ten minutes. Don't you figure we ought to mount up and make like we're fixing to rob the U.S. Army?"

Tom climbed up after Brixton. He'd never thought he'd welcome an interruption from Breed.

"Goodness me, what has become of our poor frail moth? He's grown into an eagle."

Cornelius Ragland, so hailed, stepped down from the vestibule into the embrace of Little Nell, Lady Macbeth, and Joan of Arc, distilled into one intoxicating beverage. One sip of April Clay and he felt himself floating above the train platform.

"Ponce de León was misled," he said, when he managed to land. "The fountain of youth was in the Old World all along; and you have come fresh from it."

"Such a pretty compliment."

"And uncannily specific," said Johnny, placing his stick on his shoulder. "How did you know she was in Europe?"

"I sent him a postcard from Paris. Don't be cross; I didn't write anything on it. What's the point of going abroad if no one envies you?"

"The culture, perhaps. The history, the museums, Queen Victoria, the crème brûlée at Le Grand Véfour. If envy was your aim, you could have bought a French postcard in Kansas City and posted it from there."

"With a Kansas City postmark? The effect would suffer, don't you think?"

"But how would you know where to send it? We all took special care not to tell the others where we were staying." He took the stick off his shoulder and tapped Cornelius on his.

"You needn't try to beat information out of Corny with your silly club. Where else would he spend his holiday, if not Hot Springs? He talked for months of taking the cure. Honestly, Johnny, you'll never make a successful criminal if you don't learn to think like a detective." She lowered her voice to a husky whisper on the last point, although the crowd had thinned out from around them.

"It was the coastal circuit for us." Major Davies, attired eccentrically in a deerstalker cap and travel-worn Inverness, wrung Cornelius' hand. "We were forced to steal out of Eureka in disguise to avoid a horde of well-wishers."

"Steal we did. They were quite eager to detain us. Welcome to the wilderness, young man. You indeed look fit." Mme. Mort-Davies leaned forward for a kiss on the cheek, a service he performed with some discomfort. The cheek was leathery and cold.

A porter appeared and asked him if he had any luggage to be unloaded. He shook his head, holding up his valise and fat leather portfolio. When the railroad employee withdrew, touching his visor, Cornelius asked Johnny if the costumes and properties had arrived from Denver.

"I had them placed in storage in the theater basement. We'll go through it all for damage later. You look to have nothing less than the complete works of Shakespeare stuffed in that case."

"The complete works of Ragland, at any rate. I finished mutilating the merry wives on the train. Directly I'm settled in I'll begin transcribing copies."

April pouted. "What of St. Joan? Don't tell me you've given her up."

He smiled and drummed his fingers on the portfolio. "I wouldn't do that, so soon after the French. She's *en deshabille* at present, I'm afraid; not fit for your eyes."

"You're overestimating her exposure to the language," Johnny said. "All she managed to pick up in Paris were a few phrases and forty-four boxes of hats and parasols. She's been stuck on page ten of a biography of Joan for a month. He means to dress her in ribbons, dear, so you'll know her for a saint and not a scrubwoman."

"Oh, please don't torment me. I shall make allowances. I must read it right away or perish."

Johnny nodded. "I'd comply. She's pigheaded enough to do what she says, and then we'll be out our Anne Page."

Cornelius set down his valise, untied the portfolio, and handed her a thick sheaf of paper bound with faded ribbon. She seized it in both gloved hands and read the title page. "Oh! It's in English."

"I thought it best," he said. "In this country you can sing opera in any language but English. The reverse is true in drama."

They turned and drifted toward the station. Johnny placed a hand on Cornelius' shoulder. "I'm happy to see you. The Prairie Rose is back in bloom."

The Mexicans, who agreed without exception that Matagordo was a general of uncommon brilliance, had to confess that for a gringo, *Señor* Brixton was no slouch when it came to tactics and strategy.

First, he had set them to work with their machetes, hacking away undergrowth in the tall stand of trees north of the Arkansas River, leaving only a shallow fringe at the edge visible from the Kansas Pacific tracks so that it would appear not to have been tampered with. Then he had stationed them a dozen abreast on horse-back among the trees where they would not be seen, far enough apart so that as the train approached the trestle they could slide through the spaces between as smoothly as water. When *Señor* Tomás, the man with all the words and an understanding of dynamite, touched off his two charges, destroying the trestle before the train and the tracks behind it, sealing it between, they would emerge, galloping and shooting and pinning the gringo soldiers in the crossfire from their guns and those of *El Jefe* Brixton's men on the other side of the tracks. When enough of the soldiers had been slain, and a number of single sticks of dynamite flung at the train from horseback in order to complete the confusion, both forces would converge, kill or stay the hands of the remaining defenders, and remove the payroll, to be divided among them when they assembled later at a place called Cimarron, in the panhandle of the Indian Nations across the Kansas border. It was a plan worthy of Juárez, only this time with gold rather than glory awaiting them at the end. A man could not eat glory after all, nor use it to bind his bare feet against rattlesnakes and cactus. These *Norteamericanos* were not so dull and slow-witted as they appeared when they came to the border towns to drink tequila and catch the clap.

Now the sons of Mexico sat on their tough, grass-fed mounts with carbines unshipped, listening to the clarinet whistle of the train and waiting for the first explosion, which was the signal to put the spurs to their flanks. Even the horses were wound tight as watches, snorting and tossing their manes and pawing the ground; but horses were stupid and carried no memory of previous injuries. They were in it for the oats.

"If just one of you greaser bastards twitches his thumb, we'll scoop you all up with tortillas."

They turned their heads to a man. Not more than two or three understood English, but the flat smack of the Middle Western voice from behind them was gringo to the core. It belonged to a red-whiskered cavalry sergeant seated in the center of twenty men astride fat horses, and every one of them had a Springfield rifle trained on a Mexican back.

21

"It's a comedy of manners," Johnny explained.

The gentleman representing the *Wichita City Eagle*, a wiry fifty with a tuft of white beard at the end of his chin—the living embodiment of the character the political cartoonists of a later day would christen Uncle Sam—smiled over his glass of wine. So far he'd shown no sign of carrying a notebook on his person. "Most of our readers know the meaning of comedy," he said. "You might have to define manners."

Tim Saunders, proprietor of the variety theater, refilled the man's glass from one of a half-dozen bottles standing uncorked on the table. "You mustn't pay much heed to anything Mr. Cyrus has to say," he told Johnny. "He's determined to send the few subscribers he has left over to Mr. Dockerty."

Dockerty, publisher of the *Wichita Beacon*, took his nose out of his glass. It was a long nose, and a drop of wine quivered on the tip. "I'm not sure what good they'd do us. Most of them can't read."

Johnny laughed. "Give me a community whose newspapers are out to let each other's blood and I'll give you a well-informed populace. Briefly put, *The Merry Wives of Windsor* is the story of a scheming thief and the wondrous variety of ways he receives his comeuppance."

"I'd pay to see that."

This statement, and the voice that delivered it with a mild Irish lilt, drew Johnny's attention to a balding fellow with sleek handlebars. He wore a starched white shirt buttoned to the throat under a town coat and was the only man in the room not holding a glass. Johnny switched hands on his own glass and offered his right. "I don't think we've been introduced."

"Mike Meagher." The Irishman grasped it firmly and let go. His pale eyes held on to Johnny's afterward.

"Meagher's our city marshal," Saunders said. "His brother John is sheriff in this county. We pay them a king's ransom to keep the peace, and they earn it."

Cyrus of the *City Eagle* helped himself to the bottle. "Fortunately, we pay them a straight salary rather than a commission based on the number of men they kill in the performance of their duty. We'd be bankrupt otherwise."

An unhealthy silence followed, broken by Dockerty of the *Beacon*.

"That's the editorial policy that's shrunken the *Eagle*'s circulation and swollen ours: alienation and exaggeration. Without the brothers Meagher, we'd be burying innocent citizens by the day. We approve of cowboys, we do; they work hard, and they spend money like water, to our great benefit. But once they come out from under the harsh conditions of a long trail drive—well, a stampede would be hard put to compare with the damage to life and property. Mike and John remind them of those manners Mr. Cyrus finds so scarce among his readers."

"Yes, a corpse behaves well under most circumstances." Cyrus drank.

"Mr. Cyrus prefers to keep his collar clean without the unpleasantness of a laundry bill," Meagher said, "and so I must pay it myself. As a dramatic actor, Mr. Vermillion, how many bows do you take when your villains go unpunished?"

"None, I'm bound to say. Our audiences will have justice or nothing. However, I'm happy to add that theater is not life." Johnny took a swift sip from his glass and beckoned to April, standing next to Cornelius and the Davieses with an affectionate hand resting upon the arm of her saloonkeeper mayor. The reception was taking place in a hospitality suite at the Occidental Hotel, with the press and leaders of the community invited. April drifted over, a glittering vision in a ruby-colored Paris gown she wore off the shoulders and a crown of white feathers in her hair. Her smile radiated when Johnny introduced her to the marshal.

"Such a strong hand." She squeezed Meagher's. "I haven't felt so safe since I left Park Avenue."

Meagher held her gaze as he had Johnny's. "I'm looking forward to the play. I'm told you catch a thief in it."

"And without a shot fired. Primitive, those Elizabethans." Cyrus stumbled over the last word. He was drunk.

"We don't catch him so much as teach him a lesson," April said. Johnny couldn't tell if she was fascinated with Meagher or transfixed by him, as a hen by a snake.

"Lessons are lost on outlaws. The only way to get them to change their habits is to change them for them."

"Perhaps that's why people enjoy our little fantasies," she said. "The world is so much less—forgiving."

"That's just what I was saying," said Johnny. "Look, there is Mr. Munn. I met him when I went to the Longhorn Bank to make change. Please excuse us, gentlemen, while we mingle."

The men inclined their heads; all except Cyrus, who was draining a bottle into his glass. Johnny entwined his arm with April's and they moved away. "Munn's the manager," he murmured.

"Gracious, he's as big as a barn!"

"Not so solid as that. He has the lecher's eye. Let it rest on you a moment and he'll tell you the combination of the vault and how much he has in his wallet."

"It hardly seems possible he and that splendid marshal belong to the same gender."

"Steer clear of Meagher. I swear he suspects us of something."

They were nearing the fat bank manager, who turned toward them and away from a member of the city commission, tugging down the corners of his swollen vest. She giggled and fluttered a fan in front of her mouth; Johnny would have thought it over-the-top if she'd suggested it, but in practice it seemed to work. "Actors are always suspect," she whispered. "You've a touch of stage fright, that's all. You haven't trod the boards in months."

"You're right, I suppose. I just wish his brother weren't sheriff. They're both killers, Cyrus says. That stacks the odds a bit."

She laughed gaily and lifted her voice. "Oh, Johnny, don't be ridiculous! I'm sure Mr. Munn is much too important to offer investment advice to someone of my small means."

"Good girl," he whispered, and made the introductions. When the pair were deep in conversation he wandered over to join the rest of the troupe, where the Major insisted on addressing the mayor as "m' lord."

Philip Rittenhouse, sitting up in bed chuckling over Allan Pinkerton's *The Expressman and the Detective,* looked up at a knock on the door of his room and set aside the elaborately bound volume. He slid his revolver from under the adjoining pillow and padded over in his stocking feet. He put his ear to the panel.

"It's Meagher." The voice was muffled, but he recognized the slight brogue. He twisted back the latch and opened the door.

"I've just come from the reception," said the marshal when they were locked in. His gaze swept the room and alighted on the open book lying face down on the bed. "I hope you haven't been reading too much of that. If you hadn't told me what you have, I'd take them all for jackanapes; though the girl's a dash of ginger, I'll say that. They might pinch a watch or a poke, but as to desperadoes I'd be laughed out of town if I said that to a soul."

"That's good news. I asked you not to take anyone into your confidence, especially the bank manager. He'd tip his hand the first time he laid eyes on them, and we'd be back where we were last fall."

"I'm not so sure you shouldn't be. They seem harmless enough. I couldn't rattle them."

"These are actors. They're trained to stay in character. It isn't like buffaloing a drunken cowboy or chasing guerrillas. According to our calculations, they've stolen close to forty thousand dollars from seven places, probably with the same Colt revolver, without busting a cap. We don't even know if it's ever been loaded."

"I hope yours isn't. You're waving it around like an umbrella."

Rittenhouse returned the weapon to its hiding place. He'd forgotten he was holding it.

"They're not your usual marauding gang," he said. "Unless they've changed their method, which based upon its success so far I doubt they will, they'll send one of their actors into the bank while the rest are performing onstage, cleverly switching costumes back and forth so that no one in the audience realizes any of the cast is missing. The robber could be any one of them, even the women; both are experienced at portraying male characters."

"Not April Clay. Not even a bank cashier is that stupid."

"Pioneers are hard to deceive, yet she's managed to convince several hundred of them she's a boy. It's even easier for Elizabeth Mort-Davies; she needs her corsets and ruffles just to convince people she's a woman. She has a bosom, but it's easier to conceal than you might think. It's just flesh, after all."

"I was married, Mr. Rittenhouse. It's more than that."

"Only if the woman chooses to make it so. Clearly you don't know much about the theater."

"I've never attended a performance. When that curtain goes up I'm too busy rattling doors."

"Assign a deputy to that duty Friday night. I suspect you're in for a treat, no matter how you feel about Shakespeare." As he spoke, the Pinkerton indicated that day's number of the *Wichita Beacon* on the nightstand, open to a quarter-page advertisement announcing the opening of *The Merry Wives of Windsor (An Abridgment)* at Saunders' variety theater three nights hence.

Meagher shook his head. "If what you say is true, or even if it ain't, I'll be inside the Longhorn Bank that night. They've got a coat closet just big enough for a man and a Stephens ten-gauge. I hope you're right about that Colt not being loaded, or it's one of them three men sticking the place up. I never busted a cap on a woman. It don't mean I won't, if it comes to that; but I'll lose some sleep."

"They'll choose the matinee Saturday," Rittenhouse said.

Meagher made no comment, no matter what he thought of the bald statement. The Pinkerton admired that. Some of these frontier lawmen were more than guerrillas with badges. He went on.

"The Longhorn closes at four o'clock, same as every other day of the week, and all the employees including Manager Munn go home at half past the hour. At two o'clock Saturday afternoon, Munn and Edgar English, his head cashier, lock themselves in with the week's transactions and the ledger and make sure everything balances before the bank reopens on Monday. That gives them all day Sunday to clear up any discrepancies. The guard isn't present, and no customers are flowing in and out. They're never less than two hours adding up the columns and double-checking the figures. The curtain goes up on the matinee of *The Merry Wives of Windsor* at one-thirty Saturday. If I were the Prairie Rose Repertory Theater, I'd give my audience one act to become absorbed in the genius of the Bard, then rob the Longhorn Bank shortly after intermission; say, between a quarter past two and three o'clock, when Falstaff is making his escape from the clothes basket. I'd choose Major Davies for the actual stickup, as he's invisible from the audience for most of that scene. I could be wrong on that detail."

Marshal Meagher smoothed the corner of one of his moustaches. "You wouldn't mind showing me those credentials of yours once again, Mr. Rittenhouse?"

Rittenhouse laughed and produced them from beneath the Bible in the drawer of the nightstand. "Detective work is worlds away from merely keeping the peace," he said. "You find yourself thinking more often like a criminal than like a defender of justice."

Meagher returned the badge and business card. "All the same, I hope you won't take it hard if I skip Saunders' theater and try the door of the Longhorn Friday night."

"Certainly not. I'll be in the doorway of the Occidental, just across the street."

Cornelius Ragland looked up from his pocket-size translation of Molière, realized the horse-faced waiter standing there had asked him a question, and pushed forward his glass for a refill of mineral water. The waiter carried away the empty vessel with an air as if it weighed ten pounds. Cornelius considered withholding his gratuity, or perhaps leaving one of preposterous size to teach the fellow humility, but knew that in either case he would have lost the battle of the classes. Johnny, he felt sure, would have sent the fellow after some impossible vintage of French wine, and regardless of whether the waiter was successful, reduced him to his station by leaving a banknote of an unconscionably large denomination. Instead, he sighed, fished out a quarter, and slid it under his linen napkin, to be discovered after he'd drunk his water and retired upstairs. He would never be Johnny Vermillion no matter how hard he tried.

"Thank goodness I found you, Corny. I knocked and knocked at your door. I thought you'd taken a sleeping draught."

Molière was better than his press, and his press was exquisite. He'd lost himself once again in those lines, so deceptively featherweight in their grasp of the gravity of the absurd, and had missed the descent of an angel (devil?) into his world. April, still clad in the exquisite jewel-colored dress she'd worn to the reception up-stairs, stood before his table with a beautifully embroidered shawl drawn over her shoulders. She cradled the hefty manuscript of *The Tragedy of Joan of Arc* in one arm.

Quickly he closed his book and rose, nearly upsetting his glass. "I wasn't sleepy. Will you join me? May I order for you?"

But the horse-faced waiter was already there, genuflecting. April never had to wait more than a few seconds for service. She smiled. "Tea, I think. Charge it to two-oh-eight; and the gentleman's order as well."

"The gentleman is having water."

"The gentleman will have tea as well," said Cornelius; and for that one moment knew what it was like to be Johnny. "Charge both to two-sixteen. I insist," he told April firmly.

He managed to beat the waiter to her chair and held it for her, then returned to his own. She placed the stack of pages on the table in front of her and pushed her shawl back off her shoulders, seem-ingly oblivious to the male heads that turned her way from nearby tables. She spent some moments turning back sheets. Their tea came. She paid no attention as waiter and tray withdrew. Finally she paused with her finger on a line of neat cursive, then slid a gold lorgnette from between her breasts and peered through the small egg-shaped lenses. Cornelius smiled. This was a new affectation.

She lifted her eyes to his. " 'Seraphic'?"

"Angelic," he said. "Isaiah had a vision of seraphim hovering above God's eternal throne. In this case I used it as a substitute for 'pious.' It's difficult not to overemploy the term when one is writ-ing about St. Joan." He stirred his tea. "Shouldn't you be reading *Merry Wives*? We open in three days."

" 'The dinner is on the table; my father desires your worships' company.' I know it backwards and forwards. For the leading lady, it isn't a very big part. Not like Joan."

"It's much smaller in the original. I borrowed some of Mrs. Page's best lines for you; I'm afraid it altered the character. Somehow I doubt Shakespeare would object if he ever saw you in performance."

"That's charming, and quite sweet. People are always presuming to speak for Shakespeare, but I have an idea he was a tyrant in rehearsal. Look at Johnny."

"He has a lot on his mind. It's more important to him that we all behave like actors than it is to the head of the average company."

"You needn't apologize for him. I know him better than anyone. That's why I proposed marriage."

A lance went through his heart. He had to clear his throat of the butt end before he spoke. "Does that mean congratulations are in order?"

"Not just yet. He said no. I'm wearing him down, however." She shuffled pages, and remembered the lorgnette. "Joan's frocks are very simple. The scenes in armor will be stunning, but the rest of the time I might as well be one of Lizzie's nuns. This huge cross, for instance; it says here I'm to hang it around my neck. Can I not wear it a bit off the hip?"

"I'll have to consult my sources, but offhand I'd say no. It was the Dark Ages, not *La Belle Epoch*."

"I'm concerned about the waistline. There isn't one."

"We can do something about that, I suppose. Do you like the part?"

"It's fascinating. She's a bit less humble than I'd expected."

"I wrote her with you in mind. You're more interesting than Nilsson."

"You're a dear." She sprang up before he could rise and leaned down to kiss his cheek. She gathered up the pages. Her teacup was untouched. "A bit of gold braid, perhaps, around the waist; with a tassle. I almost forgot." Her voice dropped. "Johnny said to make sure the revolver's in working order."

She said good night and left, her skirts rustling like pages of gold leaf falling.

Cornelius drained his cup of a beverage for which he had no liking, then drank water to rinse the brown taste from his tongue. His face felt hot, but he didn't think it had anything to do with his old malady. He knew then that it was possible to burn with jealousy. He had no doubt April would wear Johnny down. They would marry, and she would take him away.

22

Ed Kettleman said, "Is that train slowing down?"

From the Kansas Pacific tracks, the land sloped down gently to-ward a patch of scrub oak almost directly across from the stand of trees where General Matagordo's Mexicans waited on horseback for the first of Tom Riddle's two charges to go off. Ace-in-the-Hole lay on their bellies among the stubbly growth, their horses down beside them, each with a hand on its neck to comfort it while in such an unaccustomed position. From there, every man could see the sputtering sparks and coxcombs of smoke belonging to the two fuses, the one to the left burning faster; Tom had allowed a gap of ten seconds to give them time to mount up during the confusion caused by the collapsing trestle. The frontal assault would com-mence simultaneous with the second explosion behind the train.

There were only five cars, counting the tender and caboose: a day coach where the officers rode, the strongcar containing the pay-roll for the Indian campaign, and a flatcar behind that, bristling with armed troops, made up the rest. With the troops exposed in the crossfire from the Mexicans and Brixton's men, and Tom hurling more dynamite from horseback as they charged, the cargo would be theirs for the taking. But Ed had been right. The train was definitely throttling down as it approached the trestle, and the brakes were being applied; the wheels screeched, spouting geysers of orange sparks from the friction. The chugging slowed.

"Maybe the engineer don't trust the bridge," Ed Kettleman said.

Tom chuckled. "He don't know the half of it."

"Pipe down and get ready." Brixton's voice was tight.

The trestle went up in a huge blossom of smoke and fire and dirt and sawdust and twisted girders; they felt the rumble beneath their sternums and rose as one, scrambling into their saddles even as the horses struggled upright, galvanized by their training under battlefield conditions. The troopers aboard the flatcar, well trained also, assumed combat positions, some kneeling, the rest standing to clear their field of fire. When the second explosion came, erupting in a dome of earth and steel like an elephant-size mole bursting through the surface, Ace-in-the-Hole was galloping full speed up the slope, spreading out and firing their pistols with rebel yells. Tom, carrying a coil of unattached fuse burning at the end, used it to light a stick of dynamite, whirled it over his head by a loop of fuse like a lasso, and flung it toward the flatcar, then lit another and threw that after the first. They discharged short of their target, but threw up a screen of dirt and smoke, through which the gang rode, shrieking and shooting, like demons through brimstone.

The returning fire, however, was heavy. Ed Kettleman yelled and fell off his horse. Breed's mount went down with a squeal of pain; the rider got his feet out of the stirrups in time to land running, caught Ed's riderless horse, and swung a leg over without losing momentum or his grip on his revolver. A bullet split the air next to Brixton's right ear with a crack.

"Where in hell's the Mexicans?" he shouted.

Just then he broke through the smoke into the open—and hauled back on the reins hard enough to throw it onto its haunches had not that splendid animal the instinct and experience to adjust to the abrupt change. As it was, it reared and clawed the air, twisting for balance and nearly unseating its rider. Mysterious Bob, reacting even faster, spun his sorrel into a wide circle to slow it down and take himself out of the main path.

The rest saw the danger too late. Charlie Kettleman, Tom Riddle, and Breed were still charging hard when the big side door on the strongcar finished sliding open. When the sun struck the brass-bound barrels of the Gatling gun mounted inside, they tried to change course, but the chattering lead found them all and flung Ace-in-the-Hole in every direction like so many bloody cards.

It's not for nothing that professional thespians are so often referred to as players. When the trunks were brought up from the basement of the variety theater and the Prairie Rose dove inside to retrieve costumes and properties they hadn't laid eyes on in months, they laughed and jostled one another like children opening a chest filled with toys.

Major Davies, who was as fast as any of them once he got his bulk into motion, clawed out Falstaff's sword belt and doublet (these had served as well for *Twelfth Night*'s Sir Toby Belch, and would in fact suffice for all of the Bard's older gentlemen of gravity and healthy appetite, except perhaps the Romans), and had them fastened in place while Cornelius was still looking for Dr. Caius among the jumble and April and Lizzie were each tugging at a sleeve of the same ornate frock. Johnny, aloof to the scavenger hunt, waited until the congestion had cleared, then stepped forward and claimed his prize: a fencing foil with an elegantly rounded guard, fashioned from tin but painted to resemble gold.

Holding it at shoulder level, he peered down its length, frowned, exerted pressure with both hands to straighten a bend in the blade, then went into fighting stance and described a swift figure eight with the blunted point. At the swish, Cornelius looked up from the bit of lint he was removing from the plumed crown of the French physician's hat. He read the eager expression on Johnny's face, then shrugged, clapped the hat onto his head, and drew another foil from the same trunk compartment. They squared off.

Two minutes later, Cornelius stood pinned against a stack of leaning canvas flats with his foil lying on the floor six feet away and the button tip of Johnny's weapon pressing against his throat. The cast, distracted from their bright scraps of cloth, applauded.

The loser swallowed against the pressure. "Where did you learn that?"

"In Paris; where else? From the finest swordsman in France; who else? Also the one with the least pleasant personality. Which says a great deal when one is speaking of the French." Johnny withdrew his foil, described a bright whizzing pattern in the air, and slung the blade into an imaginary scabbard on his hip. It seemed to have left a thin blue phosphorescence in its wake.

Cornelius enjoyed once again the unobstructed motion of his Adam's apple. "You realize there is no swordplay in *Merry Wives*."

"I thought I might persuade you to write some in. I need the practice, and I don't think dear Will would object."

"With whom will you fight?"

"With you, of course. We represent two sides of a love triangle, do we not?"

The other hesitated. Of course Johnny was speaking of their characters in the play. "I won't be able to offer you much contest. All the fencing masters in Hot Springs left their hardware at home."

"You'll have lessons from the finest swordsman in Wichita. We'll work them into rehearsals."

"But, who will, er—"

Johnny smiled. "You'll make love to the fair Anne in Act Three, Scene Four. I'd thought of sending forth the Major after the clothes-basket business, but he's on probation for Salt Lake City. You've filled out, Corny; my costume will fit you this time without padding. Just wear your hat low and mind your moustaches are stuck on tight. Where is the revolver?"

Cornelius got the bundle from the chair where he'd hung his street coat, unwound the cloth, and handed him the Forehand & Wadsworth that Lizzie had found on the ground after she was assaulted outside Salt Lake City.

"I forgot we'd lost the Colt," Johnny said. "I hope we didn't make a poor trade. What did you do with the cartridges?"

"I took them out to clean it. Do you want it loaded?"

"God, no. Why change our luck now? April can tell you what kind of sharpshooter I am. I just wanted to make sure you didn't leave the shells lying around for the chambermaid to find."

"I threw them out the window into the alley."

"You aren't usually so foolish, Corny." April, who'd won the tug-of-war with Lizzie, held the frock against the front of her person, looking at herself in a dusty cheval glass with a crack down its center. "What if someone stumbles upon them?"

"This is Wichita, dear," Johnny reminded her. "The duellists don't allow each other much time to reload. There is bound to be spillage."

"I should take out my bicycle once or twice before Saturday," said Lizzie, fingering a loose paste diamond on a tiara. "I haven't ridden all year."

"That won't be necessary. I've made other arrangements to recover the money."

April looked up. "Without consulting us?"

"The details would only distract you. Our blocking needs work." Johnny tossed up the revolver, caught its trigger guard on the end of his foil, and extended it toward Cornelius. "Put away this fowling piece, good sir, and take up your weapon from the ground. This is an affair between gentlemen."

Cornelius returned the Forehand & Wadsworth to its cloth and bent to retrieve his foil. As he did so, a projectile the size and shape of a percussion ball grazed the back of his neck and struck the wall backstage with a sharp *ping*.

"Oh, damn!" said the Major. "I've popped a button off my doublet."

The best of it was Tom Riddle had found a cure for his euphoria. The worst of it was he was dying.

He'd been struck, he reckoned, three times by the Gatling. The hunk of meat he'd lost from his left upper arm could be patched up, and he'd done that after a fashion by tearing off his sleeve and knotting it in place with his teeth as he rode away. The broken collarbone was more serious, but the bullet had passed straight through, and Mysterious Bob, who knew a thing or two about stopping up wounds from the fighting in Missouri, had stuffed more rags into the holes that would keep Tom from bleeding out until he could get to a doctor. But there was nothing anyone could do about the slug in his belly. That was the payoff.

It hurt plenty bad, but not as much as he'd always heard. Mostly he was cold. The fire they'd built in the kitchen hearth belonging to the first farmhouse they'd come to couldn't reach as far as his insides, and that was the source of the chill. He lay on his back on the plank table where the farmer and his wife took their meals with his legs dangling off the end, staring up at a squirrel hole in the ceiling and trying not to move. He didn't know what Bob and Black Jack had done with the couple. Shot them, he supposed, or gagged and hog-tied them and put them in the barn.

Something gurgled. Tom didn't turn his head to see what it was. Brixton had probably found a jug. He and Bob stood guard at the windows near the opposite end of the house facing the road, in case the troopers came trailing them. It was a long open building, with no interior walls to divide it up into separate rooms. So far as Tom knew, they three were what was left of Ace-in-the-Hole.

"They knew we was coming," Brixton said. "You sure you took care of that greaser general?"

"I took care of him."

"Maybe it was his men. They never came out of them trees."

"They stood to profit better if the job came off. Somebody got the drop on them."

"Well, it sure wasn't Breed or Charlie or Tom, there; he's gone as the Confederacy. What about Ed?"

"Ed got it first. If he wasn't dead when he hit the ground, he was by the time we finished riding over him on the way out."

"It was that woman."

There was a little silence. Tom wasn't sure they'd heard him; it had come out in a croak.

"What woman's that, Tom?" Brixton's voice was so close it made him jerk. A fresh wave of cold swept through him, followed by a pain like a toothache in the pit of his belly. Sweat pricked his forehead like fire ants. He gathered up spit to take out the croak.

"That Prairie Rose woman. The tall one Charlie jumped in Salt Lake. I seen her that time in Denver and again in Wichita just before we rode out. At the train station it was. I was as close to her as I am to you."

He saw Brixton's face then, looking down at him from up near the ceiling, and knew he'd miscalculated the distance between them. Black Jack seemed to be peeping through the squirrel hole. The hole was too small and his face too far away to see what was on it. But then Black Jack always looked sore.

"You seen her at the station?"

"She was with a fat jasper, probably the one stuck up the freight office. I didn't say nothing, 'cause you got a mad on against that there Prairie Rose, and we had us a train to rob. I was fixing to tell you about it after."

He breathed in and out a couple of times. He never thought talking would ever take so much out of him. That was one thing he'd always been able to do, even when he was stuck underground and drawing in a peck of dirt with every breath. "I reckon she must of saw me too, though I didn't think she'd know me," he said.

"You reckon?" Something squeaked; metal against leather, or maybe the squirrel was back.

"She must of went to the law for the bounty, and they told the army, and the army figured out the rest," Tom said. "That's how I see it. Thing is—"

"Shut up, Tom." The muzzle of Brixton's big American was as big as the squirrel hole. It swallowed Tom up.

23

The Wichita Variety Theater provided only a single dressing room for its visiting artists, but it was large enough to accommodate a company larger than the Prairie Rose, with a cheerful buffalo-plaid blanket suspended from a rope tied across the middle for the modesty of the female players. Tim Saunders had added a second entrance for the ladies and planned to construct a permanent partition by next season. Cornelius, who shared space with Johnny and Major Davies, entered that side without knocking and found the head of the company filling two crystal glasses from a stout black bottle, using the top of an upright trunk for a table. The Major plucked one up and sniffed at the contents. Sir John Falstaff's cotton burnsides still adhered to his scarlet face, and nineteenth-century galluses held up Johnny's puffed Elizabethan pantaloons, the straps resting on shoulders clad in a white linen undervest.

The newcomer bore the Saturday editions of both the *City Eagle* and the *Beacon,* containing excellent reviews of the Friday-night opening; but as he was sure the others had seen neither, he drew the obvious conclusion.

"I take it things went smoothly at the bank."

For answer, Johnny tilted the neck of the bottle in the direction of the oilcloth sack slumped heavily on the chair of the dressing table; it was the twin of the one that had been taken from Lizzie in Utah, along with the money the Major had robbed from the Overland office there. Johnny filled a third glass and held it out.

"You brought it *here*? What if there's a search?" Cornelius took the offering and swallowed half. His face flushed as from fever.

"Easy, old man; that port slumbered a quarter-century below ground before I woke it up and carried it across the sea. It's a bit touchy. As for the sack, I told you I'd made other arrangements."

"What sort of—"

"Goodness, what's the fight about? I should have thought you lads had spent all your energies playing at swords." April emerged from behind the blanket, brushing her hair. She wore a green silk dressing gown with matching slippers and her face glistened with residue from the cream she used to remove her makeup. Without paint and powder she looked as fresh as a child.

"Corny thinks we're about to be pinched. I say, this is capital stuff." The Major took another drink.

Lizzie emerged in a faded-pink terry robe, veteran of a dozen tours, took the glass from his hand, and helped herself to a healthy sip. "Evie, this is far too rich for you. You'll be down with gout before dark."

Johnny poured another and handed it to April. "I was just explaining that a new season calls for a new system. Especially since it's our last. As of today, the Prairie Rose Repertory Company has taken its final curtain call."

Eyebrows shot up all around. Cornelius was first to find his voice. "Did we do so well, then?"

"I hadn't time to count, of course, but I've gotten to be a fair judge of weight since we opened in St. Louis. It seems an excellent year for the United States beef industry. We should clearly sixty thousand after expenses."

The members of the company began chattering all at once. April threw her arms around Johnny's neck, spilling port down his back. He disengaged himself and called for quiet. "Come, come. The reviews can't be *that* good; drowning out the cowboys will only lead to suspicion."

Cornelius said, "It's a bit late for caution, isn't it? We haven't even begun packing, and that blasted sack's a prison sentence for us all."

"Dear old fellow." Johnny set down his glass. "What exactly do you think is in it?"

"Empty ink bottles, or I've misjudged my source."

This was a new voice, coming from the opposite end of the room. The company turned in a body to look at the stranger who'd appeared from behind the hanging blanket. He was an ugly toad of a man with a polished bald head, wearing a suit that needed a press and a brush.

"Good Lord, it's Ruskin! What are you doing so far from— Barbary?"

The Major's voice trailed off on the last word. Lizzie had placed a hand on his arm, silencing him.

"Philip Rittenhouse. I represent the Pinkerton National Detective Agency." With the air of a man somewhat ashamed of its gaudiness, the stranger opened a leather folder to which was pinned a golden orb engraved on a shield.

No one moved. Rittenhouse pocketed the badge and stepped forward to seize Johnny's hand. "I can't tell you what a pleasure it is to meet you. I've followed your career with keen interest ever since Nebraska. I'm sorry I missed both performances here. Last night I was busy, but I did manage to catch a piece of your act this afternoon; from the back row, as it were. You were in and out of the bank so fast I almost missed you."

When he let go of Johnny's hand, it fell to his side like an empty sleeve. Rittenhouse walked around the silent half circle as if it were a reception line, shaking masculine hands and bowing crisply over feminine ones. "Miss Clay: Brava. Major Davies: I apologize for misrepresenting myself in San Francisco, but thank you for the splendid review. I'd hardly hoped to impress so experienced a pair of thespians as you and Madame Mort-Davies. Madame. Mr. Ragland: Perhaps when Mr. Pinkerton publishes his account of his investigation you'll consent to look at the galley proof and provide comment. The reading public responds favorably to endorsements by other famous writers."

Johnny cleared his throat. The Pinkerton looked at him. There was something beyond amusement in the reptilian face. It was almost the proprietary pride of a sincere admirer watching him step back into character after a profound shock.

"Mr. Rusthouse—"

"Rittenhouse; but I think you knew that. You've a reputation for committing pages of dialogue to memory swiftly. Floor plans as well."

"Rittenhouse. You've made an honest blunder. You overheard us rehearsing Mr. Ragland's new play and drawn the obvious conclusion."

"Please pardon the interruption." Rittenhouse raised his voice. "Come in, Marshal. You have the key."

No one but the Pinkerton appeared to have noticed the knock at the door. It opened and Marshal Meager entered, carrying a short-barreled shotgun.

"I doubt you'll need that." Rittenhouse took a step past the chair where the oilcloth sack rested, lifted the Forehand & Wadsworth from the table, and inspected the chambers. "Empty. Stage pistols usually are, unless the script requires blanks to be fired. But then there are no revolvers in Shakespeare." He slid it into his right side pocket. From the left he drew April's Remington derringer, balanced it on his palm a moment, then returned it. "Two rounds there, but a lady needs protection. All the more reason not to leave her reticule lying around."

April stepped up to Rittenhouse and slapped his cheek. Meagher said, "Hey!" and palmed back the shotgun's hammers.

The Pinkerton raised a hand to calm him, then used it to rub the red patch on his sallow skin. "I'll cherish that, Miss Clay. No woman's even kissed me, let alone struck me for a cad."

"You're worse than a cad. You're a detective."

"Haw-haw!" barked the Major. "If I had my stick, I'd give him another memory to press between his pages."

Rittenhouse picked up the sack suddenly and shook out its contents. They clattered to the floor with a noise that rattled eardrums, but none of the hundred or so squat ink bottles shattered. They were made of thick glass, and although many had no stoppers, no ink spilled out.

"LaVern Munn, the Longhorn manager, is a frugal man," he said. "The bank goes through a lot of ink in six months' time, but he saves the bottles and returns them to a man who comes through twice a year to collect them for the ink company to refill. The company pays him ten cents a pound for the service." He looked around. "I can tell by your expressions that Mr. Vermillion didn't take you into his confidence. He seems to enjoy surprising people."

"Who told *you?*" demanded Cornelius.

"Mr. Munn, when I confronted him with what I'd learned about him from my colleagues in Chicago. Before he emigrated West, our banker friend ran odd jobs there for the late Scipio Africanus McNear, principally delivering graft to the heads of various city departments. He failed to deliver some of it, and fled here to invest his new fortune. Would you care to provide the rest, Mr. McNear?"

"Vermillion," Johnny corrected. "There's no law against being a politician's son. What's the penalty for stealing fifty dollars' worth of empty bottles?"

"I think we can persuade Marshal Meagher to waive that charge. That is, if his people caught the shipment?" Rittenhouse looked at the lawman.

"I just got the wire. Dodge City's got its hands full with a train robbery, but they took it off the nine-fifteen from Wichita. They're holding it."

Johnny seemed to remember then he was still holding his glass of port. He drained it, but the color barely stained his pale cheeks before receding. It was the first time the company had seen him other than saturated with his own confidence. Cornelius turned his head away.

"Munn's agreed to testify in return for a shorter sentence," Rittenhouse went on. "Vermillion threatened to expose his past if he didn't agree to turn over all the gold and silver in the vault. He was reluctant to bring up the five percent fee Vermillion allowed him for the service, but when I suggested searching the bank and his home, he volunteered that information as well. Once all the figures are tabulated, the examiners will find that Munn has embezzled no small amount on his own from his depositors. That's why Vermillion staged the robbery, so the sum could be rolled into the loss.

"The ink bottles were supplied merely to weight the sack and convince any chance eyewitnesses that a robbery had taken place. Munn gave Vermillion the money before the bank opened this morning, and Vermillion put it on the first train, addressed to the Coronet Hotel in Denver, to be held for the Prairie Rose Repertory Company. I got that much from the station agent, who saw to it personally that the large parcel was placed aboard."

"You're all under arrest," Meagher said.

Major Davies said, "I fail to see why. I knew nothing about any stolen money being placed aboard a train. My wife did not, and you've given me no reason to suspect either Miss Clay or Mr. Ragland. Actions taken by Mr. Vermillion without the knowledge of the rest of us reflect only upon himself. We are actors, not thieves."

"Oh, Evelyn," said Lizzie. "You really are the most contemptible creature."

Rittenhouse smiled at the Major. "I wasn't being untruthful when I told you in San Francisco I admired your talent. You'll have the opportunity to play before an appreciative audience when your case comes to trial; you all will. Just in case the witnesses I've established fail to identify each of you positively as a bandit in a series of robberies from Missouri to Utah, I have a preponderance of evidence that the Prairie Rose was performing in each of those places at the time of the outrage and a stack of glowing reviews testifying to your ability to assume disparate roles at the drop of a hat. It shouldn't be hard for a competent prosecutor to prove the possibility of so talented a crew to appear in two places at once."

"That won't be necessary in my case," April said. "I helped plan the robbery of the Longhorn Bank."

Johnny laughed his old laugh; once again he was back in character. "If you believe that, Rittenhouse, you belong to a legion. Miss Clay is a gifted actress."

"I helped as well," Cornelius said.

Lizzie said, "We all did. Stop spluttering, Evie. You know perfectly well you can't survive without me."

"Oh, blast." The Major dropped onto the dressing-table chair and emptied his glass. "I suppose I'll play Sidney Carton if I must. I despise Dickens."

Rittenhouse rubbed his hands. "Since you're all so willing, I'll ask the marshal to manacle Vermillion only. I doubt he brought enough for the entire troupe."

Meagher grunted and fell to the floor, sprawled facedown on top of his shotgun. Every eye in the room rose from the bloodied back of his head to the man standing in the open doorway behind him, holding a large yellow-handled revolver by its barrel. He spun it on his finger, palming the butt with a smack and thumbing back the hammer. His long granite face was burned as dark as his hat and his worn and faded clothes were streaked with lather. He stank of horse and spent powder. "Everybody stay put!" he barked. "This here's a snake that bites from both ends."

"Who the devil are you?" said the Major.

"Black Jack Brixton."

The newcomer swung his gaze on Rittenhouse. "Last man

called me that wound up right where your friend is. Put them hands high. I heard enough to know you're heeled."

The Pinkerton raised his hands.

"You're Brixton?" Johnny said. "I thought you'd be taller."

"I'll look plenty tall when you're all bleeding out on the floor. This is the second time this herd of yours cost me a payroll train."

"What train?" April stepped in front of Johnny, who grasped her shoulders to hold her back.

Brixton lunged and took her wrist in his free hand, tearing her out of Johnny's grip. Johnny stepped forward. A harsh metallic clack stopped him. Heads turned toward a tall man standing in front of the blanket that divided the room, holding a Winchester against his hip with the barrel level and a fresh round racked into the chamber. He was burned as deeply as Brixton, his clothes stained from the same hard ride.

"That there's Mysterious Bob." Brixton spun April to face the others, twisting her arm behind her back. She cried out. "We call him that on account of nobody knows just when he'll cut loose with that repeater."

"What do you want?" Rittenhouse asked.

"I want you to wire Dodge City and get me that bank money I heard you squawking about," Brixton said. "But that can wait till we settle with these five."

"Why do you want to kill us?" Lizzie sounded as calm as the chambermaid in *The Diplomat Deposes*. "You got back all the money from the safe in Salt Lake City."

"That's spent. We had to quit Denver when you spotted Charlie Kettleman there. We was all fixed to hit the army train headed for the mint. Then we got ourselves shot to hell out by Fort Dodge on account of you seen Tom Riddle here and told the army. I think maybe I'll shoot that fat husband of yours first so you know what's coming."

"I don't know what you mean," she said. "I don't know any Tom Riddle."

Brixton made a movement that drew a gasp from April and rested the barrel of his revolver on her shoulder, pointing it at the Major, who sat holding up his empty glass as if waiting for a refill.

Johnny made a long stride to his right. As the revolver pivoted that way, he swept up a fencing foil leaning in the corner and swirled the blade in a lazy *S*. On the upstroke, the button point snagged the inside of the muzzle and tore the weapon from Brixton's grasp. It made a slow arc and struck the floor near the outside wall, jarring loose the hammer. The report rang like a huge iron bell. A piece of gilded wood jumped off the frame of the dressing table mirror.

"Bob!" Brixton's shout was muffled in the echo of the shot.

Mysterious Bob placed the muzzle of his carbine against the back of Johnny's head. The foil dropped to the floor with a clank.

Rittenhouse had his hand in the pocket where he'd put April's derringer.

Brixton gave April's arm a yank. She screamed. "Take it out and drop it or I'll snap her arm clean off."

"Let her go first."

She screamed again. The Pinkerton drew the pistol out slowly and let it fall.

"You, sir, are a knave," said the Major.

Brixton let go of April's arm and shoved. She stumbled forward. Johnny caught her in his arms. Brixton went over and picked up his revolver. "I got five more in the cylinder. That's one for each of you and I'll let Bob finish this one." He kicked Meagher in the temple. The fallen marshal, who had begun to stir, groaned again and fell silent.

"What about me?" Rittenhouse said.

"I ain't got that far in my figuring. If you do a good job getting me that bank money maybe I'll let you see Chicago again."

Johnny said, "Someone must have heard that shot. The sheriff is the marshal's brother. He's probably on his way here with deputies."

Brixton grinned. "Well, then, I reckon I better get to it. Stand up, you." He turned his barrel on the Major.

"No!" Lizzie took a step. The Major flung out an arm, stopping her. He placed his glass carefully on the dressing table and heaved himself to his feet with a grunt.

"Tomorrow, and tomorrow, and tomorrow," he said. "I should have died hereafter."

Brixton thumbed back the hammer and took aim at the Major's broad middle.

An explosion shuddered the room. The Major winced and fell back against the dressing table. He groped at himself, opened his eyes.

The impact of the bullet had slammed Black Jack Brixton into the wall behind him, jarring the revolver from his grasp. This time it struck the floor without discharging. He slid down the wall with a look of wonder on his face. Then his chin fell to his chest and his hat tilted forward over his eyes.

Mysterious Bob lowered his smoking carbine. His unreadable face turned toward Rittenhouse's. "You'll have to take my word on it," he said. "I threw my badge away in sixty-five. You can't ride and camp with the same men for ten years and keep a thing like that hid."

· V ·
The Comeback

24

Allan Pinkerton made three attempts to write *The Prairie Rose and the Detectives* and gave up after fifty pages. Although General Matagordo, a paid Pinkerton informant of years standing, was alive and well and mourning the death of his favorite carrier pigeon in San Diablo, Robert Jules "Mysterious Bob" Craidlaw had committed many questionable acts in his efforts to win the trust of Black Jack Brixton and the Ace-in-the-Hole Gang, and no amount of literary license could guarantee that the attention would not blacken the all-seeing eye of the Pinkerton National Detective Agency. His publishers, G. W. Carleton & Co., agreed to accept a substitute case history, and *The Spiritualists and the Detectives* appeared in 1877.

For this reason, and the fact that numerous legal maneuvers delayed the trial of the members of the Prairie Rose until June 1876, when news of the massacre of George Armstrong Custer and the Seventh Cavalry at the Little Big Horn crowded every other story out of the lead columns, the larcenous adventures of Johnny Vermillion and his company of artists occupy no more than a line in the few histories of the West that take notice of them. Yellowing documents of court proceedings report the following:

Evelyn Beverly Davies, referred to variously as "the Major," "Old Porky," and, in England, "Sir Rot Rotter of Rotting Lane," was released by the State of Kansas for lack of evidence connecting him to the embezzlement of the Longhorn Bank in Wichita, but ordered to stand trial in Salt Lake City for the lone robbery of the Holladay Overland Mail & Express Company office. Daniel Oberlin, the Overland manager, identified him positively—mostly by his "plummy" voice—as the masked fat man who had commanded him to "hand over the swag." He was convicted and sentenced to serve three years at hard labor, which the judge reduced to probation because of the defendant's age and physical condition and the fact that it was his first offense.

Elizabeth Jane Mort-Davies, his wife, née Janey Timble, formerly of the Ten Tumbling Timbles, withdrew her confession to complicity in the Longhorn case on the grounds that it was made under duress. The charge was dropped against her as well, and although the Pinkerton National Detective Agency attempted to have her held pending the result of its investigation of the other robberies in which the Prairie Rose was suspected, none of the eyewitnesses who were questioned would submit that the "tall bandit wearing a bandanna" was a woman. She was released.

April Clay, alias Emma April Klauswidcsz, did not retract her confession, but her tearful appearance in the witness box, dressed fetchingly in widow's black lace, convinced the twelve men of the jury in Wichita that she was innocent. They acquitted her.

(No records exist to indicate that any attempt was made to try April Clay elsewhere. It's believed all such plans were abandoned after the case collapsed against Mme. Mort-Davies.)

Cornelius Ragland was convicted on the evidence of his confession in the presence of Marshal Mike Meagher and Agent Philip Rittenhouse. The judge rejected the defense team's plea for clemency on the grounds of his delicate health, but suspended his two-year sentence because it was his first offense. He was immediately extradited to Wyoming Territory, where he was convicted of the robbery of the Cattleman's Bank in Cheyenne. He served eight months at hard labor in the territorial penitentiary and was released four months early for good behavior; guards told parole authorities he was an industrious worker "for a skinny feller," who gave them each a sample of the poetry he wrote in his cell.

LaVern Munn, charged with embezzlement and conspiracy to embezzle funds from depositors' accounts in the Longhorn Bank of Wichita, did not stand trial. He pleaded guilty to the lesser charge of conspiracy and received a sentence of six months. The sentence was suspended, with a warning never again to seek employment with a financial institution.

Johnny Vermillion, alias John Tyler McNear, spent nearly two years on trial in Kansas, Missouri, Nebraska, and the territories of Idaho, Wyoming, and Utah. He was convicted of all charges and sentenced to serve a total of forty years at hard labor, beginning in Kansas.

Topeka Daily Capital, Tuesday, March 8, 1878:

Authorities throughout the state have joined the hunt for five convicts who escaped last night from the Kansas State Penitentiary while Warden Lawler, many of his guards, and the majority of the convict population were gathered in the prison cafeteria to watch a theatrical presentation of *The Count of Monte Cristo,* performed by members of the incarcerated community. All of the men who are reported missing belonged to the cast.

Staff and penal servers alike appeared to be entertained by the play, adapted from the novel by M. Alexandre Dumas the Elder (ironically, about an escape from prison) by one John T. McNear—known also by the name Johnny Vermillion—who was also its director and lead player. So engrossed were the spectators that they sat for several moments staring at the crudely painted set after the makeshift curtain rose on the last act before realizing that the dramatis personae had fled.

Subsequent investigation revealed that each of the players had practiced assuming one another's role, and that by changing costumes created the illusion that no member of the cast was out of sight of the hundreds assembled for longer than two or three minutes. By this ruse they managed to take their leave of the prison piecemeal by means of a homemade rope ladder slung over a section of wall rendered invisible to the guards in the corner towers by deep shadow. Those still remaining took advantage of the brief interval between the second and third acts to follow in their path. The trusty who pulled the rope to raise the curtain has been isolated for questioning, but as of this writing continues to maintain his ignorance either of the plan or of the whereabouts of its practitioners.

All of the escapees are characterized as dangerous felons sentenced to periods of long servitude. McNear, who is believed to be the ringleader, is a convicted bank robber, described as . . .

Philip Rittenhouse, seated comfortably in his spartan office in Chicago, scanned the item quickly when it took its due place on top of his stack; then read it again slowly and with the pleasure of a man enjoying a good book. Then he picked up his shears and began to cut.